No [...]

Be fresh

HIDING

A novel by Rachel Runnalls

Be real

Change the world

paramedic publishing

www.rachelrunnalls.com

HIDING

Copyright © 2014 by Rachel Runnalls
'Undragoning' © 2014 by Kendra Medak
Cover design by Jess Wiberg
All rights reserved.

Second edition.

No part of this book may be used or reproduced in any manner
whatsoever without the prior written permission of the author,
except in the case of brief quotations embodied in reviews.

This is a work of fiction. Names, characters, places and
incidents are the products of the author's imagination or are used
fictitiously. Any resemblance to actual events or persons, living
or dead, is coincidental.

https://www.facebook.com/hiding.everyscarhasastory

Library and archives Canada Cataloguing in Publication data
is available upon request.

Scripture quotations are from the THE HOLY BIBLE, NEW
INTERNATIONAL VERSION®, NIV® Copyright © 1973,
1978, 1984, 2011 by Biblica, Inc.™ Used by permission. All
rights reserved worldwide.

ISBN-10: 1503372561

ISBN-13: 978-1503372566

For my father,

who taught me what a good dad loves like.

HIDING

every scar has a story

It's in these dry times that I realize
That evil is still at large
A long time ago
I figured out the more you try to hold onto innocence
The more it slips through your fingers...
We have forgotten how to love
And it's killing the dreams of our children
What does a child learn when love is shown in
bruises?

(Kendra Medak, *Undragoning*)

ONE

Blessed are those who have regard for the weak;
The LORD delivers them in times of trouble.

(Psalm 41:1)

1

Just one person.

{Jon}

Jon stepped into the drafting classroom, bracing himself with a deep breath of fresh pine smell from the woodworking shop next door. Today was the day he needed to find a partner for the midterm project. And since there was only one other kid with a drafting table to himself, today was the day he needed to speak to Ciaran Douglas.

Jon froze a second, his hands sweating on his books. Ciaran was in his seat already, his dark head bent and his arm curved around his sketchbook. He had the sleeves of his army jacket pushed up and he was drawing with fierce intensity. Ciaran's hard face and bulky jacket made him look like the kind of kid who knew how to hurt you in secret, terrible ways.

Jon swallowed, hunching his shoulders. *Keer-an,* Jon rehearsed his name silently. He couldn't mess that up if he wanted Ciaran to say yes. He went down the aisle and dropped his books on the table next to Ciaran.

The 'bang' made the other boy jump, then flash Jon a glare. "Sorry," Jon said hastily. He put on a smile and stuck out his hand. "Hi, Ciaran right? I don't have a table partner so... I'm Jon."

Ciaran's dark eyebrows lifted, looking at Jon's outstretched hand. He didn't move to take it, and their teacher, Mr. Ryerson, called for attention at the front of the room. Jon dropped into his chair, sliding down low. He'd been friends with everyone at his old school—it would have been unimaginable to not have a single friend in a class. He closed his eyes briefly. *Would it be so hard to find just one person who cares I exist?*

Are you even listening to me?

He was starting to wonder why he still prayed, when God was obviously so far from answering him.

They were supposed to be working on the problem outlined on the board. Jon snuck a look at the sketchbook open on Ciaran's side of the table. It was a blueprint, neatly done and almost complete. In the bottom corner, pressed so firmly the ball-point pen had left ridges on the page, was a boy in a box, his head ducked between his knees, his elbows and knees jutting out of the confines of the square at awkward angles.

"That's really good," Jon blurted.

Ciaran spread his hand over the deep blue lines of the sketch, frowning at him like he'd forgotten he was sitting there. With the cuff of his jacket pushed back, Jon could see a thick, pink scar running over the bone of his wrist. "I mean your drawing," Jon said, flushing.

Ciaran dropped his eyes to the page. He flipped the cuff of his jacket down quick and crossed his arms. The scar was gone.

Jon was starting to wonder if there was something wrong with him, if he was deaf or couldn't speak. "Sorry," he muttered.

"Nobody calls me that," Ciaran said in a flat voice.

"Calls you what?" Jon's voice squeaked with surprise.

"Ciaran," Ciaran said. "It's Cary."

"Cary," Jon repeated. "Oh. I'm… I'm still Jon." Then he could have bitten his tongue off for sounding so stupidly uncool.

Cary shot him a look under the straight line of his lowered brows. "What do you want?"

Sweat was running down Jon's ribs like someone turned on the taps under his arms. He took a breath. "I was just wondering if you had a partner for the midterm project."

Cary blinked. "What midterm project."

"The one we got last class. Maybe you weren't here that day." Jon dug through his backpack and pulled out the handout.

Cary read it slowly, then pushed the handout back to Jon's side of the table. "Why?"

Jon had not prepared for this question. "Um, because you're good at this class. And I really don't…" He caught himself. He'd been about to say it out loud: *I really don't have any friends.* "I really don't know anyone else."

Cary wasn't even making eye contact. He hurried on. "And we're kind of out of time this week to write up our idea and hand it in."

Cary swore under his breath, sitting back in his chair.

"I was thinking we could do Frank Lloyd Wright, his four-square house," Jon said. "We could be done in, like one afternoon." *Please God.*

"Fine," Cary said. He put out his hand to shake and Jon took it. Cary's grip was hard and the skin on his palm felt rough. "Don't fuck this up for me." His soft, even tone made Jon want to run back to his previous seat.

Instead he put on his most winning smile. "I won't. Thanks." He scribbled his phone number and address onto the handout. "Tomorrow and Wednesday work for me, if you want to come over to my place. My mom will do snacks for us."

Cary's eyebrows crept up again, like Jon had started speaking in Greek instead of plain English. "I'll see," he said.

"Great," Jon said.

When the end of class bell rang Jon was on his feet and out the door, a surge of relief carrying him down the hall. Another crappy day, over.

He just had a second to register the yellow and purple football jacket in the corner of his eye before the guy checked him hard into the lockers. An oncoming freshman collided with Jon, dropping her books and notes everywhere. Raucous laughter and "Faggot!" floated over the hallway.

Jon was breathless from the hit as he said, "Sorry, I'm really sorry," and bent to help the other kid pick up her stuff. She shot him a glare, grabbed up her books and fled up the hall.

Jon kept his back against the lockers as he picked up his own books, but the pack of footballers had already gone. Hit and run.

Jon made it to his locker, grabbed his coat and got out of the school. He'd never thought about what an easy target new kids were until he become one himself: he didn't have a group of friends around him to create a buffer zone of protection. His first three months here had been a hell of picking spit wads out of his hair and getting shoved into lockers.

While he was standing on the sidewalk waiting for his mom's van to pull into the parking lot, he saw Cary come out the school doors. Cary didn't need a group, kids just got out of the way. Jon watched him duck into the back of a shiny BMW sedan and wished to God that was him.

2

Promise.

{Cary}

Cary slid down low in the leather backseat, wishing for the thousandth time he could make himself invisible. His mother turned in the passenger seat, smiling. "How was your day, sweetie?"

He saw his father's eyes on him in the rearview mirror and ducked his head to hide his face. "Fine." He played with the volume on the iPod in his jacket pocket until he could just make out her words, bubbling along the top of the roar of his music.

"Ciaran, your mother asked you a question." His father's voice punched through, and Cary flicked the earbuds out of his ears and let them drop down the collar of his jacket. His mother was looking over her shoulder at him, still smiling brightly.

"The homework is in my backpack," Cary said. "I'm doing the reading tonight."

"What are you reading?" His father's eyes found him again, and Cary held still, his hands closing beside his legs.

"Hatchet."

"The same book you've been working on since the beginning of the year?"

"The words get jumbled," Cary muttered, and then wished he'd kept his mouth shut.

His father snorted. "Don't blame the words, boy. It's your mind that makes them jumbled. Come to my study after dinner. Bring your novel. We'll see if I can straighten out those unruly words."

Cary's ears rang faintly and he swallowed. "Yes Father." On a good day, he could make it from supper to bedtime without giving his father a reason to notice or speak to him. Today was not going to be a good day. Cary turned his face to the window, catching the rays of the setting sun slicing between the buildings. He pressed one earbud back into his ear so the screams of his music would drown out the noise in his own head.

His father disappeared into his study when they got home. His mother made a face at Cary in the hall. "Ciaran, that awful jacket."

"You never told me he was coming to pick me up," Cary said. He jerked it off, stuffing it in the back of the closet. It was useless protection here anyways.

His mother followed him to the kitchen, hefting herself onto a stool at the island counter while he washed his hands. The cut of her stylish clothes could no longer conceal the swollen curves of her pregnant body. "We went to the ultrasound appointment together." He could hear the smile in her voice without turning to look. "You should have seen your father's face when they told us it's a boy."

Cary shut off the tap, hard. "What do you want me to make for supper?"

She tipped her head, tapping one manicured fingernail on the counter-top. "Aren't you excited about having a brother?"

"Sure, it's fine." He took out a package of chicken breasts out of the fridge, his fingers sticking to the chilled plastic. "I'm fine."

Her smile returned and she nestled her hand around the curve of her belly. "Good."

Cary set the pan on the stovetop and dropped olive oil onto its gleaming surface to heat. He'd learned to lie from her, she was the best. Either he'd gotten so good at it that she couldn't tell he was lying anymore, or she just didn't care to look.

"Everything is going to be different when the baby comes," she said. Her face had softened as she watched him. "Everything will be better. Your father has never been so happy, Cary. He always wanted to have another child, and so did I. I was hoping for a little girl, but the ultrasound definitely showed a boy. A son for your father to love."

Cary dropped the chicken breasts into the pan with a 'hiss' and the smell of olive oil and garlic filled the kitchen. His shoulders were braced while her words fell like blows. *A son for your father to love.* With his jacket off, the scars on his wrists were plain on his skin, running over the bones of his wrists that had been broken. "How many weeks left?" He asked.

"Four. You could meet your brother any day now."

He took a mouthful of the fragrant smell of the chicken and swallowed back nausea. In the sizzle and the sound of the overhead fan he missed his mother crossing the kitchen until she wrapped her hand around the bare skin just below his shirt sleeve. The muscles in his arm jumped with tension.

"Ciaran?" His mother's voice was soft and strange. "Your brother is going to need you. I need you. You know that, right?"

He looked in her face. She was smiling uncertainly. "I know that," he said roughly.

Fear shadowed her wide grey eyes and her hand tightened on his arm. "You can't run away again. You can't leave me."

He looked away, his face heating to tell the truth the way it never did when he lied. "I promised already. I won't leave."

He heard her relieved sigh and she put her arm around his shoulders to hug him for a second. She said she loved him. He used the wooden spatula to push the chicken over onto their raw pink sides. That word didn't mean anything to him.

3

Supposed to be happy.

{Jon}

Both Jon's sisters were in the van when his mom arrived to pick him up from school. His mom had thrown a sweater over her pyjama shirt and track pants, and her hair was held back from her face in an elastic band. She spared Jon a smile as he got in.

"Hi Jonee!" His littlest sister Bea called from her car seat in the back.

Jon turned and found a smile for her. "Hi Honey Bee. How was your day at preschool?"

"Good." She held out a piece of construction paper, showering the seat back in front of her with glitter. "Look what I made!"

Her older sister, Tabitha, shoved her hand away. "Get that outta my face, Bea." She flicked her long pigtails, as if they might have gotten glittered too. "What is that even supposed to be?"

Bea took the paper back, looking at it with her lower lip sticking out. "It's a rainbow zebra."

"Oh." Tabitha sounded pacified. "It's nice then."

Bea's smile returned. "Thank you."

Jon turned back, slumping tiredly in his seat. "How was your day, mom?" he asked without looking at her.

She gave him a distracted smile. "Oh you know, the usual. What about you? Did you make any friends at school today?"

Like he was six years old and could just make friends in a day. He tried to make his face smile. "Yeah, kind of. I got a partner for that drafting project I was worried about. Ciaran—um, Cary."

"That's nice."

He turned his face to the window hoping she wouldn't ask anything more about that. He'd prayed every day for a friend at school—for *anyone* to notice him for a reason other than his size, or his clothes, or whatever it was that made him a loser to the guys on the football team. Cary was hardly the answer to that prayer.

When they pulled into the driveway Tabitha reached back and unbuckled her sister from her seat and they jumped out of the van one after the other, chattering about their plans. Jon watched them run into the house together with an ache like a fist in his side. It was still hard not to think about a time when he had been as small as Bea and had a brother to do everything with. For all his sister's petty disagreements with each other, their best friend had made the move with them.

Jon took his soccer ball to the backyard. He dribbled and practiced his footwork, then slammed the ball into the house as hard as he could, over and over. He was supposed to be happy; he knew that. He was supposed to be happy his dad was doing God's work and helping people in a new church. He was supposed to be happy even if he didn't have friends or a brother because he had God.

The ball smacked against the wall and shot back at him, making his hands sting when he caught it. He rubbed his palms over the familiar black and white shapes on its skin, then threw it in the grass again. He could hide from his parents, but he couldn't hide his thoughts from God. He imagined Him on his throne up there, rolling his eyes at yet another teenage temper tantrum from the faithless Jon White.

His next kick made the basement window rattle, and he let the ball roll into the grass, running to check the window frame. Nothing broken. He straightened with a sigh of relief.

His dad was stepping off the back deck, coming toward him, the sun picking glints of red out of his brown hair. Jon stayed where he was, biting his lip. Hopefully Pete hadn't seen that stupid move.

Pete tapped the soccer ball back to Jon. He was still wearing his dress shirt and slacks from the church office. "Saw you out here giving the goalie a beating," he said, with a smile in his beard. "Mind if I play in?"

Jon stopped the ball with his foot, then passed it back. His dad made the ball dance between his feet, and they were playing the old game of 'keep-away.' Jon was grateful not to have to talk or do anything except push his feet deep in the grass to out-run his dad.

Finally Pete threw himself onto the steps of the deck, laughing. "Okay, I'm beat."

Jon stopped the ball under his foot, watching his dad sideways. His anger felt smaller, with the smell of grass and the sound of his dad's laugh in the air.

"Ready to head in and wash up?"

Jon nodded, tossing the ball against the house one more time to let it lie where it fell. His dad ruffled up his hair, and Jon pulled his head away, smiling in spite of himself. "Don't— I'm all sweaty."

"Good day today, son?" Pete asked, his shoulder bumping against Jon's.

Jon shrugged. It was easier to lie now that the school day wasn't so fresh in his mind. "Yeah, really good."

In the clamour of the girls getting into their chairs and his mother bringing the steaming casserole out of the oven Jon's quiet went unnoticed. He cut Bea's food down to size and poured Tabitha's milk, since a full gallon jug was still too heavy for her to handle. He held Bea's hand on one side and Pete's on the other when they bowed their heads for prayer. He'd decided a long time ago that his parents were never going to know how much the hole still hurt him. Judah had left him this job, to be the oldest and the only son and Jon worked hard to fill it. His parents talked and laughed like a normal mom and dad again and he figured that made it worth the effort to be as good as two sons would be. Even if the lie didn't work on him.

4

Got you.

{Cary}

After dinner, Cary got his book from his bag and went down the hall to his father's study. His stomach was turning in slow flips; he had only managed a few bites of the meal. At his father's closed door Cary breathed in through his nose and out through his mouth, shutting the sick feeling away with everything else. He was stone. He knocked on the door.

"Come in."

Cary's father, Conall, was a professor at the university. His study was lined with shelves full of leather-bound books. There was a tall granite fireplace on one wall, its mantelpiece cluttered with academic awards and discarded pipe stems. Conall was in his leather desk chair, bent over his desk, marking. His broad shoulders were framed by two stacks of papers. He finished grading with a slash of his pen, turning the sheets onto the left-handed pile and said without looking up:

"Ciaran. Pour us some coffee."

A metal coffee urn stood on the sideboard, a few mugs stacked around it. Cary tucked his book under his arm to pour him a cup.

Behind him, Conall's desk chair creaked as he leaned back, stretching his long arms and fingers until his knuckles popped. Cary flinched, splashing the coffee over the rim of the cup. *Shit.* He drew his shoulders up to his ears and quickly wiped up the spill with the hem of his shirt.

"Pour one for yourself too, if you like."

Cary shot him a glance. His father was clearing the low table which stood between the two chairs in front of the fireplace. He seemed a little abstracted, but relaxed. Cary guessed he had a chance of keeping his father that way if he was careful. Maybe. He was always careful.

He set the cup of coffee on the corner of the table, holding it steady with both hands. Conall pulled up an arm chair, catching him with dark, intent eyes. "Sit."

Cary sat. Conall unlatched a small, flat case and opened it on the side table. Inside, the case was patterned with white and black triangles. Conall let the leather dice cup fall into his hand.

"Have you ever played backgammon, Ciaran?"

Cary shook his head. "No, sir."

"It's a man's game. Take these pieces." Conall poured the shiny disks onto the table in front of Cary. "Set them on the board like this."

Cary paid close attention to his father's instructions. As the evening wore on his father's mood showed no signs of breaking and Cary's fear ebbed away, leaving only his habitual caution. His inevitable mistakes were met with a brisk "Tactical error, Ciaran" as his father moved the pieces into their proper place.

When the game was done, his father the victor, Conall sat back in his chair with a grunt of satisfaction and fished in his pockets for his pipe and matches. Cary gathered the game pieces back into the box, aware of the movements of his father's hands on the edge of his vision. He couldn't think of the last time he'd spent more than an hour alone in a room with Conall like this. He was exhausted from being on high alert all evening, and he needed a cigarette. He wished his father would forget the book and let him go.

The match lit with a 'hiss' and Conall pulled the flame into the bowl of his pipe. The sweet-strong smell of tobacco stung the inside of Cary's nose. "You brought your novel?" His father asked.

Cary swallowed and brought it out from where he had stuck it under his leg. Conall gestured to the fireplace. "Stand up there. Read me the first chapter."

Cary got to his feet and his head seemed to get up faster than the rest of him. He planted his feet on the granite floor and braced his legs to keep them from shaking. His father sat back in the leather armchair, his long-fingered hands folded in front of his chest. He watched Cary through half-closed eyes, sucking on his pipe stem.

When he opened the book the words jumped and danced on the page. Cary made the first word come into focus and stuttered through the opening sentences until his father cut his hand across the air.

"Stop." Conall frowned. "I can't understand a word you're saying. Don't they make you read like this in school?"

Cary shook his head, watching his father sideways. He gripped his book so tightly he could feel the corners bite into the palms of his hands.

"Can you tell me anything you just read?" Cary went to open the book again and Conall sat forward suddenly, catching it in his hand and holding it closed. "From memory."

Cary went still. "I can't."

Conall let the book go. "Of course not. You're only seeing a word at a time. Look at the sentence."

Cary took a breath and opened the book again.

"Read it to yourself. Silently. Now – read it to me."

Cary obeyed. His voice was flat with tension, but the words came out more smoothly.

Conall nodded. "Good. Do the same with the next paragraph."

With a glance at his father, Cary obeyed.

When he was finished he looked at his father for a cue.

"Go on," Conall said.

Haltingly, Cary read the entire chapter to his father. When he was finished he looked up and found Conall's eyes on him.

"You see how to do it?" His father said.

Cary nodded.

"Are you passing this class?"

Cary nodded more slowly.

Conall's mouth turned down as he looked at his son. "When I was your age I could have memorized that passage in the time it took you to simply read aloud." Cary ducked his head, holding still. Conall snorted. "With a mind like yours, Ciaran, you will have to work far harder for a B plus than I ever had to work for an A."

Cary was silent, barely breathing. He would be lucky if he held onto his C in this class.

"You understand that's what I expect of you," Conall said.

"Yes father," Cary said softly.

"Finish the book by Friday. I will have some questions for you about what you have read." Conall waved him away.

Cary backed out of the room and escaped.

After that he was exhausted but too wound up to sleep. He laid in the dark of his room listening to the sounds of the water running and his parents distant footsteps. He thought about his mother putting her arm around the round weight of her stomach, and his father's hands moving the black and white game pieces on the board. Six months ago he'd been planning to run, to get on a bus and never come back. He could never have imagined an evening like this evening in this house. Maybe his mother was right. Maybe things were going to be different.

Sleep finally carried him off, and when he came to he was lying in the grass at the edge of a small body of water. It was the wilderness he'd been reading about that evening. The tail of a downed plane jutted out of the lake. It was dusk. There was a figure silhouetted against the indigo sky.

Cary started up and found he couldn't move. "Who's there?" His voice wavered.

The figure had a mouth full of light, as if there was a glow bead under his tongue. "Can you walk?"

Cary looked at himself in the gathering dark. His legs were splayed crookedly in front of him. "Both my legs are broken," he said. He set his hand on his leg. They didn't feel like anything.

The figure drew nearer, rustling through the grass. Cary was afraid.

"Don't come any closer!"

"Don't you want to leave this place?" The man asked. His face was faintly illuminated by the light in his mouth.

"I'm fine." He could feel the broken bones shift under his hand, loose in a sleeve of muscle. Distantly his mind cried a warning—if there was no pain in a break this bad something was very very wrong.

A noise reached them by the water: little coughs escalating into a drawn out wail.

"The baby's crying," the man said.

Cary tried to arrange his legs so he could stand. They flopped and bent at wrong angles. "Shit. You get it then."

The man stepped forward and scooped Cary into his arms. His face loomed over Cary, huge and distorted. Light poured from his mouth and eyes.

"GOT YOU."

Cary woke with a gasp and slapped the light switch on the wall. His room was empty. He sat forward, touching his legs under his blanket. They were reassuringly intact. He turned off his light and lay back in the dark.

5

People watching.

{Cary}

When the sky outside his window turned pale Cary got up, showered and left the house. He caught the bus to the school, then walked the rest of the way to downtown Strathcona. The morning light poured up the street, making the old brick buildings glow with warmth. There were family run cigar stores with apartments on top, next to Starbucks, next to the kind of artsy and expensive home furnishings stores his mother liked to shop at. Cary walked with his head up, his hands in his pockets, feeling the last shadows of his nightmare vanishing in the bright light of morning.

There was a big old church building on the corner, with stone steps spread out in front. A few kids were clustered there already. A boy was perched on the stair rail, smiling at the passers-by with his stubby hands clasped around his knees. An older guy, built like a brick wall with a tattoo on his neck was sitting back on the steps, sunning himself with his eyes shut.

Mike cracked his eyes a slit when Cary pulled up a seat on the bottom step. "Spare me a dart?" he rumbled.

Cary fished his crumpled cigarette pack from his jacket and silently offered it to him. "Thanks." Mike lit up with a tarnished lighter, then held the pack and the lighter out to Cary.

Cary took them and lit his own smoke. He returned the lighter to Mike without looking at him. They saw each other every day at the school doors, where the kids who didn't fit and didn't give a shit smoked in the breaks. But Cary had figured out a long time ago it was simpler if he didn't make friends.

He was startled when the boy addressed him. His voice was light and sweet as his smile. "Do you ever watch people go by and think—that person has a whole life I don't know anything about. They love things and have things happen to them same as me."

Cary blinked, looking at the few pedestrians passing on the sidewalk. "No."

"I do."

Cary frowned at the boy. There was something not right about him and his moon-round face.

"Don't mind him," Mike said. "He's always saying crazy shit like that."

The boy smiled beatifically, looking in the light of morning like one of the saints in the stained glass behind them. "You think it too, Michael." he said.

Mike rolled his eyes. "Yeah like every day I see Cary here I'm just dying to know what's in his head."

Cary huffed a laugh, surprised to find one so close to his surface.

"I'm like, what's a rich kid like that doing on the street ass-crack of dawn?"

That wiped the laugh off his face and Cary slid him a sideways look, the skin on the back of his neck prickling. This kid had noticed him, he hated being noticed.

"And then I'm like, mind your business Mike Joseph, you're here too." Mike smiled, smoke dribbling from his nose. His hands were open and loose between his knees, not looking for a fight. "So I do that. Always good to listen to my own best advice."

Cary got to his feet, rolling his tight shoulders and feeling Mike's eyes on him. There was no reason to start something here, even if the blood was thrumming in his ears like an invitation.

"You cool bro?" Mike said.

Cary nodded shortly. "Thanks for the light," he said.

The fair boy lifted a hand, smiling. "Bye Care. See you."

///

The kid from drafting class found him at his locker in the break, smiling at him with a little worried wrinkle in his forehead. "Hey, Cary." It took Cary a second to recall his name, Jon. "Did you check if tonight works? To work on our project?"

He was about to shut Jon down when he remembered the way his father had looked at him in the study last night saying *When I was your age I could have memorized that in the time it took you to read it.* He glared into the locker. "Sure." He had to get this project out of the way and finish that book report.

"Okay!" Jon's voice squeaked a little at the end, and Cary turned his frown on him. What was his problem? Jon was holding his smile on his face like it was a shield, his arms crossed tight over his body and his shoulders drawn up to his ears. Cary recognized that look in an instant. Jon expected him to punch him in the face.

Cary looked aside, wishing he had any clue how to put a person at ease. He'd learned a lot of things from his father with his university education, but that was not one of them. "So what's your mom making for snack?" he asked.

Out of the corner of his eye he saw Jon relax a little. "I don't know – whatever's in the cupboard."

Cary shrugged. "Whatever sounds good."

6

Jon's house.

{Cary}

Cary bussed home with Jon after their drafting class. His awkward attempts to not scare the crap out of Jon seemed to be working—Jon kept the conversation going almost single-handedly. Cary liked that. And he was quick. Jon had a pad of graph paper on his lap that he used to illustrate their ideas. The layout of their building was almost complete before Jon pulled the cord. The bus sighed to a stop on a residential street of older bungalows and duplexes with frayed brown siding.

"This is us," Jon said.

Cary followed Jon closely, watching everything.

Two little girls whooped and ran on the brown grass of the front yard. A whole tribe of Barbies littered the front step.

The littlest girl collided with Jon and wrapped her arms around his middle. "Jonee come and play."

Jon unwound her arms. "No Bea, we have homework."

She peered around Jon's body at Cary. "Is this your friend from school?"

Cary shot a look at Jon's back. Jon turned, smiling with just one side of his mouth like an apology. "Cary, this is my little sister Beatrice. The one on the bike is Tabitha."

Jon's sister rubbed a foot up and down her leg, looking at Cary sideways. "You can call me Bee," she said. "I like your pockets."

Cary frowned, putting his hands in the pockets of his jacket. "Thanks."

"Do you keep rocks in your pockets?"

Cary found the handle of his knife and gripped it. "No."

Bea used both hands to dig into her jeans pocket. "I keep rocks in my pockets, see? And a feather from our blackbird but it's crunched now." She held it out on her palm.

Jon stepped around her. "Okay, bye Bea."

She held out the feather to Cary with a hopeful smile. "You can have that." When he didn't move she took his wrist so quick he didn't have time to pull away. She put the feather in his hand. "Bye Cary."

He stuck the feather in his pocket and followed Jon inside, panic fluttering in his stomach. Jon's front entryway looked like someone turned a shoe store upside-down, and the roar of a vacuum cleaner filled the hallway.

Jon raised his voice to a yell. "Mom? Cary's here, we're going to my room."

The roaring noise snapped off and a woman appeared in the doorway with a vacuum in her hand. Her face was flushed and her hair escaped from the blue bandana tied around her head. Her smile made deep dimples, and her eyes went from Jon to Cary and back.

"Mom, this is Cary. We're going to my room to do homework."

She smiled right at him. "Will you be staying for supper, Cary?"

Cary glanced at Jon for his cue.

"Sure, you'll stay right?"

"Yeah, maybe." Cary said. He was having trouble drawing a full breath. Jon's house was crowded and everyone looked him in the face.

"Do you want to put your coat in the closet?"

Cary held the cuffs tight over his wrists. His jacket was the only cover he had. "No. Thanks."

The front hall went right into the kitchen, crammed full of a table and chairs. Cary looked for the dining room, then realized there was none. His parent's front entryway could have held Jon's whole house.

Framed photos of Jon's family lined the wall as they went down the hall. Cary snatched sideways looks. "How many siblings do you have?" he asked.

"Just the two you saw. Do you have brothers or sisters?"

"No." Cary checked himself. "My mom's having a baby."

Jon laughed, startled. "Wow. Was that a surprise or what?"

That seemed to not require an answer. The door to Jon's room had 'Keep Out' and 'Construction Zone' signs taped on it. Inside, it was even messier than the rest of the house.

Jon moved clothes from the floor to his bed, casually as if the disaster of his room was normal. "So boy or girl?"

Cary tore his eyes off the poster of the man outstretched, blood running from a stake through his hand. "What?"

"Did you find out? Are you having a brother or a sister?"

"Brother. A brother." It was the first time Cary had said the word and it made him feel faintly sick.

"You're lucky," Jon said.

Cary swallowed, making his face still as a stone. He had his hand on the door knob behind him. He could go. Nothing held him here.

"I had a brother." Jon wasn't looking at him, lifting papers and books to the top of his dresser. "He was sick and died when we were small. My parents don't talk about him anymore, but I remember him."

After a moment, Cary released the doorknob. He understood a house with secrets. He put Jon's secret with the others and was silent.

Jon reached deep under the twin bed and emerged with a big pad of grid paper. He looked up at Cary wearing the same hopeful smile his little sister had worn earlier. "So, ready?"

Cary joined Jon on the floor. "Pass me a pencil."

///

Cary lost track of time as they sprawled on the floor, drawing. The sound of the front door banging open made him freeze, then the voices of Jon's little sisters reached them through the door. Jon sat up with a sigh. "I'd better go help with supper. Do you want to stay?"

Cary pulled out his cell phone to check the time. There was a text message from his mother:

<dinner ready where r u?>

He shut the phone in his fist, frowning. "I gotta go. These are almost done—you want me to finish?"

Jon smiled. "Sure. I can't wait to see Mr. Ryerson's face when we hand them in."

Cary was on his feet before he realized Jon had put out his hand to help him up. Something about Jon's gesture recalled his dream from the night before, the dead weight of his legs and the man catching him up in his arms. He shivered and followed Jon out of the bedroom.

7

Blood to pay.

{Cary}

There were cars in the curving drive of Cary's house. Cary slipped in the house through the garage entrance and stood in the boot room, listening. He heard the sound of cutlery tinkling and conversation punctuated by his father's voice. His parents were entertaining tonight. Probably he should have remembered that. He went into the kitchen through the door off the hallway to forage for food.

The caterer was there, leaning against the counter with his arms crossed, looking bored. Cary kept the man between himself and the doors that swung into the dining room. He had a plate full of roast beef scraps and scrapings from the mashed potato container when the doors slapped open.

His father saw him and his face flushed.

"More gravy, sir?" The caterer lifted the gravy boat from Conall's hands.

Cary escaped to his room.

He spent the evening working on the drafting project, finishing the drawings with dark, sure strokes. He heard his mother running a bath while the conversation below rose and fell. The house didn't quiet until after eleven o'clock. Cary pulled off his headphones to listen. His father was treading up the stairs. The footsteps stopped outside of his room.

His father's hand swung the door wide and Cary held still, looking at him from the middle of the drawings spread on the floor. The smell of wine and pipe smoke wafted into the room. Conall's dark hair tumbled over one ear as if he had run his hand through it multiple times that evening.

"I told you we were hosting my students this evening." His father's voice was soft. "I expected you to understand that your presence was required."

Cary looked down at his drawings. He heard the words under the words and the back of his neck prickled.

"What is this." Conall swept up two of the drafts.

"It's a project—"

"More cartoons." Conall tore the pages down the middle, and Cary lost his breath. He scrambled away and put his shoulders on the wall as Conall shoveled up his work, Jon's work, and tore it all to pieces.

"My god you shamed me tonight slinking around in that piece of shit jacket like you came to rob the place."

Cary's hands curled on his knees. His father was right above him, and he could feel the weight of his gaze on his bent head.

"Stand up."

He got to his feet. There wasn't enough room for him; his shoulders bumped against the wall. This close, the smell of alcohol was like a physical presence between them. Cary took shallow breaths.

"Look at me." Conall's hand caught his face, tilting it up. Cary braced himself, his fists against the wall. The line of Cary's eyebrows mirrored Conall's own.

"Look at you. This face – my face." His father's fingers tightened, digging into Cary's cheek. Cary was on his toes, straining to relieve the pressure of his grip. Conall's mouth twisted. "All you have to do is walk in the room and my failure is written on you for anyone to read – here." He gave Cary's face a shake. "You don't have to say a word."

Cary bit his lips shut, shoving everything out of his head and locking the door. He was nothing. He felt nothing and nothing mattered except he must not make a sound.

Then his father's face caved in and his fingers loosened. He opened his hand on Cary's cheek, soft as a caress. "My son." His fingers rested in the corner of Cary's jaw, where Cary's pulse would have beat if his heart wasn't stopped. "I loved you. I tried." His father's voice was hoarse with unshed tears.

Cary shut his eyes, frozen. Tomorrow Conall wouldn't remember this moment, but he would. He leaned his throbbing cheek against his father's palm. "I'm sorry father," he whispered.

Conall let him go. He stumbled once, crossing the floor. He kicked the crumpled drawings out of his way. "Clean this up. It's lights out."

Cary stayed against the wall after the door shut, pinned there hearing his father's broken voice. *I loved you. I tried.* Finally he got to his knees, gathering up the drawings. They were so torn and crumpled there was no way he could hand them in tomorrow. He balled them up small and stuffed them into the wastebasket. Breathing hurt. There was a red-hot band wrapped around his chest. If he could cry that might relieve the pressure. He hadn't been able to cry since a time he couldn't remember.

He turned out the light. The moon made his window a bright square of silver. He had a wallet of razors wrapped in a hand towel in the drawer of his nightstand. Putting it in his pocket, he climbed out his window onto the roof.

This was his best hiding place. From his second floor gable, he could climb onto the sloping roof above and sit unseen, his feet braced against the slanting shingles. Cary laid his bare arm against his knees, opening and closing his hand. The band around his chest was so tight it felt like it would cut him in half. He had to cut to breathe again.

He did.

Blood to pay.

Blood to wash away.

His father's voice drowned in the sound of his own blood.

Cary fell back, arms spread against the rough shingles while the vast night sky swung over him, cold and black. He was a speck on a dot in an ocean of stars and no one knew him or cared.

He stayed on the roof until he was numb, then lowered himself back into the bowels of the house below.

{Jon}

At bedtime, Jon's father leaned in the doorway. Pete had changed into a faded sweatshirt and jeans, and there was a

{32}

smile on his face. "I missed hearing from you at supper son. How was your day?"

Jon laid aside the comic he'd been reading, avoiding his dad's eyes. "Um. Good."

"Your mom said you had someone over from school to work on a project?"

Jon imagined she had said a few other things about Cary's army jacket and tough appearance. "Yeah. Cary's really good at that class so I'm lucky he said yes."

"Cary's a friend then?" Pete looked hopeful.

Jon let out his breath. "Not really, dad. I think I'm just on my own this year." He smiled like that wasn't a huge deal and his dad didn't need to worry.

Pete came into the room and settled on the edge of his bed. His dad's weight drew Jon down towards him. "Jon, look at me."

Unwillingly, Jon brought his eyes on his father's face.

"I know it's a big deal at school about who's cool and whose group you're in."

Jon's hands closed on the blankets and he looked to the side. He was not ready to have this conversation with his dad, as if Pete even had a clue.

Pete touched his knee. "Son, you already have the most important thing. You know how to *be* a friend. I saw you do it over and over in your old school. You had so many friends there because of the kind of friend you were to them – kind and loyal and good. I was really proud of you then, and I still am."

Jon blinked, ashamed and angry to find his eyes stinging with tears. "Nobody cares about that here dad," he said in a low voice. He slid down and tugged his blankets up to his shoulders, putting his face to the wall.

Pete hesitated, then put his hand on his shoulder. "Can I pray for you tonight?"

Jon shrugged the shoulder under his father's hand. He shut his eyes, listening to his father's prayer. He didn't have anything to say to God that he hadn't said already.

After Pete said "Amen" and "Love you son," Jon could still feel where his hand had been on his shoulder. It was the only good thing he could think of that had happened all day.

{Cary}

Cary's father came into his room in the middle of the night. Cary was awake and up, shoulders against the wall, before Conall was halfway across the carpet.

"I'm taking your mother to the hospital." Conall was a bulky shape in the darkness. "You can take care of yourself for a few days?"

"Yes." Cary saw the outline of his father's shoulder and bent head as Conall turned to go. He couldn't stay silent. "Is she alright? The baby?"

"The baby's coming. They'll be fine." Conall said, as if the strength of his will could make it so. Cary listened to the front door close and the car start. He had difficulty falling back asleep.

8

Partners.

{Cary}

Cary washed and bandaged the cuts before he went to school the next morning, awkwardly pressing the tape down with one hand. Bleeding drew attention. He didn't bother changing the clothes he'd slept in, just put his jacket over everything and locked the empty house.

The north entrance of the school was paved with concrete slabs, and there was a strip of grass between the brick school wall and the wall of the rec centre beside it. This early, Cary had the north doors to himself. The sky was scraped clean, empty and blue. Light fell through the corridor and touched his jacket as he leaned against the brick and fumbled his cigarettes out with one hand.

The north doors opened and closed. Mike's biceps flexed as he cupped his hands to light his own cigarette with a tarnished lighter. He glanced at Cary and his eyebrows lifted. "Care. You look like hell."

Cary didn't bother to respond. He kept his head down and put his cigarette carefully to his lips. His face was tender and faintly shadowed with bruises the shape and size of his father's fingertips.

"I thought you'd be kicking the dust off and gone by now," Mike said.

"Mind your fucking business," Cary growled. His hand didn't work right with the palm cut up like it was and he couldn't get his cigarette to light. "Like you know anything about family."

Mike held up his hands, open to show they were empty except the cigarette dripping ash between his fingers. "Easy there bro."

Cary fumbled the lighter and dropped it with a swear, his palm smarting and burning.

Mike stooped to pick it up off the concrete. He plucked a cigarette from his own pack and lit it, then held out one long arm to offer it to Cary. Cary stood with his fists closed looking at him, looking for the trick. Mike's eyes went over his face, and Cary snatched the cigarette and lighter back and turned away.

Mike shook his head, narrowing his eyes in the sunlight coming straight at them. "Motherfucker," he said thoughtfully.

///

In the crush of the hallway during class change, a voice registered above the din: "Cary—hey Cary!" Jon jogged up to his shoulder, wearing a grin. "Hey, how'd it go last night?"

It took a second to figure out what he wanted. The project. "Find a new partner. I'm dropping the class." Cary didn't look to see the grin fall off Jon's face.

"But... you had all the drawings. You didn't finish?"

"No."

They were in the hallway outside the smoke doors. Jon turned on him, his face wide open, all confusion and hurt.

"Cary, I don't get it. Did something happen?"

Cary clenched his fist in his pocket, so tight the cuts opened. "Fuck off." He pushed past Jon and out the doors for his smoke.

Kids like Jon didn't cross the north doors. Cary smoked in fierce puffs, hunkered against the bricks. Drafting was his best class. Dropping it meant losing a whole grade point—from barely passing to completely failing. He punched his anger down and stuffed it someplace small. He'd have to beg Mr. Ryerson for a pass on this assignment, and work his ass off on the final project. Without a partner.

There was no one he could beg for a miracle in English.

He spent lunch in the library, picking his way through *'Hatchet'* word by word. For 40 minutes he was away, in the wilderness figuring out how to survive. He envied Brian, the character. Brian didn't have anyone watching.

He had to undo his stone face for Drafting. A good apology needed emotion.

"Excuse me sir, I think I made a mistake when I looked at the due date. I'm sorry to ask but could I hand the drafts in next week?" He felt his ears get hot with Mr. Ryerson and what felt like the whole class looking at him.

Mr. Ryerson pushed his reading glasses up to rest on the deep creases in his forehead and rifled through the papers on his desk. "Cary, I'm sure I have your drafts. Yes, here they are." He pulled a stack of drawings out of the pile with an amused smile. They were Jon's sketches. At the top of each sheet, Jon had written 'Jon White' and underneath 'Cary Douglas.'

Cary had trouble keeping the shock out of his face. "I forgot about those. Thank you sir." He went to his drawing table. Jon's eyes found his face and Cary frowned at him. What was his deal?

Cary's cell phone vibrated against his ribs during class. He clapped a hand over it, startled. His parents never called during school. He ducked out of class to listen to the message in the shelter of the entrance to an unused classroom.

"Ciaran, this is your father. Your mother has had the baby. A boy. Liam. They're in ICU. Don't touch anything in my office. Keep the house locked." There was a click— end of message.

Cary lowered the phone, staring at the darkened screen. He had a brother. Was he supposed to feel something about that?

The class bell rang and students rumbled into the hallway. Cary shut the phone, returned it to an inside pocket in his jacket. He saw Jon a second too late to bolt. Jon elbowed his way across the hallway and joined Cary in the concrete alcove. "Hey."

Cary looked at him under his eyebrows.

"I handed in the drawings we did on the bus."

"Why did you do that?" Cary asked.

"I was hoping you would change your mind." Jon tried a smile. "I need you for a partner."

Cary was silent.

"I thought your drafts were really good." There was a question in Jon's face as he looked at Cary.

"I don't have them." Cary looked aside from that open face. He needed to keep Jon from looking at him like that, with questions. Usually the most insulting story worked. This kid needed something different. He touched the cell phone inside his jacket and picked the closest thing to the truth he could make himself say out loud. "My mom went to the hospital last night. She had the baby."

Jon's mouth went round. "Oh wow. Was that supposed to happen?"

"No. Early. They're still there."

Jon's forehead wrinkled. "How many weeks?"

Cary shrugged.

"Bea was early. She's okay. I'm sure your brother is okay." There was a pause while Jon looked at him. "So are we still partners?"

"Looks that way."

Jon smile warmed. "Good. Thanks."

Cary frowned after him as he walked away, thinking maybe that thanks should have gone the other direction.

9

Guts.

{Cary}

Cary stayed up half the night writing a page of something for his book report. He hadn't finished the book. He moved through the empty house like a dreamer.

"Liam. I have a brother," he said in the dark when he couldn't sleep.

He dragged himself to school with his assignment in his backpack and fell asleep in Mrs. Somers' class. The class bell woke him, and he joined the crush of students in the hall.

A little space had cleared for the mugging that was under way: a pack of guys in boarder brands were dumping the contents of their victim's backpack on the floor.

"Seriously, give it back." It was Jon's voice, protesting. One of the guys gave him a careless shove, and Jon's hands slapped against the floor. They tossed Jon's wallet back, bouncing it off the back of his head, and left laughing.

Cary was frozen for a second, buried in the crowd of bystanders. He made his feet turn and walk the other way.

He couldn't afford to care about someone else's problems; he had enough of his own.

///

He was sitting against the sun-warm bricks, thinking about skipping the afternoon when Jon stepped out the north doors. His face lit up when he saw Cary and he headed across the concrete towards him.

"What are you doing here?" Cary's feet scraped on the concrete as he shoved himself up.

Jon's smile wavered. "I just saw you out here and I thought I'd say hi."

Cary was silent. How did this kid not get tired of finding a smile for him?

"So… I brought my English notes from this morning," Jon said. "Mrs. Somers talked about our final essays. Um, while you were sleeping."

Cary frowned. "Thanks."

Mike shoved out the doors, the tattoo rippling on his massive neck. "Care." He sounded like he was chewing rocks. "Gotta dart? I'm out."

Cary silently passed Mike the pack. Mike stared at Jon, standing on the cigarette-littered concrete in his pressed khakis and collared shirt.

Jon gave him his best smile. "Hi, I'm Jon."

Cary's eyebrows lifted. Credit for guts.

A corner of Mike's mouth went up in sardonic amusement. "What're you in for Jon?"

"Pardon?"

"Grade. What grade are you in?"

"Ten. You?"

"Same. I haven't seen you around."

Jon blinked at Mike, a whole head taller than him. "Um... we just moved."

"Aw, that's hell."

Jon crossed his arms. "Yeah." It took him a second to retrieve his smile. "You move around a bit?"

Mike huffed a laugh. "No one keeps me for long. Missed a whole grade—five. That foster uncle beat the shit outta me."

There was a beat of silence. Jon wasn't smiling now. "That's terrible," he said.

Mike narrowed his eyes as he sucked his cigarette to the filter. "That's life Jon. Everybody has to eat shit sometimes. You'll figure that out."

Cary saw Jon run a hand up the back of his head. He had a feeling Jon knew already. "Well, I'm sorry," Jon said.

Mike put his head back and laughed. "Kid, you're killing me." He wiped his eyes with a meaty hand. "Where did you find this one Care?"

Cary gave him a flat look. He didn't give a crap how big Mike was, that was not his name.

Mike was still chuckling as he went back into the school. When he was gone, Cary said, "You don't have to hang around me just because we're partners."

Jon shrugged. His mouth was unhappy. "I needed someplace to be." He looked around the yard like it wasn't what he'd expected. "You wanna come over for supper tonight? We could work on the project, or just, whatever."

When he looked back at Cary, his smile came back, as hopeful as the first day they met.

Maybe that smile was why Cary said, "Sure. Meet you here."

10

No more ouch.

{Cary}

"I'm home!" Jon called as he came in the door. He kicked his shoes to the side and dropped his bag on top of them. "I brought Cary with me."

Jon's mom was in the kitchen looking flushed. "Hi honey, hello Cary." She spared Cary a smile. "I hope you don't mind if supper is kind of thrown together."

Cary shook his head. He had neatly left his shoes in the bottom of the closet and he kept his jacket on.

Jon's littlest sister sat on the kitchen floor, her bare legs splayed in front of her. She waved a long striped sock. "Help please!"

Jon bent to tug it up to her knee. "Soccer tonight?"

His mom nodded. "Can you help set the table?"

"Jonee, where's my shoes?" Bea asked.

"I can set," Cary said. He washed his hands before he filled his arms with plates, navigating around Jon's mom with care.

Cary heard the front door open and Bea squeal, "Daddy!"

A man's voice said, "I'm home! Hey, my little soccer princess."

Cary set the last glass and backed up against the counter.

Jon's dad came into the kitchen with Jon's littlest sister laughing in his arms. He set her down to give Jon's mom a quick kiss on her cheek. "Hey love, smells good." Cary sized him up in a glance: middleweight and fit, Jon's dad had sixty pounds on him, easy.

"Dad, this is Cary," Jon said.

The man came toward him and Cary barely managed to hold his ground. The kitchen suddenly seemed cramped and full of hard edges.

Jon's dad had a smile in his rust-colored beard. "Nice to meet you Cary. I understand you and Jon have a project you're working on?"

"Yes sir."

The man laughed. "We're not in the army here. Just call me Pete."

Cary's eyes widened and he ducked his head in a nod. New rules. He edged behind Jon's shoulder, keeping him close for cover.

Jon's mom flipped grilled cheese sandwiches onto a serving plate and set it on the table with a pot of tomato soup, and everyone scraped their chairs back to sit down. Pete held out his hands to his wife on his right and his son on his left. Bea held out her small hand to Cary, wiggling her fingers. Across the table, Tabitha frowned at him. "Take it silly. We're praying."

Bea's hand was feather-light in Cary's own and damp. Jon's father bowed his head and closed his eyes. Cary bent his head to hide his frown.

"Father, thank you for all the good things you have given us today. Thank you that Cary could be with us tonight. Bless him out of your love. Bless this food to our bodies' use and bless the hands that prepared it. Amen."

"Amen," Bea said and let Cary's hand go.

Cary watched Jon's father out of the corner of his eye. Pete was serving up his daughters' plates. Cary had never seen a father like Jon's except on TV.

Dinner at Jon's house was noisy—Jon's sisters and their chatter seemed to fill every possible opening. Jon's father turned his head from Tabby to Bea, doing his best to listen to both at once. Cary ate quickly, watching Jon's family for the cracks, the signs of danger he knew so well. He saw the shadow of sadness in Jon's mom's face. He saw the tired lines Pete's smile couldn't lift. But something was missing.

"Do you like your 'girled' cheese sand-itches?"

Cary glanced sideways at Bea, startled that she had spoken to him. "Yeah, they're good."

"You should take some ketchup for them." She had to use both hands to lift the bottle. "That's how they're best."

"Thanks." Cary put a little on his plate. For a second he felt hysterical laughter bubbling behind his lips, picturing his mother serving a plate of grilled cheese sandwiches and ketchup for dinner. He glanced at Jon, who met his eyes with a questioning smile. Fear. That's what was missing. No one was afraid.

///

When the meal was over, Cary slipped out to the back porch for a smoke. Tabitha and Bea found him on the step and sat down on either side. Tabby watched him put the cigarette to his lips.

"What are you doing?" she asked.

He glanced sideways at her. "Something for grown-ups only."

"Why?"

"Because it's bad for you."

"Is it bad for you?"

"Yes, but I'm bigger." He saw her put her fingers to her mouth as if holding a cigarette and blow out. He caught her hands in one of his. "Don't do that." He immediately regretted his need for a smoke.

Tabby took her hand back, frowning at him. "I don't think you should either. My mom says cigarettes are dirty."

Cary lifted his shoulders. "Bug off then."

Tabby flounced into the house, but Bea attached herself to Cary's free arm. She unfolded his hand palm up like a fortune teller, the one she had held at supper. "Cary, you're hurt?"

Cary quickly closed his fingers. She concentrated, trying to open them again, one by one. After a moment, Cary let her, watching her serious expression as she ran a finger along the cuts.

"Owie," she said softly. She turned her palm up in his own. Her skin was smooth and perfect. "I scraped my hand when I fell off my bike. Daddy kissed it better and put Band-Aids on." She bent and planted a kiss in the middle of Cary's palm. "There. No more ouch."

Jon swung the back door open. "Bea, time to go, mom's waiting in the van for you."

She scrambled to her feet, throwing Cary a smile. "Bye."

Jon joined him, standing on the grass with his hands in his pockets. "Sorry about that. I didn't know my sisters were out here bugging you."

Cary closed his hand around Bea's kiss, frowning. "That's okay."

Dusk was falling, cool and dim. "How late can you stay?"

Cary looked up at him and realized he didn't want a reason to leave. "There's no one at my house."

Jon smiled. "You want to stay the night? My dad does pancakes Saturday morning."

Cary laughed, and then realized Jon was serious. "Sure."

///

They found Pete up to his elbows in dishes.

"Hey dad, is it okay if Cary sleeps over?"

Pete looked over at Cary, smile lines crinkling around his eyes. "That okay with your parents Cary?"

"I'll see." Cary said. He went into the hall to check his cell phone. No messages. He frowned, then dialed his home number. No answer. He looked at the screen, about to do a search for the number of the hospital when Jon's angry voice stopped him.

"If I have to go to make the pastor's family look good then just say so."

Cary dropped back against the wall in the darkened hallway. All he could see was the lit rectangle of the kitchen entrance.

"It's not a question of appearances Jon." Pete's voice was quiet. "You made a commitment to that worship team and now I want you to follow through."

That answer seemed to make Jon angrier. "The only reason they asked me is because I'm the pastor's kid. They don't even need a guitar player—Curtis is twice is good. I am tired of trying to please everyone for you. If you want me to go, then make me."

Cary held still, measuring the distance between himself and the front door. In the silence he could hear sirens passing on the road behind the house.

"Jon. I'm not going to make you." Pete sounded tired. "Would you at least call Grant to tell him you're not coming."

Jon came in to sight. His face was flushed. He had a fistful of cutlery and a towel in his hands. "Fine," he said. He scraped the cutlery drawer open.

Cary took a breath and stepped into the kitchen. "They say it's okay."

Pete found a smile. It was like watching someone stand up under a weight. "Good. I'll make pancakes tomorrow morning."

Cary helped Jon finish putting the dishes away, stealing quick glances first at him, then at his dad. They moved around each other with unfailing politeness, not speaking, not touching.

When the dishes were done, Cary and Jon headed out of the kitchen. Jon turned back to his dad in the doorway. In a low voice, he said, "I'm sorry I yelled at you."

Pete's shoulders were bowed as he stood at the counter. "Jon, I forgive you. I'm sorry."

Jon tried to laugh. "What for?"

"I wanted this move to be easy for you. It hasn't been." Pete looked at him, his hands spread on the counter. "I wish I could take that for you."

Jon's smile looked forced. "Dad, I'm fine. Okay? You have enough to worry about. Don't worry about me."

From the hall, Cary saw the look Jon's father gave his son as Jon left. Pete's face was naked, pain and longing and love right there in the open for anyone to see. Jon didn't look.

///

"What does your father do?" Cary was on Jon's bed while Jon moved mountains of clothing and books into his closet to make room for Cary to sleep on the floor.

Jon glanced at him, wary. "He's a pastor."

Cary frowned. His mother went to church most Sundays. "Is that like a minister?"

"Yeah. He works for a church."

Cary couldn't imagine what Jon's dad did all day. Were there transactions to be made with God? Did that make Pete like a holy day trader? "So he talks to God a lot or what?"

"Yeah. He preaches on Sundays. And visits people. It's his job to take care of everyone in the church."

Maybe that explained Jon's persistent friendliness. "Is that what you want to do too?"

"No." Jon said it flat. "Bad enough to be a pastor's kid. When I grow up I want to live somewhere no one knows me and no one checks what I do every day for mistakes."

"Huh." Cary watched him sideways. "So you don't believe all that stuff about God."

He saw Jon's face crack with misery before he turned aside to cram the closet doors shut. "Yeah I do. I just don't always get it. Why he lets stuff happen."

Cary looked down at his wrists, crossed with scars under his jacket. His hands closed. "I think he's just not there."

Jon turned. He put his misery away to pay attention to Cary. "Really? You don't believe in God?"

"No." Cary agreed.

"Wow. I've never met anyone who didn't believe in God." Jon looked like he was trying to do a complicated math problem in his head. "I don't think I could do that. Stop believing that he's real. Stuff like space and our bodies…" He opened and closed his fingers. "The world is just too amazing not to be created by someone amazing."

Cary frowned, rubbing his fingertips over the cut inside the curl of his hand. It was already sealed. How did his body know how to do that? "That is weird," he said.

Jon laughed, almost surprising a smile into Cary's face.

"Weird. Thanks a lot."

11

Pete's pancakes.

{Cary}

Cary woke up to the sound of someone passing in the hallway outside his door. He lay still a second, looking up at the pin holes of light coming through an unfamiliar curtain, trying to remember where he was. He untangled himself from the nest of blankets on the floor and got up, fully dressed. He'd gone to sleep in his clothes even though he knew in this house probably nothing would wake him up in the night. He left Jon, still asleep in his bed, to get a smoke.

Jon's dad was in the kitchen, at the stove, dropping pancake batter onto a hot griddle. It sizzled as it hit the pan. He looked around and smiled when he saw Cary. "An early riser. Did you have a good sleep?"

"Yes sir." The shadows under Pete's eyes told Cary not to ask how he slept in return. He didn't know how to have a conversation with a father, so he edged out the door.

Dew bent the grass in Jon's backyard. Cary buttoned his jacket against the chill and lit his smoke, watching the dew steam off the grass, as the sun lifted over the trees.

He tried to imagine what it would be like to be Jon, waking up in this tiny house every day. Safe. Cary drew a breath. He'd been afraid for so long it had started to feel like normal. He felt fifty pounds lighter at Jon's house— like he could leave off the stone face and just be Cary. If he even knew how.

He stubbed his cigarette and went back into the house. Jon was sitting at the kitchen table; his hair stood straight up over his cowlick. He smiled. "Morning."

The kitchen was warm and fragrant with the smell of pancakes. Cary hunched his shoulders, suddenly conscious of the stink of cigarettes in his jacket. "Okay if I shower?"

"These pancakes'll be ready in five minutes." Pete said.

"I'll be fast." Cary said.

Jon took him to find towels and shampoo. "You sleep okay on my floor?" Jon said.

One side of Cary's mouth pulled up. Almost a smile. "Yup, nice and soft."

"So what do you want to do today?"

Cary hesitated. "My mom had the baby yesterday. I think I should go see her."

"Wow, okay." Jon thought a second. "Things might get a little crazy with a new baby at your house. If you need a place to crash, you know you can come here right?"

Cary looked him in the face. He couldn't say the words for how much he would like that. He said, "Sure, thanks."

///

He came out of the bathroom in his shirtsleeves. Jon was lying on the couch watching cartoons. "Dad says pancakes are ready for us."

Cary closed his hands, feeling naked with the open air touching the skin on his arms. "Do you have a sweater I could borrow?"

Jon swung his legs off the couch. "Yeah sure, in my room."

Jon waited for him to pull the sweater on, sitting on top of his desk. "Your scars. What happened?"

Cary checked his arms for what was showing. Just his wrists. "Skate accident. Hit the concrete. Broke to shit." The lie came easy; he'd been doing it his whole life. "There's pins in them now." That part at least was true.

Jon grimaced. "Yikes. I guess that'll teach you not to wear wrist guards."

Tuck and roll, Cary thought. That's what he'd learned that time. His face was hot. "Sorry for swearing."

Jon lifted a shoulder with a laugh. "Like I haven't heard it before."

They went upstairs for pancakes.

12

Pop quiz.

{Cary}

It took two phone calls and a bus ride to find his mother's hospital. The lady at the desk waved him through. Cary tapped on the door of his mother's room and slid inside.

Beverly was in bed, wrapped in a shiny bed coat. She smiled at him and held out her hands. "Sweetheart. I missed you." The hospital smell was stronger when he leaned over to brush her cheeks with his lips, and it put him on edge. It reminded him of things he didn't like to remember.

"Are you okay?" Cary said.

"Of course baby." Her jaw was set under her smile. She would never say different.

Cary still felt naked from being at Jon's house. He needed to get tough. Now. "Where's the baby?"

"He's too small to be in the room with me. The nurses will bring him."

Conall brought the baby, cradling a cloth-wrapped bundle in his arms. Cary had never seen his father's face look so tender.

Conall looked up at Cary and his usual, razor sharp expression returned. "Ciaran. Have you come to meet your brother?"

Cary nodded. The bundle stirred, one tiny hand stretched up and opened. Cary backed up against the foot of the bed. His father drew back the flannel blanket so Cary could see the baby's face. Liam was sleeping with his lips parted.

"Do you want to hold him?" Beverly said. Cary was aware of every shift of his father's expression. He felt like he'd walked into a pop quiz.

"Yes please," he whispered.

He made a cradle with his arms and Conall passed the baby into them. Liam's warm weight settled against Cary's chest. He was soft as the inside of an egg and just as fragile. Cary could see the throb of his heartbeat on top of his head. He sank onto the foot of the bed, staring into his brother's face. Maybe if he hadn't just been at Jon's house it wouldn't have felt like being kicked in the chest.

When the baby had been a bump under his mother's clothing, Cary had been able to hope it would die. Better for them both. He looked up at his mother. She was watching him. A moment's understanding passed between them: Nothing could ever, ever hurt Liam.

Liam stirred, opening his mouth in a yawn—a perfect pink shell. Cary froze.

"I'll take him," Beverly said.

When his arms were empty Cary fled the room. He stood in the waiting room staring blindly at the pastel prints of flowers. He could still feel Liam's warmth against his chest. That soft, floppy body was coming to live at their house. How could he possibly keep his brother safe?

13

How he made peace.

{Cary}

Monday LA class, Cary looked for Jon. He found Jon's bent head a few rows up. He was wearing different clothes: a hooded sweatshirt and black cargo pants. The sweatshirt had a skull on the back, printed in dark red. Cary knew camouflage tactics when he saw them.

Three of the boys who had mugged Jon were in the back row with Cary, flicking elastics at each other and playing games on their cell phones under cover of their desks. Cary held still. At class bell, they flanked Jon and caught him in the hall again.

"Hey Jon, you owe us twenty bucks today."

Jon's face was flat, as close to angry as Cary had seen him. "Actually Todd, I think you're the one who owes me. I'd like my fifty dollars back."

That made them laugh. "Let's make it another fifty." They shoved Jon against the lockers and dumped his backpack on the floor. There was nothing in his wallet, so they pushed him around a bit and left.

Jon's bag lunch was strewn on the hall floor all the way to Cary's feet. Cary put everything back in the paper bag and held it out to Jon, who was shoving his books back into his backpack.

Jon looked up quickly to see who was standing over him.

"Nothing's squished." Cary said.

Jon took it, color rising in his face. "Thanks."

"Coming to the doors for lunch?"

"Sure."

///

Cary stretched his legs on the grass having a smoke while Jon ate his lunch. He glanced sideways at Jon. "You gonna fight those kids?"

Jon crumpled his lunch bag and tossed it. "Are you kidding? No."

Cary frowned. "The one in front, who knew you—"

"Todd." Jon turned his face aside.

"If you got him alone you could take him."

Jon looked like someone had thrown a bag over his head and rubbed out his smile. "I doubt it."

"You could hurt him anyways," Cary said.

Jon shrugged. He wasn't looking at him. "I was hoping I could talk to him. Figure something out."

Cary frowned. "Don't do that. Keep your head down like you are. He'll get bored."

Jon crossed his arms tight, like something was hurting him. "It's been two months."

Anger sparked hot in Cary's chest. Probably cutting Todd open to let his guts fall out wasn't an option. But for a second, he considered it. He looked at Jon's downturned face and wondered why he didn't tell his dad. He didn't ask.

He looked up the narrow alley between the school and the rec center, looking for a change of subject. "I've been thinking about our project."

Jon smiled. It looked like the real thing, if a little dimmed. "Yeah?"

"I thought we could make it so when you look inside, you see some rooms and stuff."

Jon laughed a bit. "How would I get a project that big on the bus to hand in?"

"Maybe 1 to 250 scale?" Cary showed with his hands how wide and tall the model would be.

"Do we have to wait until Mr. Ryerson hands our drafts back?"

"No. Let's start now."

Jon sighed. "I can't tonight. I have youth group at the church. I'm supposed to bring a friend."

That hung in the air a second while Cary waited for him to ask. He didn't ask. "I could come."

Jon looked at him with that open, hopeful face. Cary looked back. It was an easy thing if it made Jon feel better. "Or whatever." Cary said.

"Okay." Jon said. "I don't know if you'll like it."

This seemed funny to Cary. "Why are you supposed to bring a friend then?"

"It's like an outreach event." The word didn't mean anything to Cary. "Pastor Grant said we'll watch a movie about Jesus and then talk about who he is and why that matters."

This actually interested Cary. Conall talked a lot about God and other religions, but Cary had never had a chance to hear from someone else on the topic. "Tell me how to get to your church."

///

Jon's church was a large stucco building in a residential area, stained by decades of rain and snowfall. Cary went in the double front doors the way he saw other kids do. Jon was waiting beside a coat rack, smiling and saying hi to the kids who passed. His smile slipped when he saw Cary. "Hey, you made it."

Jon was still wearing his clothes from school. Cary had changed into the sweater and dress pants his mother made him wear to her church. He watched the other kids in the foyer warily. "You have friends here?"

"Sort of." Jon said.

The double doors opened on a pair of boys. One was carrying a guitar case. The other was Todd. He had a pair of drumsticks in his hands, and he clattered on the handrail and the coatrack as he passed. He flashed Jon a grin and did a drumroll on his forehead before Jon could jerk away. "Hey Whitey."

"Hey Todd, hey Curtis." Jon's voice was distantly friendly, like they hadn't just seen each other at lunch.

Cary watched the boys pass, wishing he had his knife in his pocket. When they were out of earshot, Cary said, "He goes to your church."

Jon nodded. He didn't look at Cary. "So this thing is in the gym; I'll take you there."

Cary stuffed his anger under his stone face, ready for anything.

The gym was dimly lit with lamps and Christmas lights strung from basket to basket. Kids milled around a table of chips and boxes of donuts. Todd was at one end of the juice table, the center of a group of older guys. By unspoken agreement, neither Jon nor Cary went for snacks.

There was a stage with lights and a big screen, and folding chairs set up. Cary found them seats at the end of the back row where he could see everything. An older man was threading his way toward them. Cary braced his legs against the floor. Jon's smile looked strained.

"Hey Pastor Grant."

"Good to see you here Jon." Pastor Grant had trendy, thick-framed glasses and greying hair buzzed up the sides. "You brought a friend?"

"Yup, this is Cary."

Pastor Grant turned a chair around to join them before Cary could figure out if he was supposed to stand and shake hands or what. "Glad you could come Cary. Where do you go to school?"

"Eastglen. With Jon."

"Okay, awesome."

Cary had been trying to interpret Pastor Grant's careful expression. He realized that of the two of them, Jon looked like the punk kid. Cary's church clothes fit right in.

"So Cary, if you have any questions after, Jon's your answer-man."

"Sure, thanks," Cary said.

They sat in silence when Pastor Grant left, watching girls with shiny hair find seats together. Other guys stood around in awkward groups. Lights came up on the stage and everyone took their places in a hurry. Cary thought he recognized Todd behind the drum set. The band played songs Cary didn't know, nothing like the hymns at his mother's church. The kids sang and lifted their hands up. Jon didn't. Sometimes Cary could hear him singing softly, like it was just to himself.

The band was tight and Cary liked the way the woman leading the singing closed her eyes and tipped her head like she was totally, beautifully high. If he hadn't been aware of Todd in the room all the time he might have let his stone face down. When the woman prayed at the end with her hand up, Cary felt something loosen inside. He was sorry when that part was done and Pastor Grant bounded onto the stage.

Pastor Grant talked a lot, and even told some funny stories. Mostly he talked about Jesus and how He healed people and taught people about God. Jesus collected a bunch of working class guys to tramp all over the country with him. Jesus was smart about words like Conall, but so easy to be with crowds followed him and children climbed into his lap.

Cary listened for the part that might explain the way Jon's house was so full of peace, that even when Jon got mad nothing got broke. He thought Jesus sounded like a man who made peace wherever He went.

At the end of the talk Pastor Grant said he wanted to show them a clip from a movie about Jesus' life. "Guys, if Jesus was just a good man who said some good things and lived a good life, I wouldn't be standing up here talking to you. Jesus didn't just talk the talk, he walked the walk all the way to death on a cross. Jesus' death changed everything."

The lights went out and the screen came to life with a dusty road and a crowd in robes and sandals. They were yelling, their faces were twisted with anger. A man's face filled the screen. His eye was swollen shut. After a minute of watching Cary had to conclude it was Jesus. He had no idea why everyone was so angry at him or why his hands were tied.

When they stretched Jesus over a post and stripped him to the waist, Cary stopped breathing. The whip crack bounced against the concrete walls of the gym. They beat Jesus' skin off, then put a massive piece of lumber on his bleeding back. Cary was frozen in his seat. Jesus stumbled up a dusty road under the weight of the crossbeam. By the time the soldiers hammered stakes into Jesus' hands Cary didn't feel anything. Jesus hung on that piece of wood from the nails in his hands. He cried out and he died.

Cary got up and walked out. He kept going until he hit a door that opened to the outside. He didn't have a smoke, so he just sat with his knees drawn up, his mind a blank. When the door behind him opened, he turned his face aside.

Someone joined him on the step. Black cargo pants. Jon White. The gears of Cary's thoughts started to grind again. "What. The hell. Was that." His voice was all flat.

"What… what part?"

Cary still didn't feel anything, just like when his father pulled his belt free of his waistband. "The part where they beat the shit out of Jesus and killed him on a piece of wood."

He saw Jon clench his hands together like he was praying. His knuckles showed white. "I guess Jesus was a threat to them. Politically. And religiously. So the leaders of his people wanted to get rid of him. And that's the way they killed people then. On a cross."

"He was the son of God? That's what Pastor Grant said?"

"Yes."

"He could have stopped them. God could have stopped them."

"Yeah, that's true. Jesus chose to come and die that way. To get to us, that had to happen."

Feeling returned. Anger prickled like a foot that had fallen asleep. "You let your sisters watch that?"

"No."

"But that's what you believe—that's the story they'll hear when they grow up. Jesus dying like that."

"That's what really happened."

Cary turned on him. "I know it's *real.* I don't know why you would – make a religion out of it. I would rather believe in nothing."

Jon's forehead creased. He was white-faced in the twilight. "Cary, that's not how the story ends. Jesus didn't stay dead—he rose again. He's alive."

Cary looked for the lie. Jon believed that. "That's a kids' story Jon. Dead is dead." He got up and walked to the bus stop.

14

Love your enemies.

{Jon}

When Cary was gone, Jon put his face on his knees. The things Cary said stuck in his chest. Whatever Pastor Grant said, Jon didn't have answers. Or maybe his answers didn't work anymore because he was too angry to believe them. He didn't know why Jesus' good life was rewarded with a brutal death and he had no idea why Jesus didn't seem to care that Todd was everywhere, on him all the time. When Jon's family moved he had believed Jesus would listen to his prayers for friends and give him a good year in a new place.

But here he was, on the steps of his dad's church, losing his only friend over a stupid youth group event. Jon took a deep breath, fighting tears. He would not cry at church. He was the pastor's son.

He went to find his dad. Pete's office door was closed. Jon was about to knock when he heard raised voices–one yelling, and his father's, quiet and even as he answered. Jon stepped back from the door and sat on a pew in the darkened church foyer to wait.

After a few minutes, Pete's door opened and a stocky man in a crisp white dress shirt stormed out. Jon knew the names of everyone in the church, so he recognized Todd's dad even though he'd never had the pleasure of meeting him. They seemed to have quite a bit in common.

Jon went and tapped on his father's open door. Pete glanced up and offered him a smile that didn't make it to his eyes. "Hey, how'd it go tonight?"

"I'm ready to go home."

"Okay. Just let me send an email and I'll be right with you." Pete glanced behind Jon like he was missing something. "Does Cary not need a ride home?"

"No," Jon said.

Pete hesitated, then shut his laptop without typing a word. "What happened?"

Jon hunched his shoulders. "He was upset. Grant showed a clip with Jesus dying and Cary left."

"Did you have a chance to talk with him after?"

"Yeah I gave him all the answers I knew." That snapped with more of his anger than he had intended for his dad to hear. Pete was quiet, looking at him.

Jon turned his face aside, afraid his dad would see all the things he wasn't telling him. "So I'll just get my things and we can go?"

Pete was quiet. He always saw too much. "Yeah," he said. "I'm ready when you are Jon."

///

Curtis was still in the gym, packing up his guitar and cords when Jon came in to pick up his Bible and backpack. When he saw Jon come over, he vaulted off the stage, shaking his hair off his face. "Hey Jon, missed you at worship practice."

Jon held his Bible against his chest like a shield. "Sorry, something came up." It wasn't Curtis' fault his little brother was an asshole. In fact, he seemed oblivious to Todd.

Curtis stood loosely, with his hands in his pockets. "I wanted to ask you—can you play for Friday night with me? Grant asked me to put together a band for the Jr. High event and everyone's bailing on me."

"You want another guitar?" Hope fluttered in Jon's chest. It was one thing for Grant to pay attention to him— he was the youth pastor, he had to. Curtis didn't have to, and Jon had been trying to make friends his own age at youth group for months.

"I can play bass or keys, whatever," Curtis said.

"Me too," Jon said.

Curtis smiled. "Cool. So you're in?"

Jon tried not to let how much it mattered show in his face. "Who's your drummer?"

Curtis rolled his eyes. "No idea—Todd has football. You know someone?"

"Nope, sorry." He couldn't keep the grin off his face.

"Practice is Wednesday, that work?"

"Totally," Jon said.

"Very cool. See you then."

Jon walked out of the gymnasium feeling a foot taller.

///

That evening, Jon sat cross-legged on his bed with his Bible open in front of him, reading it for the first time in weeks. He was in Luke, the part where Jesus sat on a hill teaching a crowd about the way things are in God's kingdom. Jesus' words practically jumped off the page:

"But I tell you who hear me, love your enemies. Do good to those who hate you, bless those who curse you, pray for those who mistreat you... Then your reward will be great and you will be children of the Most High because he is kind to the ungrateful and wicked. Be merciful as your Father is merciful." (Luke 6:27-28, 35b-36)

It sounded like Jesus wanted him to be Todd's punching bag. The little bubble of happiness he'd been riding since Curtis talked to him at youth group burst. How could he ever pray for Todd? He doubted Jesus meant for him to pray that Todd would suffer a terrible accident and never come back to school.

Jon pushed the Bible aside and lay back with his arm slung over his face. The house was quiet; his sisters were already in bed. He pictured his room the way it was and Jesus there, in the flesh. This had been one of his favourite ways to pray when he had prayed every day, throughout the day.

Jesus was leaning against his desk, looking at him with a smile like a question in his face. His feet were bare, and his toes were long and brown.

Jon drew in his breath. He hadn't expected to be afraid to see Jesus. And it felt like really seeing Jesus, not just pretending he was there.

"Hey," Jon said. What was there to say, anyways? Jesus had been there for everything; he already knew about Todd and Cary and youth group.

"Jon." Jesus said. His voice was warm, like he was glad to see him. "I love when you share your stories with me."

Jon lifted a shoulder. "No good stories to tell. You know that."

Jesus' hand rested on the edge of the desk. His scar was white against his brown skin. "You could tell me your bad stories."

Jon made his mouth lift with a smile. "Thanks for sending Curtis to me tonight. I've wanted to make friends with him ever since we came to this church."

Jesus was quiet.

It was Jon's imagination—he could pretend Jesus didn't say anything.

But Jesus words still hummed in his ears: "What about Todd?"

"What about Todd?" Jon finally responded.

"I gave you Todd," Jesus said.

Jon's whole body tensed and he turned his face away. "This is why we're not talking. You say things like that." Humiliation and anger made his skin prickle when he remembered the things Todd said to him when he pushed him around. "Does it make you happy that I'm not happy?" he asked Jesus.

"No," Jesus said. "I wish you knew me better than that Jon." He was looking Jon in the face; Jon couldn't hold His eyes.

"I thought I did," Jon said. He had loved Jesus so wholeheartedly it hurt him now to remember. He had given Jesus everything, completely trusting that Jesus would take care of him.

And Jesus gave him Todd.

Jon pushed the picture with Jesus in it aside and sat up, crossing his arms over the place that hurt. He still felt Jesus close, and that rubbed like sandpaper on his skin.

"Please just leave me alone," he said softly. And he wished he could believe Jesus would listen and take his painful, nonsense way of loving somewhere else.

///

Jon was deep in a stack of comic books when his father tapped on his open door.

"Ready for bed?"

Jon nodded and slid under the covers.

"Can I pray for you son?"

The last thing Jon wanted was to waste any more words on the person who gave him Todd. "If you want," he said, without looking at his dad.

Jon felt the weight of his father settling on the side of his bed and in spite of himself, he remembered all the nights Pete's prayers had chased away monsters and he had gone to sleep knowing nothing bad would happen to him because his father loved him.

"Is there anything in particular you want me to pray for tonight?"

Jon made his mouth smile but he couldn't look Pete in the face. "Curtis asked me to play for worship Friday. So that's cool."

The lines in Pete's face lifted with his smile. "That's an answer to prayer."

Jon could feel his dad's eyes on his face. He picked at the blanket on his lap. "What did Mr. Klassen want?"

Pete tried to speak lightly. "He's a board member." Jon understood that meant that he was like Pete's boss. "There are some things he's not happy about."

"Things about you?"

Pete met Jon's frown with a wry smile. "Well I'm not perfect."

Jon looked aside, anger bubbling in his gut. "You've done everything for this church. If you're working so hard to take care of God's people, he should make your job easier."

Pete laughed softly. "We've had that conversation."

Jon glared at his blankets. He had an idea of how that conversation had ended. "I just don't get why crappy things happen when all you want to do is serve God and do the right thing. That doesn't make any sense."

Pete bent his head. "I guess I don't... try to make things make sense anymore. God promised to work all things for our good, but he's God and his way of working is way beyond me."

Jon stared at him. He'd been hoping when he was as old as his father he'd have better answers.

"There's good parts though, right?" Pete asked. He put his hand on Jon's. It was still big enough for Jon's hand to fit inside. "I hang onto the signs that say God is

{72}

still working, still listening. Coming home to you and the girls—you are my good part right now, Jon." He smiled into Jon's face and Jon was overwhelmed by how warm and open Pete was, compared to how Jon felt inside.

Pete bowed his head to pray and addressed God as their Heavenly Father. Jon kept his eyes open and his heart shut.

15

If he could carry it.

{Cary}

Cary couldn't fall asleep that night. Liam was home. He listened to the sound of his brother crying and his parents talking and walking back and forth in the hall. He could feel tension in the air like a thread about to snap. Finally he pulled the blanket off his bed and climbed out his window.

It was quiet on the roof—nothing but wind in the leaves and the distant hush of traffic. He lay stretched under the star pricked sky, looking up. He thought of the man, arms stretched out on a cross as he died.

From the way Jon was so unused to hurt, Cary had expected a Jesus with no marks on him. Cary could have watched that Jesus live his perfect life and float up to the clouds without feeling anything. A God like that had nothing to do with him.

The image of Jesus carrying that massive hunk of wood on his bloody back glowed hot and red behind his eyes. How could he have chosen that? Why would he?

Cary heard a disturbance in the house. He dropped back through his window and crouched in his darkened room, listening. The baby was crying again. Light footsteps went up the hall and in a moment the crying stopped. Cary crept to Liam's room and pushed open the door.

His mother was in the rocking chair giving Liam a bottle. The shadows under her eyes were so dark they looked like bruises.

"Do you want me to feed him?" Cary asked.

Her eyes closed as she nodded. "You were never this difficult."

Cary carefully took Liam into his arms. Liam gave a squawk as the bottle nipple popped out. Cary nudged the bottle back into his mouth. "It's okay, here you go."

Beverly got to her feet with difficulty. "Don't forget to burp him or he'll just wake up again."

"Okay," Cary said. "Go back to bed mom. Have a good sleep."

She turned in the doorway, a pale shape in her housecoat. "Be careful around your father tomorrow. You know how he gets when he's stressed."

Cary watched her go, his chest tightening. He looked back down at his brother, trying to draw a breath. Liam had his eyes open, frowning as he sucked. Cary found a smile.

"Hey. Why the frowny face?" Liam's eyes tracked up to Cary's face, sucking more intently. Cary touched the crease in Liam's forehead with a finger. "Your bottle is here. I'm here. You're safe."

Liam ate until he fell back asleep, milk dribbling from his mouth. Cary put him on his shoulder and rubbed his tiny back up and down, up and down. Liam burped and sighed. His breath was warm on Cary's neck.

The realization grew on him gradually, looming up in the dark. There was a thing he could do to keep Liam safe. If he was strong enough to pick it up and carry it.

He laid Liam, sleeping, in his crib, then went downstairs to his father's study. Books—his father's most precious belongings—lined the walls. He lit a fire in the grate, listening for movement in the hall. When the fire was hot, Cary pulled a stack of leather-bound volumes off his father's bookshelf and threw them on the fire. When they didn't burn fast enough, he used the poker to flip them open so the greedy flames could lick the pages.

He checked that the flue was open in the fireplace and crept back upstairs and into his bed, leaving the books to burn. He was shaking. He buried his face in his pillow. Seven hours until his father went into his study to get ready for school. Maybe fifteen if his briefcase was still in the car and he just went straight to the university. Then, if it was enough, the tension would snap and leave the air in the house loose and easy again.

Cary laid awake a long time before getting up and helping himself to his mother's sleeping pills. Then he slept like a dead man.

16

Cary puts it all together.

{Jon}

The next morning Todd cornered Jon in the locker room after gym class. "Hey Whitey—looking good out there. Must be tough having to work twice as hard to keep up with the rest of the girls."

Todd's friends laughed. Jon hunched his shoulders and kept shoving his gym clothes into his locker.

Todd whipped him around with a hand on his arm. "Hey faggot, I'm talking to you."

Jon's hands made fists against his legs. "So? What do you want?"

Todd gave him a shove, grinning. "Why don't you show me what you've got?"

For a second Jon wanted to smash Todd's face in. Curtis and Pete and Jesus in his bedroom held him against the lockers. "I'm not going to fight you Todd. Maybe you should get a hobby."

That was how, ten minutes later, the gym teacher found Jon wedged into one of the lockers with a bloody nose.

"White," the man barked. "Get outta there—it's time for class."

Jon stumbled free, putting a hand under his nose to catch the bleeding. "Okay, I'm going," he said thickly.

The man looked more closely at him. "Aw for Christ sake. I suppose you need to see the nurse."

Jon was edging past him to get to the door. "No thank you, I'm fine."

The halls were empty; class had already started. Jon hurried to the nearest washroom and bent over the sink, pinching the bridge of his nose hard enough to hurt. The bleeding slowed and stopped. He rinsed his face and straightened, looking at himself in the mirror. There was a cut above his eyebrow where his face hit the locker room bench. He didn't think anyone who didn't know to look would notice.

He shivered, sick with anger and fear that Todd would corner him again. He had forty minutes until his next class. He went to the north doors.

///

Cary was there in his faded army jacket, hunkered against the warm brick of the school. Jon put his shoulders against the brick a little distance away. He crossed his arms, fixing his eyes on the cigarette strewn concrete.

"Does smoking make you feel better?" Jon asked.

"Yuh," Cary said.

"Do you think I could get a cigarette off you?"

Cary seemed to absorb that, looking at him. He took his pack of smokes out of his jacket and got to his feet. "There's blood on your shirt."

Jon couldn't look at him. "Todd cornered me after gym."

Cary lit him a cigarette and passed it to him. Jon drew on it and coughed, then drew deeper and coughed again. He couldn't make his hands stop shaking.

"You don't want to report that?" Cary asked.

Jon saw his dad's warm, open face when he said, *You are my good part right now Jon,* and felt his tongue freeze to the roof of his mouth. He looked at Cary, silent and desperate.

Everything went out of Cary's face, diving deep. "'Kay," Cary said.

Jon lowered himself onto the concrete and Cary hunkered beside him without saying anything or doing anything or even looking at him. That helped. After a few more sips on the cigarette, Jon felt lifted a little above himself and able to speak again.

"Last night, I asked my dad about why… why crap happens." He knuckled his unbruised eye. It was stinging and he told himself it was the smoke. "He said that God is working everything for our good even if we can't see how. He really believes that." His throat closed a moment and he spread his hand over his face. His fingers were cool against the heat of his bruise. "I wanted to—I thought I could be the son he wanted, no mistakes. I lie every day and I can't—Cary I can't—"

His words caught, tripping over a sob tearing out of his chest. He hadn't meant to cry and then he couldn't stop. Cary crouched beside him, catching each word the way Jon had cupped his hands in the locker to catch his own blood.

When it was over, Jon wiped his face, humiliated. "Crap. At least I didn't cry like this for Todd."

"That won't happen again," Cary said. His voice was as hard as the look on his face.

Afterward, Jon wished he had never opened his mouth so Cary wouldn't have made such a promise.

///

In English class, Todd came in with his usual swagger, the usual friends and took his usual seat. Jon didn't hear a word of Mrs. Somers' lecture. He sat, rigid with tension in his seat, as the minute hand crawled around the clock face until the class bell rang.

Todd caught him in the jostle of students in the hallway, blocking Jon's escape. He was laughing, high on the morning. "Hey, who let the runt out?"

Someone planted a hand on Jon's chest and shoved him against the lockers. It was Cary, launching himself at Todd. Jon's breath was gone. Todd's friends fell back and the crowd opened for Todd to hit the floor flat on his back. Cary was on him before Todd quit skidding.

In the roar of crowd noise, Jon could still hear the thick smack of Cary's fists hitting Todd's face. It didn't take a minute—Cary jerked Todd's stunned, bleeding face toward him. "There's more where that came from." He dropped Todd on the floor and got off his chest.

A disappointed noise rippled through the hallway. It had ended too soon. Todd got to his hands and knees, spitting blood, then stood.

"Douglas," he called warningly after Cary.

Cary turned and Jon heard a little *'snick'* he didn't recognize. Cary had a knife open in his hand. The four-inch blade looked deadly in a hallway packed with warm bodies. Cary didn't say anything, just gave Todd a black look. Todd turned and pushed through the ring of onlookers. His friends were gone, he ran after them down the hall.

Cary folded the knife and made it disappear in his jacket. He joined Jon, ducking his head at the way kids looked wide-eyed at him as they passed. "You got your lunch?" he asked.

Jon nodded, swallowing.

"Then let's go."

///

Jon wasn't hungry. He sat on the grass outside the north doors with his ham sandwich open in front of him and his stomach doing flips. He finally crumpled the sandwich into its wrapper and threw it in the garbage. Cary watched him. There was nothing in Cary's face today; he was hard and flat as stone. Jon thought he wasn't angry with him anymore but he couldn't really tell.

"Cary, I don't think you should have done that."

Cary shrugged. His fingers were busy plucking up the grass in front of him blade by blade. "It's done. You think he'll touch you again?"

"I think he'll get you in trouble."

"Like how?" That careful look was the only thing Jon could read.

"Like get you suspended for pulling your knife."

Cary laughed. It was the first laugh Jon had ever heard from him. Cary covered his mouth as if he wanted to wipe it off when he was done. "Jon, you're so…" Cary's voice trailed off and he shook his head. A fragment of the smile was still in the corner of his mouth. "Whatever. I don't care about getting suspended. Quit worrying about it."

Jon was quiet a bit. This was exactly the kind of trouble he had wanted to protect his dad from. "What would you say? If they ask you why you did it?"

"I didn't like his fucking face."

Jon shot him a surprised look. Cary's voice had changed, like he was doing an imitation of someone angry and careless. There was no anger in his face. Cary ripped up a whole handful of grass and tossed it in the gravel. "Anyways, I think I'm taking a couple days off. Family stuff."

Mike came out the doors, his eyes bright with amusement. "Care—they're calling your name in there. Better make tracks."

Cary got to his feet, knocking grass off his pants with a quick motion of his hand. He went into the school without a word. Jon watched him go, then found Mike watching him. Mike's mouth twisted like the joke was on him. "Someone's looking for trouble today," Mike said.

Jon looked away. His stomach triple flipped and he thought he might puke.

He should have been relieved. Todd was off his back and he didn't have to tell his dad, or face Todd and Mr. Klassen in the principal's office. He could let it all slide into the past as if it had never happened.

Jon was barely on speaking terms with God but his sense of right and wrong was keen as it had ever been. He was gripped with the conviction that if he kept this to himself and let Cary walk into a suspension that would be wrong.

He took out his cellphone and called his dad.

The church secretary was distant and polite. Jon waited on hold for his dad to pick up. By the time Pete said "Hello?" he was out of breath, like he'd been running.

"Dad, I think I'm in trouble, and I don't know what to do."

"Jon, are you calling from school? Is everything okay?"

Jon shut his eyes. He felt like he'd been stuffed in the locker again and there wasn't any air to breathe. He had to tell his dad but he couldn't over the phone. "Can you come? Pick me up?"

There was barely a pause for thought. "I'll be there in fifteen minutes," Pete said.

///

Jon leaned against the radiator inside the school's main entrance, watching for his dad's car to pull into the parking lot. Lunch hour was over, and the hallways were empty. Jon's science class with its buzzing fluorescents seemed a long way away. He heard a man's voice approaching behind him and he glanced over his shoulder.

There was Cary, propelled in front of a larger man with dark hair like him. The man was leaning over to speak low, one hand gripping the back of Cary's neck.

"You pulled me out of class for that?" Cary had no jacket. His shoulders were hunched like he wanted to duck and run.

As they went out the doors, Mr. Douglas' gaze went over Jon like he wasn't there. His face was hard and closed, like Cary's.

Jon watched them cross the parking lot to a shiny BMW. Cary's father jerked open the rear door. Cary was a moment too slow, and his father took him by the front of his shirt and shoved him into the backseat of the car. Jon was on his feet. He saw Cary wrap his arms around his head as he went down, narrowly missing striking his head on the frame of the car. His father leaned in through the open door and for a moment Jon couldn't comprehend what was happening. His dad leaned in like that to help the girls buckle into their car seats. Cary's father swung his fist and the car rocked. His shoulders moved with the same pounding rhythm Cary used on Todd.

Jon's mouth opened but he couldn't make a sound. He fumbled with the door handle, pressing his hand flat on the glass. That was Cary in there, he couldn't see it but he was sure those fists were connecting with Cary in the back seat.

Cary's father slammed the rear door shut and went around to the driver's side. Jon put his hands over his mouth. There was nothing he could do. The BMW peeled out of the parking lot and was gone.

17

The Jon he knew.

{Pete}

Pete could see his son pacing on the school steps as soon as he turned into the parking lot. Jon came towards the car and swung inside before Pete could get out.

"I signed out sick." Jon said. His face was a thunderhead. Pete registered the smell of cigarettes.

"Are you sick?"

"I had a nosebleed." Jon plucked his shirt. There was blood on the front. "I need to change."

"Okay." Pete pulled away from the curb, anger prickling his skin. It was like this a lot now with Jon: anger and fear and love all mixed up and lodged deep. "I got a call from Rob Klassen before I left. He said you and Cary were involved in a fight this morning, and Cary threatened his son with a knife. Is that true?"

"Did he mention the part where Todd gave me a bloody nose and crammed me into a locker?"

Pete's hands tightened on the steering wheel. "No, he didn't." They were at a red light. Pete looked over at his son. Jon had his fists clenched and his arms crossed. His face was turned away but Pete could hear from his breathing that he was crying.

Father have mercy, Pete prayed, taking a breath. *I don't know what to do here.*

That moment made it possible to speak without anger. "Have you had lunch yet?"

Jon slapped tears out of his eyes. "I couldn't eat."

"Let's get a burger."

///

Pete ordered for them both. Jon stared up at the Dairy Queen menu boards with his arms tightly crossed, not speaking. Pete eyed the skull on the back of Jon's hooded sweatshirt as they made their way to a table. The Jon he knew was still inside that sweater, right? How was it possible that a few months could have changed his son beyond recognition?

At the table Jon picked at his food, putting his eyes on his fries or the kids coming in the door—anywhere but Pete's face.

"Jon, can you start from the beginning?"

Jon shot him a look. His eyes were red-rimmed and his freckles stood out on his white face.

"What happened today?" Pete asked.

"It was my fault." Jon's fingers tore one of his fries into smaller and smaller pieces. "Cary was fighting Todd because I wouldn't. Because Todd wouldn't leave me alone."

Pete tried to catch his eyes. "Todd has been bullying you?"

Jon nodded. "Him and his friends. Since we moved."

Pete's mouth opened but for a moment no sound came out. "Jon—why didn't you tell us?"

Jon made himself small inside his sweater. "I didn't want to stress you out. I wanted you and mom to be happy and to think that I was happy."

Pete sat back, angry with himself. He should have known this was more than a rough transition to a new school. He should have seen something was really wrong. Pete asked the questions he used when he counselled people in his office, but anger churned away in his gut. "Was he just calling you names, or has he been physically hurting you?"

"Both." Jon didn't look at his dad. The bruise above his eyebrow looked green in the bright restaurant lighting. "He stuck me in a locker today. Hit me a bunch. Called me a faggot."

The pieces snapped together for Pete. The sick days. The time Jon came home with a black eye and said it happened in gym class. For a moment Pete's anger flared so white-hot he could have destroyed the kid who had done this to his son. It took all his strength to wrestle that anger into submission.

"Is that how the fight started?"

"No." Jon sheltered his face with his hands like the light was too bright above their table. "Cary wasn't there. He saw the blood after. I shouldn't have said anything. I don't know why he took it up except that he knew that I wouldn't." A shudder went through Jon's body and he went silent. When his voice finally came out, it was pressed with strain.

"We have LA class together—Cary and me, and Todd. That's how I lost my birthday money—Todd stole it after class a couple weeks ago. Today Todd started in like normal and Cary knocked him down. He punched him a couple times and let him go. Just to make a point. But Todd wouldn't give it up. He kept coming. So Cary pulled his knife. He just stood there holding it and Todd ran." There was a long silence. "That's it." Jon finished in a whisper.

Pete closed his eyes. He had prayed every day for good friends for Jon. This was so far from what he had in mind. He spoke without thinking, right out of his anger and fear. "Jon, Cary could be expelled."

"I know."

"The Klassen's could press charges; he could be arrested."

"I know!" Jon snapped, the tendons standing out on his neck. "That's why I'm telling you this—that's not what he should get for what he did. It wasn't his fight, it was my fight."

"It was his knife. Someone could have been really hurt."

Jon covered his face with his hands. Pete took a breath. This wasn't just anyone who had come to him for counselling; this was his only son. He held onto his awareness of Jesus' presence like a lifeline. "I have a meeting with your principal tomorrow morning."

Jon dropped his hands, clenched into fists. "You can tell her it wasn't Cary's fault."

"Jon, it's about you." Pete met his eyes, afraid he would see Jon lie. "Is there anything she's going to tell me that I haven't heard yet?"

"Like what?" Jon looked guarded.

"Have you been using drugs?"

Jon drew back. "No."

"Have you been around other kids while they were using drugs or dealing drugs?"

Jon frowned at him. "Dad, I haven't. Is Todd saying that about me?"

Pete lifted his hands, exasperated. "Jon, I can smell the cigarettes on you."

Jon fell silent, looking at him.

"Is there anything else I need to know?"

"No. I had one smoke. That's all. If you want to search my backpack, go ahead."

Pete searched his son's closed, angry face. He used to feel sorry for parents of kids like Cary. "I'm not going to search your backpack. I'm just... afraid for you. When we moved you left behind a really positive friend group. Now except for Cary, I don't know who you spend your time with."

Jon crossed his arms, glaring at the soft serve ice cream ad on the wall. "Except for Cary, there's no one I spend time with. Your youth group wouldn't give me the time of day if I was lying by the side of the road." He jabbed a finger at the bruise over his eye. "Okay? Literally. So I'm sorry if you're disappointed that I picked a friend who smokes and who's not a Christian, but there is no one I'd rather have at my back than Cary."

"Did Cary give you that cigarette?" Pete asked.

Jon didn't say anything. His mouth was a flat, miserable line.

Pete touched his thumb to the place on his index finger that had been stained yellow for years. He sighed.

"Jon, I'm not—disappointed that you're friends with someone who's not a Christian. I wasn't a Christian when I was your age." He could see from Jon's face that this had slipped his mind. "If I didn't have friends who were Christians—who were different than I was—I don't know where I'd be. But I hope you remember that you're different than Cary. You have a hope and a reason to live, and that attracts people to you. If you quit looking any different and your friends can't see Jesus through you, what kind of friend are you really to them?"

Pete realized he was preaching and shut up. Jon was jigging his knee up and down, focused deep inside himself. Something was wrong, out of joint and hurting him, and Pete was certain their conversation hadn't touched that part yet. He wished for a way to launch his words over Jon's defenses so they could hit him right in the heart. But all he could do was say the thing he most wanted Jon to hear and hope it stuck.

"Jon, I love you. I don't want you to quit telling me things. I would rather know the crappy truth than have you lie to me."

"I told you the truth," Jon said. "Will you talk to my principal?"

Pete hesitated, hearing Rob Klassen screaming in his ear over the phone just half an hour ago.

"Please dad." Jon's voice broke.

"Yes," Pete said. "I will."

"Thank you." Jon pressed his hand over his eyes before tears could fall. "This has been such a horrible year."

If Pete could have transfused joy and confidence back into Jon with his own blood he would have done it. "I wish things had been different for you."

Jon got up abruptly. "I guess it could be worse." He dumped his meal in the garbage. When he came back his face was closed and shadowed with something like shame. He waited with his arms crossed and his body turned aside. "I can't talk about this anymore. Thanks for lunch."

18

The basement (red).

{Cary}

The basement of Cary's house was not finished. There was one room sketched in with drywall, but the rest stretched open and dim, with plastic draping from the ceiling to the floor. The floor was bare concrete, cool and rough against Cary's forehead.

The kiss of a lit match and the crinkle of a cigarette lighting seemed loud in the silence.

"Get up Ciaran."

Cary found his hands, and spread them on the concrete to obey his father. He couldn't get up any further than his knees. Conall was limp and damp with sweat, sitting on the bottom step, smoking. Cary dragged his shirt over his skin, tasting blood and his father's cigarette. He was shaking—deep shock shakes he couldn't control. Adrenaline had left him a long time ago.

Conall folded his belt into four in his hands. "I wanted to start new with you, boy." There was no anger left in his voice. He thumbed sweat out of his eye, leaving a smear of blood on his temple. "I wish I knew how to start new."

There was one thing left to finish it. Cary made spit with his mouth and said, "I'm sorry, Father."

Conall looked at him from under his eyebrows. "If I didn't know better, I would have said you wanted me to do that."

Cary tipped against the drywall, closing his eyes. He was going to black out in a minute. His throat made a soft sound he couldn't help. He wanted black.

His father's feet scraped the concrete and Cary's eyes opened and he swayed back. Conall was right in front of him, huge and dark. His father's arms closed around him and he was lifted off the floor. Black.

He came to on the stairs, rocking in his father's arms in time to his father's climbing feet. The walls rippled like falling water. The water was red. Cary shut his eyes, opened them. Everything was red; there was blood running down the walls and down the steps.

He was red, shaking like a flame. Every step shook him; one more step and he would crush in a mess of no more Cary—just pain pain pain.

///

It was night. The sky rippled with stars, so close Cary thought he could feel the cool touch of their light on his skin. He was lying in a grassland under the vast curtain of the night sky.

There was a campfire. He turned his face towards its heat as a log collapsed with a sigh and a cloud of sparks went up into the night.

A figure crouched on the other side of the flames. His eyes found Cary, the firelight reflecting gold in their depths. Cary held still, heart hammering. He couldn't make his body get up and run.

The man looked away, using a stick of kindling to stir up the fire. The flames seemed to lick Cary's skin and he curled with a cry, drawing his arms over his head to press the pain out. But it ate the starlight and the fire and everything he knew about himself with a red mouth full of knives.

"Cary."

That was his name. He came through the teeth in shreds, gasping. The man was watching him with his face tipped, firelight and shadow flickering across his expression. It was quiet here.

Cary's throat hurt. "I'm thirsty."

The man stood and Cary was afraid.

"Don't," Cary begged. "Don't send me back."

The night wrapped around him like a great sheet of cloth, soft and cool as satin.

///

Cary woke up once. He was lying on top of his blankets in his clothes, and he didn't know what day it was. Sunlight fell through his window and bounced off the water in the glass beside his bed.

He dragged himself up and reached for the glass. He drank it all, whimpering when the water spilled and ran down onto the welts on his chest.

He had one clear thought: water made blood. He needed blood to mend, make scars, get up again. He dropped back onto the bed and fell back out of consciousness.

TWO

Where can I go from your Spirit?
Where can I flee from your presence?
If I say, "Surely the darkness will hide me
And the light become night around me,"
Even the darkness will not be dark to you.

(Psalm 139:7, 11-12)

1

Darkness.

{Jon}

Jon was silent at dinnertime. Family conversation washed around him like a river around a stone. He got up, cleared his dishes, and ran hot, soapy water into the sink, barely hearing the clamour of his sisters at the table behind him. His ears were full of the silence of the school hallway between classes, the hiss of the radiator and the sound of Cary's footsteps hurrying in front of his father.

His stomach was a sick, hard knot. He should never have let Cary fight his fight for him. He should have hit Todd back. At the very least he should have tattled to the principal—the shame of that would have been less than the shame he was feeling now. He'd told his dad too late.

When he was finished the dishes he went to his room without speaking to his family. He shut the door and sat at his desk, opening a schoolbook at random. Math. He sat with his pencil in his hand and couldn't write a single sum. Shutting his eyes, he saw Cary without his jacket. He saw Cary put his arms up as he fell into the car. He saw the car rock and the door slam shut.

Jon's door opened. "Jonee?" Bea hung onto the handle, a picture book stuck under her arm.

"Out Bea," Jon said.

"I wanted you to read my bedtime story to me."

"I have homework. Get out."

She came in, looking around his arm at his desk. "What are you doing?"

He slapped his notebook shut and grabbed her under her arms. Swinging her over his doorway, he dropped her back in the hall. "Get the fuck outta my room!"

He slammed the door on her white face and trembling lip.

That felt good for half a second, and then he had to listen to her crying for the next ten minutes. Hunched with tension, he waited for his dad to come speak to him. No one came.

Jon heard his mother finally settle Bea, and the rise and fall of her voice reading their bedtime story came through the wall between their rooms. When it got quiet, Jon went down the hall to his sisters' room.

He knocked, watching his shadow stretch over the floor as the door swung open. "Bea?"

"She doesn't want to talk to you," Tabby said.

In the silence, Jon heard a little sniffle from Bea's bed.

"I'm sorry," he said.

"Why are you so mad at me?" Her voice was still watery with tears.

Jon put his shoulder against the doorframe and shut his eyes a second. "I'm not mad at you."

"Who are you mad at then?"

Jon didn't say anything.

Bea turned her face to him. "Will you give me a night-night kiss?"

Jon came into the room, knelt by her bed and kissed her cheek the way he had when she was much smaller. When he was much smaller. She was soft and smelled like lotion. Bea took hold of a handful of hair behind his ears and pulled his forehead against hers. "You scared me Jonee. I was scared."

Jon gently opened her fingers. "I'm sorry Bea. That was very wrong of me to scare you."

"Okay." She nestled into her pillows with her arms around Mr. Rabbit. "I forgive you. Love you." Her words were sleepy and slurred and her eyes were already closed.

The curl of her lashes against her round cheek hurt him. Something that pure and fragile should not exist in the same world as Todd and Cary's father.

"Love you." He got up. "Night Tabby." He left the door open a little so the light would keep them company as they fell asleep.

His dad found him in the basement blasting asteroids on their old Nintendo. Jon didn't look at him or quit punching the buttons on his controller. "I already said sorry to Bea."

"It's a school night," Pete said. "Time to head to bed."

"I'll be up in a minute."

"Now, Jon."

Jon ended his game and tossed the controller onto the floor. He brushed past his dad on the stairs, close enough to smell the laundry soap on Pete's sweatshirt. For a second he thought Pete would grab his arm on the way by. Jon was so tense his shoulder blades felt pinned together.

He got ready for bed, slamming cupboards in the bathroom and kicking dirty laundry aside in the hall.

He was lying in bed, glaring at the ceiling when his father tapped on his open door. Underneath his beard, Pete's mouth was lined with fatigue. He leaned in the doorway, looking at Jon. "Cary's father and Rob Klassen were in the meeting with your principal today. I told them what you told me—that Cary was defending you."

Jon's hands closed on his blankets.

"Cary's suspended at home until the end of the week and suspended in school for the rest of next week."

Anger went off like a firework in Jon's chest. "He didn't start that fight."

"Todd is suspended too," Pete said. He measured Jon with his look. "You understand that there is never, ever a good time to use violence as a solution, right?"

"I knew you would say that," Jon muttered.

"Okay. Do you know why I would say that?"

"Because it's God's job." Jon didn't look at his dad, but he knew exactly where he was standing. If Pete took one step over the line into his room, he thought he would explode.

"That's part of it," Pete finally said. The silence that followed was painful but Pete still didn't leave. "Can I pray with you tonight?"

Jon turned his face away. "No," he whispered.

After a moment he heard his father turn to go. "Good night then son. Love you."

When Pete turned the lights out, it was as dark in the room as it was inside Jon. He shut his eyes and realized he was crying. He thought of Cary and as soon as he thought of him, he prayed for him. It was like a reflex—reaching out even when no one seemed to be listening. God hadn't kept him safe, God hadn't kept Cary safe, and there was nothing he could hold onto anymore. He wanted to go back to being as small as Bea hugging Mr. Rabbit in her bed.

I have done everything you wanted my whole life. You said you were Love. Where are you?

2

Jon's business.

{Jon}

In the following days at school, Jon kept looking for Cary and then remembering he was suspended. At lunchtime he opened his sandwich bag on the grassy strip beside the north doors, the spring sunlight hot on his head. Halfway through his sandwich he thought about where Cary might be, and he wasn't hungry anymore. He threw his half-finished lunch away.

During the afternoon break everyone at the north doors was talking about the locker searches that had happened during class. Jon listened, slumped against the brick wall.

A fierce-faced girl was taking a poll. "Did they search your locker for drugs?" When she came to Jon he shrugged.

"Yeah. Mine and Cary's."

Mike huffed a laugh. "You got something you want to tell us Jon? You planning to do some business here?"

"No," Jon said.

"Where is Cary?" Mike looked around the yard.

"He's suspended," Fierce Girl said. "For fighting."

Mike's eyebrows went up. "Someone stupid enough to fuck with him?"

She lifted a bony shoulder, bare except for the strap of her tank top. "And he had a knife. That's what I heard."

"I bet they bled all over the hallway," another kid giggled. "Sliced and diced."

Fierce Girl rolled her eyes. "You get expelled for that."

"Huh." Mike crossed his arms over his massive chest. "Care's too smart for that."

Jon's eyes burned and he bent his head so no one could see his face. If he had climbed out of the gym locker, bled into the washroom sink and then gone to the library to keep his hurt to himself, Cary would not be in trouble now.

When the three minute bell rang, Mike and Jon were the only ones left standing on the concrete.

"You were there for the fight?" Mike asked.

Jon nodded. "Cary pulled his knife. He didn't use it."

Mike huffed a laugh. "He didn't have to. I bet the other kid was shittin' his pants."

Jon didn't say anything, looking sideways at Mike's broad face and crooked nose. He wasn't afraid of Mike now.

"How did you get out—that place you lived in grade five?" Jon asked.

Mike's eyebrows lifted. "I called the cops. They dragged that motherfucker out in cuffs." He laughed again, short and hard. "Best thing I ever did in my life."

Jon wrapped his arms around himself, thinking about that—calling the police to rescue Cary from wherever he was.

Mike's eye's narrowed. "This about Care?"

Jon looked at him sideways, longing for the relief of telling someone. His throat was so tight that he could barely get the words out. "I saw his dad hit him, when he came to pick him up. I think he's in trouble."

Mike was quiet a second. Then the tattoo on his neck rippled with his shrug. "Some days Cary comes to school beat to shit under his jacket. It's his skin." The words were like a rockslide.

Jon could hardly speak. "What? Why haven't you told someone?"

Mike frowned. "I figure he has his reasons for keeping quiet. You're the first person I know ever got him to talk." Mike considered him. "You know anything about this shit, Jon?"

Jon shook his head.

"Well, I'm going to tell you. You open your mouth on Care and his life is ended. Cops pull up to his house and put cuffs on his step-dad or whoever, and nothing is the same again. I say that's his call."

"Do you think he's okay?" Jon asked in a small voice.

Mike laughed. "You're giving yourself a hernia kid. Care is tough. That guy he fought is lucky he didn't gut him from here to here." He drew his thumb from his waist to his throat. "He doesn't want help so I leave that shit alone. You should too." He shrugged his big shoulders.

Jon wanted to believe him. Mike would know. He tried to forget the way Cary looked half his normal size without his jacket on. Probably Cary was at home playing video games and eating cereal. Probably he was laughing about how stupid his suspension was. Probably he hadn't felt a thing because Cary was tough like stone.

3

Mouth shut.

{Cary}

Cary woke up to the smell of pancakes. For a second, lying still, he thought he was at Jon's house. He bent his knees to roll out of bed and his bruises kicked him wide awake.

His house. Time to get up.

Standing wrenched a sound out of him and he hung onto the desk, waiting for his vision to clear. His stomach's hungry clench demanded he eat, and the smell of pancakes could not be his imagination.

The walk downstairs to the kitchen took a long time. When he got there, he found his father standing at the stove, flipping pancakes in his jacket and pleated pants for teaching.

Cary blinked and ducked into the hall to hide. Had he ever seen Conall making pancakes?

His mother was gliding up the hall, the baby in her arms. She smiled when she saw Cary, her eyebrows coming together like a question mark. Liam's eyes were open; his little face was propped on his mother's shoulder looking at where they had been. Cary watched his brother watch him as Beverly went into the kitchen. His father turned with a smile for his mother and put his hand around Liam's soft head.

"I think Ciaran might like to join us for pancakes," Beverly said.

"Of course," Conall said, turning two fresh onto the stack on the plate. "There's plenty."

His mother looked into the hall. Cary didn't move from where he watched through the crack in the door. She came out to him, smiling. "Ciaran, your father has made us pancakes." She brushed a hand over his shirt, and he shied back.

"Honestly, did you sleep in your clothes again? Come in and have breakfast before you go to school," she said.

He couldn't tell if she even knew she was lying anymore. "I'll eat in the kitchen."

The mood of the morning made her generous. "Alright honey. I'll make you a plate."

She told Conall he wasn't feeling well. Cary saw his father lift his head to look out the door. There was no sharp edge on his expression. Cary drew a full breath and his shaking stopped. That look told him he'd bought a kind of safety for himself as well as Liam—for now.

When his parents had gone into the dining room, Cary stood at the counter in the kitchen with a plate of pancakes stacked six high. He ate quickly, washing the food down with milk from the carton. In the dining room, his parents were laughing and making easy conversation about getting a nanny. Cary looked at his last pancake, golden and soaked with syrup on his plate. There had never been a morning like this in his memory.

He had never tried to touch the bottom of Conall's anger and leave him empty.

Cary set his plate in the sink and leaned on the counter. He had done it. He had taken it all. In a handful of days he would have his body back for himself—not healed exactly, but close. He heard Liam's contented chuckle in the dining room, talking to himself under the sound of his parent's voices.

Worth it.

Cary gathered the dirty dishes off the counter and started to load the dishwasher. He heard his father leave and his mother settling Liam for a nap.

He was drying the griddle when Beverly came into the kitchen. She put a hand on the counter, smiling with half her face. The other half was doing something he didn't recognize. "I'll run the bath." she said.

///

When he went upstairs his mother had the tub full, as hot as he could stand and grainy with Epsom salt in the bottom. Cary locked the bathroom door and stripped without looking at himself in the mirror. He lowered himself into the steaming bath, gasping, then slid his head under. The water boomed in his ears and was hot on his eyes and face.

He saw his father make his hand soft for his brother, cupping Liam's downy head. Something hurt Cary inside, deeper than his bruises. He stayed under the water, eyes open, mouth shut.

Mouth shut. He could stay under a long time, almost two minutes. He sat up. There was another soft tap on the door.

"Cary?" His mother's voice sounded different, plain like her face without make-up. "Do you need your back done?"

He looked at the water, already pinkish. He cleared the water out of his ears, took a breath to steady himself and reached a dripping arm to the knob of the door behind him to turn it open.

They didn't look at each others' faces or speak. His mother scrubbed his back in quick, smooth movements, then poured water over his shoulders, a double bowlful, to wash the torn, dead skin away. Cary pressed his face against his knees, his hands clenching the hair at the back of his neck hard enough to hurt.

The bathroom door clicked shut.

He splayed his hand against the tile wall, feeling himself tipping into black. A minute or two, a drumline of heartbeats and the feeling passed. He reached back to lock the door, then lifted himself out of the tub.

He caught a look at himself in the mirror. Shit. He blinked and in the black of his eyelid falling he was in the basement again—holy hell Conall was angry, swinging so hard he couldn't move fast enough—and then Cary was looking at himself again, his white face and black eyes in the mirror. Mouth shut.

///

On his way out of the house, he stopped in his brother's room. Liam was sleeping, curled like a little peanut under his blankets. Cary reached into the crib and put his hand around the back of Liam's soft head. His brother's skin was warm under his cold fingers. Liam stirred and sighed. Cary withdrew his hand, gripping the crib rail to just look.

He wasn't a kid anymore. He knew Conall would be angry again in a week or three or five. His father's anger would fill the house until the air crackled with its dark electricity and his mother tiptoed around the edges of rooms, white and quiet.

He would have to do this again. The realization pressed on his face like water. He held still, not breathing.

In that moment he thought of the God Jon prayed to, if there was such a person for him. If not for him, then for Liam. His mouth was shut but the words came out somehow:

If You are real, keep him safe.

(not like you kept me.)

Cary went to his mother's bathroom, made himself a cocktail of painkillers, and went out.

4

Gazebo Park.

{Jon}

The next day at lunch, Jon joined the circle of smokers at the north doors. He wasn't hungry, and there was something about standing shoulder to shoulder with Mike and his friends and smoking a borrowed cigarette, that covered up the stuff that was hurting so bad. When the class bell rang, Mike nudged him and said, "We're heading downtown to hang in Gazebo park. Coming?"

Jon turned from the school doors, feeling interested in something for the first time that day. "Yeah. Heck yeah."

They piled onto the city bus: Mike, Fierce Girl and her friend, a skinny kid with a beanbag, and Jon. It felt good to be in a crowd, kind of like he belonged.

Gazebo Park was a lush, grassy space flanked by old buildings whose worn sandstone still retained some dignity. There was, in fact, a gazebo as well as some picnic tables—all with flaking brown paint and fresh graffiti scrawl. The girls spread themselves out on the grass, exposing as much skin to the sun as possible. Mike and the skinny kid started to kick the hacky sack, taking turns getting as many hits as they could before the hacky hit the ground.

Jon watched until Mike hucked the hacky into his chest with a ricey *'thunk.'*

"Quit spectating," Mike said.

Jon tossed the hacky back and joined them, a smile tugging at his lips. He had quick hands and feet; he picked the game up fast.

When they took a break, sprawling on the grass, the skinny kid dug into his backpack and brought out a hand-rolled cigarette to share. Jon passed it to Fierce Girl without putting it to his lips. He wasn't sure that was tobacco inside the twist of paper. Mike kept the cigarette, lying back in the grass to finish it. Jon drew his knees up, uncomfortable for the first time. A couple months ago he had never even seen a joint up close. Looking up, he saw another kid sitting on the steps of the church. He recognized Cary's jacket.

He got to his feet and went over, feeling lighter already. Cary was hunched over his drawing book, working intently.

"Hey, Cary."

Cary looked up and his face relaxed when he saw Jon. It was almost a smile.

"What are you doing here?" Jon asked.

Cary turned his notebook around and showed it to Jon. "Our project."

Jon took it in his hands, sitting on the step below Cary to look more closely. It was a drawing of the side of their house. A child was running in the foreground laughing. Jon's mouth turned up. "Is that Bea?"

Cary ducked his head, his face colouring. "No."

The building was completed in dark, sure pencil-strokes against a clear sky. "Wow, this is beautiful."

Cary took the sketchbook back and Jon put his back against the cold stone banister. "They searched our lockers yesterday. Yours and mine."

Cary frowned at him. "Why did they search your locker?"

Jon shrugged to cover how mad he was about it. "Looking for drugs."

"That's stupid."

"Yup," Jon said. He picked a stone up off the step and held it in his fist. "This you serving your at-home suspension?"

"Yup."

Cary's blank, innocent expression made Jon laugh. "Huh." He looked at Cary again. There was nothing to tell where Cary's dad hit him—except Jon was in his shirtsleeves and the sun was warm on his skin, while Cary still had his jacket on. Jon hucked the stone, made it *'ping'* on the wooden bench a few feet away. "You get in trouble when you got home?"

Cary shook his head once. Jon couldn't see his face. "You?" Cary asked.

Jon gripped his hands together, looking at Cary's shoulder. After a second he shrugged. "Yeah. My dad took me to Dairy Queen. He talked about how he's worried my friends are dragging me down."

Cary didn't say anything. Jon dropped his eyes to his sneakers, turning them in. "I told him how Todd is an asshole. And that you're the best friend I could have asked for."

Cary frowned at him like he thought Jon was making fun.

Jon couldn't look him in the face. He was red to the roots of his hair. "I'm really sorry Cary. I should have fought Todd back or told someone and you got in trouble for that."

Cary shrugged his shoulders, one stiff movement up and down. "Nothing happened. I got grounded for a day. Quit worrying about it."

Jon tasted sick in his mouth and swallowed. He was silent for a moment, looking at the north door kids, who had every available inch of skin exposed to soak up the sun.

"You're a really good liar Cary. Better than me. I think you've had more practice."

{Cary}

Cary went still, his heart thudding in his chest.

Jon said, "I saw your dad hit you in the parking lot. I assume—there was more when you got home. And that's why you always wear your jacket."

Cary gripped the edge of the step to keep his hands from shaking. He had been stupid. He never should have let Jon close. Now it felt like Jon had a hold of him, and one good yank would tear him wide open. "You tell your dad?"

"No." Jon wouldn't stop looking at him. "*You* should tell someone. You told me to tell—when I was getting hurt. You didn't do anything that deserves—"

Cary slapped his hand over Jon's mouth and drove him against the stone. "Shut it," he said. Jon was hanging onto Cary's arm, wide-eyed and white-faced. Cary's lips pulled back from his teeth. "If you think you know shit about my family—you can go to hell, Jon White."

He felt Jon swallow, and something warm and wet ran down his wrist. Tears. His fingers were biting into Jon's cheek. His hands flew free and he backed up until his shoulders hit the stone bannister on the other side of the steps. His brain jabbered with panic. He was fucked now. He couldn't make his hands hurt Jon badly enough to shut his mouth for good. He needed Jon to keep his mouth shut.

Jon put his face against his knees, his hands clenched over his head.

Cary swallowed with a mouth dry as stone. The torn place inside him was shaking like a flag in the wind. "I didn't mean to hurt you."

Jon shook his head. When he lifted his face the white prints from Cary's fingers were still around his mouth. "Are you okay? Are you safe?"

Cary drew back, holding still. He could feel every wrinkle and seam of his shirt pressed against his back. *They're safe. That's what matters.* His mouth was frozen shut but Jon's eyes read his face like the words were written there.

"Shit, Cary." Jon's voice broke. He looked away, wiping tears from his eyes again and again.

Cary didn't know what to do to make him stop crying. He frowned, fishing in his pockets for his cigarettes and lighter. He burned his thumb lighting the first smoke. He swore and sucked his finger before lighting the second smoke from the first and sliding across the step. He touched Jon's arm with his fist holding the cigarette.

Jon gave him a quick look, then took the cigarette. He smoked it with his head down. Finally, he said in a low voice, "You know what would have happened if I had punched Todd and landed in the principal's office?"

Cary shook his head.

"Pretty much it already did. My dad would have made me talk about it and apologize. He would have given me this look he gets when he's hurt, like he's so disappointed that I'm not—" Jon tripped on the words, "—that I'm not the son he wanted."

Jon's voice sank to a whisper. "That's all I was afraid of. A look." He covered his eyes. "You should have left it on me, Cary."

Cary drew the smoke from his cigarette deep into his chest and held it there, his mouth shut. He felt like he was falling down the stairs—that terrifying moment when it's all air and flying before hitting the steps. He exhaled.

"It wasn't about Todd." He couldn't look Jon in the face. "I wrecked some of my father's stuff. If I never laid a finger on Todd he still would have…" He blinked and couldn't say another word, like there was something broken in his brain, between what he could see behind his eyes and what he could make his mouth say. Cary put his head down, fumbled another smoke out of his pack and lit it. His fingers were shaking.

"Nothing would have been different," he said finally. "Todd was just—a bonus."

Jon made a sound that could have been a laugh. Cary looked at him from under his eyebrows. He couldn't say the words to make Jon understand about Liam and pancakes the next morning. He needed Jon to understand. He needed Jon to keep his mouth shut.

"You cutting the rest of the day?"

Jon took a moment to speak. "Yup. Think so."

Tuck and roll, Cary thought. He straightened, stretching carefully. "I left more drawings at my house. Let's go."

5

The last place he wanted to be.

{Jon}

Jon rode the bus to Cary's house in silence. Cary swayed with the turns, leaning on his knees. Watching buildings pass, Jon felt as if grief had stretched him as tight and thin as a guitar string. The bus turned into a residential subdivision and strip malls gave way to houses, each one bigger than the last. Cary reached across to pull the cord. Startled, Jon got up and followed him off the bus. The house in front of them was set back on its own loop of road, guarded by a tall hedge.

"You live here?" Jon couldn't help asking.

Cary gave the house a look, with no appreciation in his face. "Yuh."

Jon trailed up the drive behind Cary's shoulder, staying close to the hedge as if he might need to leap in for cover at a moment's notice. Cary didn't use the double front doors with the steps marching half-way up the house. Instead, he led Jon around to a sheltered side entrance, took a key out of his jacket pocket and let them into what appeared to be a boot room. Utility shelves lined the walls, and hooks held out-of-season coats and hats.

Cary stood still a moment, listening, before peeling his jacket off. He balled it up small, stashing it inside the shoe bench under the coat hooks. He looked at Jon, who was still standing in the doorway.

"You can come in."

Jon stepped inside and followed Cary down the hall. He couldn't help staring. Cary's house was nothing like what he had expected. The walls went up and up, gleaming white and hung with real paintings, not prints—blocks and lines of color in dark, massive frames. At the end of the hallway, suspended above the tile floor was an enormous glass sculpture, throwing shards of light against the high walls and sweeping staircase. Glancing into the rooms that opened off the hallway, Jon saw the strong shapes of modern furniture and more glass on display. Everything was as immaculate as a show home.

A woman tapped down the hall towards them. Her blond hair was swept back from her face, emphasizing her astonishing cheekbones and large gray eyes.

"Ciaran, you're home." She smiled and put her arms around him.

Cary held still for her embrace, his hands closed at his sides. She pulled back, her nose wrinkling. "You reek of cigarettes."

"I'll change," Cary said. Her eyes went over his shoulder to Jon. "Mom, I asked a friend over to work on some homework."

She spared Jon a smile, getting her coat from the hall closet. "Your father will be home in an hour. I'm stepping out for a few minutes."

"Liam?" Cary said.

"He's sleeping."

Cary nodded.

"Nice to meet you, Jon." She swept out the door. The *thump* of it closing made the chandelier above them shiver and scatter light over their faces.

"My room is upstairs," Cary said.

Cary was stiff and slow going up the stairs. Jon opened his mouth to ask if he was okay, then shut it again, looking away. He was sure Cary didn't often have friends over after school. Never on a day like this. So what was he doing here?

He talked to make the whole thing seem normal, but what came out of his mouth was mostly nonsense. "So are your parents artists or millionaires or what? This place is amazing."

Cary said, "Grandpa Douglas' money." He put a hand on a door, swinging it open. "This is my brother's room."

Jon saw the edge of a crib, curtains with giraffes in blue bow ties. He felt Cary watching him as he leaned around the door. Cary's brother was curled in his crib, asleep with one fist clenched against his cheek. His blue cap had slipped over his eyes so only his parted lips were visible.

"He's okay?" Jon asked.

"Yup." Cary's face was fierce.

Jon followed Cary down the hall. Cary's bedroom was as big as everything else in the house, but it seemed empty: a neatly made up bed sat against one wall, and a desk stood beside the door. Jon could see the stripes where the vacuum cleaner had crossed back and forth over the rug. There were no posters or pictures, just a flatscreen TV mounted across from the bed. There was a laptop folded on the desk, an MP3 player in a cradle with speakers on the nightstand and a handheld DVD player on a shelf above the desk. To Jon's inexperienced eye, everything looked expensive and brand new.

"That's a lot of gear," he said.

"My mom buys me that stuff." Cary leaned a hand on his desk and pulled open the drawer. "This is for us." He passed Jon a roll of drawings and straightened with effort.

Jon slid the drawings out and spread them on the floor. They were pattern pieces for the walls and roof of their house, on heavyweight paper and to scale. "Jeez Cary, you've done everything." He leafed through the drawings, taking in the detail around the windows, and the bricks drawn onto the outer walls.

"We still need to assemble them." Cary was at the sink in the bathroom adjoining his room. He shook a couple pills into his palm, then ducked his head to drink from his hands and wash his face.

"That'll take no time at all," Jon said.

Cary closed the door most of the way to change behind it. "You did all the work on the drafts," he said. "It's fair."

"Like hell it is," Jon said, glancing up. He lost his breath. He could see Cary's back in the mirror. His skin was solid bruises, moving with his shoulders as he pulled a shirt over his head.

Jon nailed his eyeballs to the drawings on the floor. He lifted one sheet of paper, then another.

Cary came out in a clean sweater, his dark hair pulled back from his pale face. He was frowning, but his mouth looked like it might smile. "What do you want me to do—

tear them up and start again? They're done. Enjoy your free ride."

Jon's laugh was strangled. "Yeah right."

They both became aware of the sound of a baby crying at the same time.

"Just a sec." Cary disappeared out the door.

Jon sat back on his heels, covering his eyes. He really wanted to get out of this house. He heard Cary speaking in a soft voice he had never heard him use before: "I'm here, don't cry. Ready to wake up? "

The thing Jon had taken for a walkie-talkie on top of the desk was a baby monitor. Jon got up and snapped it off, embarrassed to be eavesdropping on Cary.

Cary returned a few minutes later with his brother in his arms and a bottle in one hand. He settled on his bed, cradling Liam to feed him. Liam had a shock of black hair standing up on his head like a blackbird wing. His blue eyes were focused on Cary's face as he sucked intently.

"So this is your brother."

Cary nodded.

Jon couldn't keep his mouth from running. "Thirteen years—that's a big gap. There's seven years between me and Tabby but... there was supposed to be another baby in-between us."

"Was there?" Cary glanced at him from the corner of his eye.

"No." Jon shifted. "Not after my brother got sick." He didn't know why he was talking about this.

Cary frowned. "I'm sorry."

"I don't remember him much." Which was easier than the truth. He could never forget the hole where Judah was supposed to be.

He watched Cary settle Liam on his shoulder to pat his back after the bottle was done. He'd never seen Cary look so... human. All the regular stuff was in his face: first he looked tired and worried, and then with his cheek against Liam's, he looked almost happy.

Cary looked at Jon with that open face. "Do you want to hold him?"

What else could he do? Jon took the baby carefully, one hand cupping Liam's head like he remembered from when Bea was born. The guitar string in his chest tightened, ringing wordlessly. He watched Liam fight his drooping eyelids and knew that if he were Cary, he would do anything—*anything*—for his baby brother to fall asleep like this, safe.

A door slammed shut on the main floor. Cary pivoted toward the sound as if he could see through walls.

"Your mom?" Jon asked.

There were footsteps treading up the stairs. A man's deep voice called, "Beverly?"

Jon's arms tightened around the baby. Liam squirmed and chirped in protest.

Cary put out his hands, snapping his fingers. "Give him to me."

Jon handed Liam over, sweating all over his body. Cary glared at him. "Smile Jon," he said.

The door swung open, and Conall Douglas stepped into the room. He seemed bigger in this enclosed space than he had in the school hallway. He swept a look around and frowned. "Where is your mother?"

Cary held out the baby. "She had an appointment, father."

Conall took Liam out of his arms and his eyes raked over Cary's face like a searchlight. "You should not be left alone with him."

The hairs on Jon's neck stood up. Cary turned, his face blank as stone. "Father, this is Jon White. We have a school project together."

Jon's face ached he was smiling so hard. "Hello, Mr. Douglas." He put out his hand without thinking, conditioned by hundreds of mornings in his father's church. Cary's father tucked Liam into the crook of one arm to give Jon's hand a firm shake. The corner of his mouth twisted with amusement.

"Jon, I believe I met your father at the school the other day."

"Oh?" Jon couldn't keep worry out of his voice.

"He was quite eloquent in the defense of my boy." Conall's mouth was still twisted, and Jon couldn't tell what it meant. "I'm grateful Ciaran has friends who can be a good influence on him."

He frowned at Cary. "Tell me about your project." When Cary said nothing, Conall swung his gaze back to Jon.

Jon felt like he was pinned in the headlights of an oncoming car. "It's for drafting class. We're building a model for drafting class."

Mr. Douglas' eyebrows lifted. "How interesting. And how do you find working with someone who is nearly incapable of speech? Or is that not a requirement of drafting class?"

Jon thought it was supposed to be a joke. He made himself smile back at Cary's father, his fists stuffed into his jeans pockets. "I guess I wouldn't know about that, sir. I picked Cary as my partner because he's the best in our class."

Conall laughed. "Shrewd boy. Are you joining us for supper, Jon?"

"No, thank you, sir." This massive house was the last place he wanted to be right now. "We were just finishing up."

"I need you downstairs in fifteen." Conall said to Cary, and left carrying Liam asleep against his chest.

When the door shut, Cary knelt and rolled up the drawings on the floor. He stuck them in a cardboard tube and capped it, handing it over to Jon. There was nothing in his face, now.

"Are you in trouble because I was here?" Jon asked.

Cary shook his head. "You were good. He likes you."

"He doesn't like you?"

Cary lifted his shoulders.

Jon yanked the backpack zipper closed around the tube of drawings. "I'm sorry." It was a totally inadequate thing to say. "Care—Cary—if there's anything I can do…"

Cary turned away. His voice was dry and soft: "Keep your mouth shut."

Jon shut his mouth and nodded. He turned to go. "He's beautiful." He looked back at Cary. "Your brother."

Cary met his eyes. His silence said everything.

6

Pastor's kid.

{Jon}

Jon huddled on the vinyl bus seat, watching the setting sun transform concrete apartment buildings into towers of gold. He was shaking. He thought he should pray for Cary. Crossing his arms tightly, he put his head down on the bus seat in front of him, but he couldn't pray.

For eight weeks, he'd lived in a constant state of dread, expecting Todd around every corner. That was Cary's everyday life. Jon got stuck thinking about how long, how many times Cary had stood there like that, taking it from his father. He tried to quit shaking, quit feeling like he was about to burst into tears.

Tears came anyways when he stepped inside the door of his home. It was cramped and filthy compared to Cary's entryway but it closed around him like a hug, the safest place he knew.

His mother came out of the kitchen. "Jon, where have you been? Supper was half an hour ago."

He bent and made a big deal of unpicking the knots in his shoelaces so she wouldn't see he'd been crying. "Cary's house. Sorry, the bus back was slow."

"Did you have supper at Cary's?'

He shook his head.

She turned aside into the kitchen. "I put a plate aside for you. I'll just warm it up."

His father's voice in the kitchen stopped him just as he was about to escape to his bedroom. "Jon, come in here please."

He went and stood in the kitchen doorway. His father was sitting at the table, his coffee cup in his hand. His mother's cup was on the table across from him. Parent conference. Jon's face heated.

"Your mother would have appreciated a phone call to let her know you wouldn't be eating with us," Pete said.

"I said I was sorry."

Pete's face was grave. "I'm not sure it's appropriate for you to be spending time at Cary's house, while he's serving a suspension at home."

Twenty minutes ago, Jon would have done anything to get out of Cary's house. Now he wanted to fight for the right to go back. "He's not under house arrest, dad," Jon said. "I think he can have friends over after school if he wants."

His parents exchanged glances. The microwave beeped and his mother set the plate at his place at the table and pulled the chair back.

Jon took the plate without looking at either of them. "I'll eat in my room."

As he walked away a part of him hoped they would call him back, sit him down, and demand to know what was wrong. He had never worked harder to keep them out.

"Curtis called," his mother said. "I think he was wondering about worship practice?"

That was supposed to be tonight. Right now. He stopped in his tracks. "Crap."

"I can take you," Pete said. "I have some things I can work on at the church."

Jon looked at his father. He couldn't say "Forget it, I'm not going. God might as well be dead." Instead he said, "I'll get my guitar."

///

Jon leafed through his binder of worship music in the van on the way to the church. He'd played most of these choruses a hundred times: *Amazing Love, Mercy is Falling, 10,000 Reasons.* He shut the binder and stared sightlessly out the window. How was he supposed to sing those songs?

Curtis just needed him to play guitar. He didn't have to sing; he used to just for the joy of it. He didn't hear himself sigh, long and shaky.

Pete glanced at him. "How was your day?"

"Fine."

"Did you have a good time at Cary's house?"

"Yeah." Jon tried to think of something his dad would appreciate. "He did a lot of work on our project while he was home."

"I'm glad he's using his time constructively."

Jon closed his eyes. He saw red, purple and black, striped like the art on the twenty foot walls. He licked his lips. "Dad?"

"Jon?"

"Can Cary still come over? To our house?"

"To work on your project?"

"Yeah."

"With his parents' permission," Pete said.

Jon looked steadily out the window. "He's not a bad influence."

"I didn't say he was."

"You were thinking it," Jon said.

Pete was silent.

///

Jon was late. The worship team was gathered in the front pews in the sanctuary, heads bowed and praying, when he arrived. He slid into the end of the third pew back, glancing at the others: a couple adults, a couple kids and Curtis. One of the girls from the youth group was praying aloud. Jon knew her name: Kadee Yoshenko. She went to his school. He had admired her straight shiny hair and brilliant smile for a couple of weeks.

Kadee was praying for a friend, earnestly asking God to save him and turn him back to the truth. Jon was jiggling his leg and not really listening until he heard his own name. Kadee was praying for him. He opened his eyes to look at her and found Curtis' eyes on him. Curtis' face turned red and he looked away. Jon sat rigidly for the rest of the prayer time, eyes open and fixed on the wood grain of the pew back in front of him.

When it was finally over, a couple of people noticed him, sliding their eyes over him quickly and getting up to go onstage. Kadee gave him a little smile. There were actually tears in her eyes.

"Hey Jon, can I talk to you a second?" Curtis asked.

Jon stood and crossed his arms, conscious of everyone on the stage shooting them glances while they plugged in their instruments and shuffled through their music. "Sorry I was late," he said.

"Yeah, I was hoping you'd call me back before you came." Curtis looked around at the pews and the light fixtures like he was searching for inspiration. "The thing is, you're off worship team."

Jon planted his feet. "Why, what did I do?"

"You know," Curtis said vaguely. "The way things are right now, I wasn't really comfortable with putting you on stage."

"The way things are."

"I mean, you're getting in fights now and the company you keep—"

"Your brother picked a fight with me, not the other way around."

Curtis lifted his hands. "It's how it looks, right? Jon, maybe you haven't figured this out yet but the kids you hang out with—they're drug dealers. Everyone knows that. This church has standards for the people in leadership. If you're going to be on stage you have to be able to set an example for the youth—a good example. The way it looks... well, you're not the kind of person you ask to lead worship."

Jon sucked in his breath, speechless for a second. "That's complete bullshit." His voice cracked on the swear.

Curtis lifted his eyebrows. That certainly hadn't changed his mind.

Jon stormed out of the sanctuary, slammed his dad's office door shut and punched it. The rattle was almost worth how badly his hand hurt afterward.

He dropped onto the couch and put his head in his hands, thinking of the brilliant things he should have said: "You don't know anything about me. You never took the trouble until there was something I could do for you. And by the way— your brother is a sick asshole who likes to hurt people."

There was a tap on the door and his dad pushed it open, looking wary. Jon thought he seemed relieved it was him. And there was something else.

"You knew," Jon said. "You knew they were kicking me off."

Pete shut the door and gathered a few books off his desk to return to his briefcase. "Rob Klassen is the head of the worship committee. They met last night." He looked up and saw Jon's white, furious expression. "I wasn't there, Jon. But when I heard—I thought something like this might happen."

"I didn't do anything. Everything they're saying about me is lies."

Pete stood still, his fingertips resting on his empty desk. "I know, son. It's going to take a few weeks for the truth to get around."

"Maybe you should call the prayer chain—see how fast it gets around then."

Pete was quiet. Jon had never known him not to meet his eyes.

"What?" Jon asked.

"They called already," Pete said. "One of the ladies called your mother today to pray with her over the phone."

Jon's ears rang, he was so angry and stunned. "They should mind their fucking business." The word made his father wince, and Jon was viciously glad.

"This isn't like other jobs," Pete said. "We talked about that a long time ago. You're held to a higher standard. So am I."

Jon jumped to his feet. "I hate your job. I hate being a pastor's kid. You had a choice. I never did."

Pete turned his cheek. "I know, Jon."

Jon's fists clenched. "You don't *know*." His voice didn't sound like his anymore, snarling through his teeth. "You have no idea what it's like to be the firstborn son of Pastor White. I wish I had died and your perfect Judah was standing here right now."

The color drained out of his father's face.

Jon's face was so hot he could feel it in his eyeballs. "I don't take it back. I know you wish he was here instead of me screwing things up. I wish he was, too. Then I could quit." He grabbed his binder of worship music and chucked it at his dad. "I quit anyways."

Pete caught the binder against his chest. It flew open, spraying chord charts all over the desk.

Jon stood, shaking, with his fists closed. Was he supposed to leave now and walk home? His dad was his ride. Pete would pass him in their van and get home before him.

His father folded the binder around the mess of its contents and laid it on his desk. "Was there anything else?" His voice was very quiet.

Jon exhaled. "No."

"Maybe if I gave you a hand with tossing that couch, we could quit together."

Jon's laugh felt close to hysteria. Or tears. He turned aside, scrubbing his hands over his face. "Whatever."

Pete got his jacket and keys, moving slowly like he might scare Jon off. "Okay. I'm finished here, and I would like to go home."

Jon picked up his guitar and followed his father out the door. They could hear the worship band playing as they passed through the foyer. Jon's guitar felt like it weighed one hundred pounds.

Pete didn't speak until their van pulled to a stop in their driveway. He left the keys in the ignition, wrapping his hands tightly around the steering wheel.

"I didn't know you felt that way," his dad said. "About your brother." Pete caught Jon's eyes and Jon was surprised by the heat and the darkness in his look.

"I would never have chosen you instead of him. Never."

That struck Jon with the same force as if Pete had tossed the couch at him. He threw the van door open and climbed out. He turned, still gripping the handle to steady himself. "That doesn't change what I want."

"To no longer be my son?" Pete was leaning across the seats to look at him.

Jon couldn't hold his father's look for long. "I'm not going back there. I'm not walking back into your church where they think I'm a drug addict and a fuck-up. So you tell me if I'm your son or not." He shut the door with a thud and went into the house.

7

Jesus was that big.

{Jon}

When Bea heard Jon come in, she shot down the hall in her footed pyjamas, holding out a storybook. "Jonee, read to me?"

Jon hung up his jacket, feeling his dad standing on the mat right behind him. "I'm tired Honey Bee," he said finally.

Her face fell.

Jon looked down on her bent head, remembering when she had been small as Liam. She had been his favorite even then. He sighed. "Just one, okay?"

Her smile beamed again. "Okay."

They sat together on her bed, the blankets over their feet. Bea burrowed under Jon's arm to use his body as a pillow. The storm of Jon's emotions smoothed out as he read. One story turned into three, and Tabby climbed into her bed across the room to listen, too. Three stories turned into five before Jon realized Bea's breathing was slow and deep, her little body totally relaxed against him.

"Is she asleep?" he said softly to Tabby.

"Yup." Tabby got up and turned out the lights.

Jon eased Bea onto her pillows, tucking her blankets in tight. He brushed her hair back from her soft cheek. The idea of someone hitting Bea, or making her afraid jolted him with anger. He would want to be big enough to protect her and hit back hard.

The thing was, Cary wasn't big. Jon couldn't stop seeing the narrow wings of Cary's shoulder blades making his skin ripple hot red and purple and black.

Jon showered and brushed his teeth, then went into his room and shut the door. When his father knocked, he stayed silent, pretending to be asleep. He couldn't erase what he knew: God let people get hurt. It changed everything—Jon could never go back to being the shiny pastor's kid he had been.

Jon rolled over, slapping his pillow back into shape.

Jesus was in the room, leaning against Jon's desk.

Jon suddenly realized whom he was really angry with. Not his dad. Not Todd or Curtis or the worship committee. Not even Cary's father. The person he wanted to hurt the most was standing with his bare, scarred feet on Jon's bedroom carpet.

Jon glared at Jesus. "What did you come here for?"

Jesus' face was covered with shadow. His eyes glittered in the city light falling through the window. "I came to answer," he said. "For what I've done."

The pile of things Jon was angry at Jesus for was heavy and hot on his head. "That's a lot."

Jesus was silent. The scar on the hand resting on Jon's desk shone in the moonlight.

Jon said the filthiest thing he could think of. "Cary's dad beat the shit out of him and you watched him do it. You *watched*."

"Jon."

The guitar string started ringing in his chest.

"Come here," Jesus said.

Jon put his feet on the floor and took a step toward Jesus, trembling.

Jesus lifted his shirt off his waistband. "Put your hand here."

There was a hole open, dark, in Jesus' side. Jon swallowed and put out his hand.

Jesus tore open. Jon's ears and eyes and mouth were full of his blood, and there was a terrible, bone-shaking cry. Jesus was full of all of it: Todd hurting him and the lies sticking to him at church, his dad's grief and Cary's stripes and more and more—all the suffering in the world. That cry went on without breath until Jon's legs couldn't hold him anymore. He fell on his knees, hiding his face on Jesus' feet, covering his ears. "What is it? What is that noise?"

It was suddenly silent, and dark. He felt Jesus wrap his arms around his body, so close he could feel the warmth of Jesus' breath when he spoke. "It's me."

The frayed edge of the cry was in his whisper. Jon turned his face to the sound of Jesus' voice. His teeth were chattering. "You were saying something—what were you saying?"

He started up when he heard Jesus' answer, falling out of his bed with a thud. He curled there gasping and crying, his cheek against the carpet where Jesus put his feet. His ears were still ringing.

Jesus said: "It is finished."

The next morning Jon woke up before the sun had done more than pale the night sky. He laid in bed, but couldn't fall back asleep. He felt raw—like he'd been scraped with salt—and his eyes were still puffy from crying. He gave up and got out of bed, digging his Bible out of a pile of comics to take it to the kitchen.

His ribbon opened to the story of Jesus' friend Lazarus, who was sick. Jon bent over its open pages while he waited for his toast to pop. Jesus' friends travelled to bring him the news of Lazarus' illness, but Jesus stayed where he was another two days, teaching and healing. When he finally set out to see his friend, Lazarus' sisters met him on the way, weeping because their brother was dead. The story said that Jesus wept.

Jon stared at those two words: Jesus wept. Jesus knew he had the power to raise Lazarus back to life. He probably knew he was hours away from seeing his friend again, alive. So why did he cry?

The toaster popped with a *'chunk.'* Jon got up and spread the toast with butter and honey. He ate it while standing at the counter, watching the clouds shout with pink and orange in the light of sunrise.

He heard Jesus' terrible cry. It had been like standing next to the amp at a rock concert, the bass shaking his guts. Jon couldn't match the Jesus he'd seen last night with the Jesus he'd thought he knew. The Jesus he'd thought he knew was big enough to overcome sin and death and make everything new: no pain, no tears.

Jon finished his toast, tasted honey in his mouth. His forehead wrinkled, seeing the other Jesus in his memory again. That Jesus was full of pain and tears. He was carrying it all. He was that big.

Jon drew a breath and knuckled his eyes. If he could just quit crying all the time. Cary didn't cry.

As if in response to this thought, he heard: *Cary has scars where his tears used to be.*

Jon pressed his hands over his face. *I didn't want to know that Jesus. I didn't want you to tell me that.*

Jesus didn't speak again. Jon put another piece of toast in the toaster and waited, watching the twisty wires glow red with heat. Something popped in his brain—a completely new thought. He was supposed to do what Jesus did. Not say a bunch of wise stuff and smile all the time at his perfect life. Stuff hurt Jesus and he cried. He took other people's hurt and carried it for them.

He could do that for Cary, if he still wanted to be Cary's friend. Cary couldn't cry and Jon could. He could do what Jesus did.

Jon bowed, gripping the counter. He couldn't say it, the "yes" Jesus wanted him to say. He was stretched so thin from holding everything, he thought he might just tear apart. *Don't you get tired of feeling so freaking helpless and hurting so much all the time?*

Jesus was quiet, but Jon knew the answer. He'd heard Jesus' cry and seen how much he could hold.

Jon ate his toast and his mouth was dry as the crumbs. Everything spread in front of him, clear in the light of day. Cary was suspended for a week and half. That was enough time for Jon to find new friends who didn't have such heavy problems, or get a hobby and join a sports team, or whatever. Anything would be easier than being Cary's friend. It wasn't like he could even do anything to help, just keep his mouth shut and watch it happen. Just cry some more. Jesus, he was sick of crying.

{Pete}

When Pete got up, he found Jon at the kitchen table. He drew in his breath, feeling the sting of Jon's words from just hours ago. He hadn't expected to have to face his son again so soon.

He tried to smile. "You're up early."

"Couldn't sleep." Jon shut his book and pushed it aside. His Bible. Pete's heart lifted. It had been weeks since he'd noticed Jon reading it.

"Should I make us some eggs and toast?"

Jon shrugged, avoiding his eyes. "I already had toast."

Pete got out the frying pan and started heating the oil. He made his voice light. "The school called. Cary's teacher was wondering if you could take him his homework today."

Jon was quiet, moving crumbs on his plate with his finger. "To his house?"

"I guess so."

Jon spread his hand on the table. "Yes. Yeah I can." He crossed his arms tight over his hoodie, looking up at the window. "I guess he doesn't have a lot of other friends to do that for him."

"I guess not."

When the eggs were done, Pete set the plates at the table and sat next to his son. He bowed his head and said grace. Jon bowed his head next to him. When he said 'Amen,' Jon lifted his fork and started to eat, still silent.

"It's good to see you reading your Bible," Pete said tentatively.

Jon chewed and swallowed. "I'm not losing my faith, dad." Color rose in his son's face. "I know Jesus is real. I still believe the things you taught me. That's not what's going on."

Pete stayed quiet while they ate. He hoped Jon would say more, but he didn't want to set him off.

Jon set his fork down. "What happens to you if I stop coming to church?"

Pete's heart sank and he grabbed on tight to his awareness of Jesus' presence. He could not lose this son too.

Careful to keep how much it mattered out of his voice, he said, "Nothing Jon. You are your own person. You're old enough to make your own choices." He tipped his head and decided to risk it. "I hope you wouldn't make a decision like that because you were afraid of someone like Todd."

Jon made a face. "No. I would have quit going weeks ago."

Pete waited, watching his son try to find the words to explain. Jon said, "I just think people in the church don't know what it's like in the real world, how bad it can be. How bad people can be hurt." Jon rolled his shoulders like they ached. "They don't wanna know. The kids I hang out with are invisible to them. But they're hurt and lost and I know Jesus cares about that. I *know* He does." He looked at his dad, his eyebrows pulled down low.

"I'm glad you care about that." Pete said. "Don't discount the church completely, Jon. There are good people there."

Jon shoved back from the table and took his dishes to the sink. "You have to say that. You're the pastor."

Pete laughed a little, sitting back. Something was different about Jon today, something had broken him open a crack and he almost recognized the Jon from before under all the anger and doubt.

Jon ran the water for their dishes. "Will the Board be angry with you if I quit?"

Pete's mouth made a flat little smile. "Not for that, no."

Jon frowned as he washed his dishes, then set his plate on the drying rack to drip. "Why do you keep doing it? You could build houses, or sell cars, or something and be way happier."

"You could be right, son." Pete shrugged. "That's not what God called me to do. I'm doing it for him."

Jon shook his head, clearly unhappy with that answer.

"And I love the church, Jon. She's the Bride. She's God's plan to be Christ in the world. There's no plan B."

"The church doesn't look anything like him." Jon's voice was rough with emotion. "I would follow him anywhere. I couldn't care less if I never see a church again."

"Would you follow him into a church?" Pete asked carefully.

Jon drew back, shutting his eyes. "You think Jesus loves the church?"

"I know he does."

Jon's eyes were still closed. For a moment nothing was hidden in his face; he looked so hurt and troubled Pete had to resist the urge to put his arms around him.

Jon's voice was small, like he was talking to himself. "I just don't see how he can hold so much hurt and keep loving people." His sigh shook his body and he turned to go.

"Jon?"

His son looked back warily.

Pete smiled, feeling happiness and sadness mixed up together. "Thanks for the talk."

A corner of Jon's mouth lifted in return. Pete watched him go, praying for him as Jon went. He remembered Jon as a little boy—how he used to climb onto his lap to plant a big kiss in his beard. He remembered how precious Jon's "Love you, Daddy" had been then. And how much easier it had been to get.

8

The truth.

{Jon}

Todd was back in school. Jon watched him from the corner of his eye while the gym teacher led their warm up. Todd's nose was smushed against his face, and his skin was mottled purple and brown where Cary had hit him. Once, Todd caught him looking and gave Jon a glare. Jon looked away.

Todd's face didn't make him feel better. He doubted if the beating Cary had given him had made Todd feel half as ashamed and afraid as Jon had felt the past eight weeks. Even if it did, was that supposed to make Jon feel better? Was he supposed to be glad that Todd had bruises like Jon, like Cary—like Jesus?

The teacher blew his whistle and they started doing wind sprints. Jon was glad to push his body and think only of the breath burning his lungs and the turn and push off the blue line at the end of the gym. It was all just too screwed up.

When class was over, Jon was changing his gym clothes alone in an aisle of lockers. Todd turned the corner, carrying his jeans and shirt, saw Jon and turned back to find another place to change. Jon smiled to himself. That, on the other hand, felt excellent.

He was about to break free of the humid locker room when he heard a commotion in the washrooms: harsh laughter and a toilet flushing repeatedly. Jon's head got hot. "Shit."

He put his hand on the washroom door and pushed it open.

Todd's friends had a kid headfirst in a toilet bowl, dunking him while they flushed. Todd was standing back with his arms crossed. When he saw Jon, he looked startled.

Jon slapped the door wide open. "Hey Mr. Martin," he yelled over his shoulder at the empty locker room. "They're in here!"

Todd jerked the nearest guy's shoulder to get his attention and the whole group piled past Jon and out of the locker room, punctuating their exit with loud swearing.

Jon laughed. He'd been sure he was about to get beat up again.

The kid left in the stall was on his hands and knees, gasping and dripping wet. Jon grabbed a couple gym towels and held them out. The kid took them, giving Jon a wide-eyed look, as if he hadn't expected someone like Jon to come to his rescue.

"Tell the principal if that happens again, okay?" Jon said. "Do you know their names?"

The kid shook his head, towelling his hair dry. Jon listed all the guys he recognized, including Todd. "I'll come with you if you need someone." He put out a hand to help the kid to his feet.

"Thank you." The kid combed his hand through his hair, flicking toilet water off his fingers and making a face. "I'm Rasheed."

Jon felt a small smile on his face. "I'm Jon. You new here?"

Rasheed nodded.

"Well, good luck." Jon left him in the washroom and hit the fresh hallway air.

///

Jon spent lunch hour at the north doors, alone. The warmth of the sun made him think of summer, though the solitary tree growing in the strip of dry, brown grass had only swollen, red buds where its leaves would be. Jon tipped his head back against the warm brick of the school and closed his eyes. He felt scrubbed clean, his skin tender enough to feel every breath of wind. He sensed Jesus' presence slip up beside him, keeping silent company. He almost fell asleep, the sun warm and heavy as a blanket on his body.

"Hey, Jon?"

Jon looked up, startled. Kadee Yoshenko was standing in the sun, looking at him with a half-smile on her lips.

"Kadee." He got to his feet. It was some effort to keep the shock out of his face. "What are you doing here?"

She flipped a strand of her straight black hair over her shoulder. "Everybody is saying all this stuff about you and when I was like— 'Has anyone actually asked Jon what happened?' —they were all like, 'Um, no.' So I decided to come talk to you myself."

Anger built like heat in his chest, but Jon kept his mouth shut, holding a non-committal smile on his face.

She glanced around the north door exit, her gaze lingering on the knot of smokers by the dumpster. "So, is it true you were in a knife fight with one of these kids?"

She was so unfairly gorgeous, standing there with the spring sunshine on her hair, the charcoal wings of her eyebrows lifting a little over her dark eyes, that Jon couldn't even hate her.

He crossed his arms. "Nope. That was Todd, actually. A friend of mine got sick of the way he was treating people, and they got into it."

She lifted her chin. "Good. Somebody should have stood up for you a month ago when Todd did that stupid 'purple nurple' thing to you at youth group."

Jon's face flushed right to the tips of his ears. He really didn't want anyone to remember that moment.

"Nobody really likes him at church, you know," Kadee said. "Everyone is just friends with him because they're afraid of what he could do."

"They're right," Jon muttered. "That's why I hang out here."

"Curtis said he thought you were doing drugs."

Jon made a noise. "His brother told him that because he's an asshole. I don't do drugs. I never have. I'm never going to. I made friends with the people who would make friends with me. That's it. So thanks for the prayer, but you kind of got it wrong."

Kadee's mouth made a round 'O.' Then her phone bleeped and her thumbs flew over the keypad. "It's Monique," Kadee said without a break in her texting. "I'm telling her Todd totally lied about you. She is going to love that. They were dating and now they hate each other." She finished her text and gave Jon a dazzling smile. "So, wow, we should have talked way before this. You never come over to say hi to me, Jon White."

Jon didn't know how to breathe or where to put his hands with Kadee Yoshenko standing right there smiling at him like that. "Hi," he said.

"Hi." She giggled. "You should come have lunch with us at the stands sometime. No way Todd is showing his face there again."

Jon looked aside. "Thanks. Yeah maybe."

He would never do that. He couldn't think of a single thing he could talk about with Kadee. She was the kind of girl who danced and lifted her hands when she led worship. He was the kid who got shoved into lockers, with a best friend in the worst family in the world. There was no way she would want to hang out with him if she knew that, even if he could tell her the truth about anything.

Her phone beeped and she turned to go. "Okay, well bye!"

"See ya." He watched her hair dance against her shoulders as she pushed through the doors into the school. He slid down the brick and put his arms around his knees, waiting for the bell to ring. Kadee's smile stayed with him, and slowly his own mouth tugged up to smile in return. So nothing would ever happen there in a hundred years. But still. Kadee Yoshenko had flirted with him. There was nothing wrong with letting that make him a little bit happy.

///

He called Cary's house after school, with a sheaf of homework in his fist. After three rings, an answering machine picked up. Jon's hand tightened on the phone and he almost hung up when heard Mr. Douglas' recorded voice. He hung on until the beep.

"Hi, Cary? It's Jon White—"

There was a click and Cary answered. "What is it."

Jon blinked. He tried to hear what was happening where Cary was—if Cary was safe. Then he realized he'd been quiet too long. "I have your homework," he said rapidly. "Ms. Somers wanted someone to bring it over so I said I would, if that's okay. But I don't remember your house number."

There was a beat of silence. "Not today."

"Okay." Jon closed his eyes. "This weekend? Do you want to come over and finish our project?"

"Yeah," Cary said.

"Sunday after church?" Jon said it without thinking. He realized the minute the words came out that he wanted to go—he wanted to see Kadee smile again. "Like two o'clock?"

"Yeah, that works," Cary said.

Jon was about to hang up when Cary said, "Jon—don't use this number. I have a cell." Cary rattled off the number, and Jon scribbled it down in a corner of his notebook.

"Okay," Jon said. "Thanks. See you Sunday."

Cary hung up.

9

Everything doesn't mend.

{Cary}

Cary's mother tapped on his door early Sunday morning.
He rolled over and frowned at the clock. After five days
stuck at home it took a second for him to figure out what
day it was, and what he was supposed to wake up for.

He showered, dressed in his church clothes and went
to his mother's room. She was sitting at her vanity table,
applying mascara. She capped the tube and frowned at
him.

"Darling, when was the last time you ran a brush
through your hair?" She got up and pressed him down on
the stool. He held still while she brushed his hair. Her
fingers felt cool on his skin.

"There." She stepped back. "Very handsome."

Cary looked up. His father's face looked back at him
in the mirror; his father's dark hair waved back from his
forehead. His eyebrows drew together and he got off the
stool. He didn't look at the mirror again.

"I'll just get my purse, and we can go."

"Liam's not coming with us?"

She smiled. "No, the nanny has him. Isn't that lovely?"

Cary didn't say anything. He didn't like the idea of a strange woman touching his brother. On the other hand, both his parents were happier when they weren't jumping at Liam's every cry.

Beverly's church made Jon's look like a parking garage. It was a large, ornate building with stained glass windows and a sweeping stone ceiling. The pews were two-thirds empty. Cary figured it was because they were so uncomfortable. He tried to shift his weight off his bruises then held still, his hands braced next to his legs.

He was practiced at rising and kneeling next to his mother for readings and prayers. The words of the service ran together like a river, making as much sense to him as the sound of water. At the end, the minister held up a small round wafer. His words rang on Cary's ear, different than the rest:

"On the night he was betrayed, the Lord Jesus took the bread and broke it saying, 'This is my body broken for you. Do this in remembrance of me.'"

Cary watched the people file out of the pews and shuffle to the front of the church for a mouthful of wafer and wine. He frowned. This was about the story of Jesus dying. He hadn't put that together before.

His mother went forward. When she slid back into the pew beside him she folded her hands and closed her eyes. He looked at the tips of her manicured fingers, which had just held Jesus' body. When the service was finished and they were settled in the leather seats of her sedan, he asked:

"What is the cracker and wine for?"

She laughed, as if she was startled by the question. "It's the Lord's Supper, Ciaran. We do it every Sunday."

"Why do you do it?"

She brushed a strand of hair off her face, stalling. "It's a way to say sorry," she said finally.

"For what?"

"For things that we've done."

Cary looked out the window. "Can I do it?"

"Take communion?" his mother asked. "What for?

"To say sorry," Cary said.

She laughed a little. "What do you have to be sorry for?"

Cary didn't reply. He felt her remember; her stillness made the air freeze and she didn't answer his question. Cary lifted his aching shoulders. Of course he couldn't do it. No amount of sorry would be enough.

///

Cary's mother dropped him off at Jon's house after lunch. Pete answered the door. His smile looked guarded. "Cary, come in. I think Jon's in his room."

Cary stepped in, taking the temperature of Jon's house without thinking. The main floor rumbled with the noise of Jon's sisters playing, and loud pop music about God poured out of the kitchen. Nothing threatened its happy din—except perhaps him.

He lifted his face to Jon's father, the way Conall liked. "Thanks for having me."

Pete nodded, but he didn't really look at him.

Cary went down the hall to Jon's room and rapped his knuckle on the door. Jon looked up, his face brightening. "Hey, you're early."

"My mom's church finished early."

"Oh." Jon was obviously surprised. Cary could practically see the questions popping out of his skin. Cary let his face relax, amused by how hard it was for Jon not to just say everything he thought. It felt good to be back— Jon's house felt good.

The templates were spread on the floor with everything they needed to cut them out and assemble them. Cary hunkered down and pushed his sweater sleeves up to his elbows. "Nice work."

Jon laughed. "Yeah, well you did them."

"Knife?"

Jon passed the utility knife into his outstretched hand. "You doing okay?"

Cary flicked him a look. "Yup. You?"

Jon lifted his shoulders. "I got my dad in trouble. A bunch of people wanted to talk to him at church today."

"What for?"

Jon made a face. "It's all blown out of proportion: the fight, the locker searches. Whatever. One of the youth group kids told me that 'a pastor's kid isn't supposed to hang out with kids who do drugs.' They don't know anything."

Cary hunched his shoulders. That's why Jon's dad looked angry with him—because he was. "I shouldn't have come over."

Jon glared at him. "Yeah, you should have. You're my friend. And I don't want to fail this project."

Cary's laugh was almost silent. "Thought so. Using me for a better grade."

Jon grinned. "Definitely."

Cary finished cutting the shapes out of one sheet of cardstock and stacked them to the side.

"I saw Todd today," Jon said.

Cary looked sharply at him.

"At church." Jon worked at assembling the pieces while Cary waited. "I never did anything, you know? To make him hate me. I wanted to make friends." There were deep, unhappy lines around Jon's mouth. "There was just something about me he didn't like—something wrong with me."

Cary's eyebrows snapped together. "There's nothing wrong with you."

Jon sat back on his heels, looking at him with that unhappy smile.

"You're good," Cary said. "Todd's the kind of asshole who likes to break good things."

Jon took a breath, and some of the tension went out of his body. "Oh. Thanks." He bent over the house again, raising the walls and pressing them into place. "Cary? Why does your dad—get so angry with you?"

Cary didn't say anything, cutting with steady pressure along the lines he had drawn.

"Does he drink?"

"No," Cary said shortly. "That's not why." His head buzzed. There was a room in his head he never went into, unless he was prepared to bleed.

Jon's forehead wrinkled as he looked at him. "There's nothing wrong with you either. There's no reason—"

"Shut up and leave it Jon."

Jon looked down. The silence was tense between them. "I just hate it," he said in a low voice.

Cary held the door of that room shut tight and put his weight against it. "Everything mends," he said.

Jon bent his head. "Right." He swore softly and jumped to his feet, turning his face so Cary couldn't see it. "I'm going to go get us some snacks. You hungry?"

Cary watched him, frowning. "Sure."

When Jon was gone, Cary straightened, stretching carefully. He took a slow breath, asking his muscles to unlock. He was safe here; that was hard to get used to.

He sprawled on his stomach on Jon's bed and pulled Jon's Bible onto the blanket beside him. There was a ribbon marking where Jon had left off, and Cary opened to there. He flipped through the pages, backwards then forwards. Jesus was all over them, speaking and doing stuff. His words were like hooks, catching on his skin and pulling him close. He flipped the book shut and pushed it away. A second later, it was stashed in his backpack.

Jon returned with a plate of sandwiches and a couple glasses of juice. Jon stretched his legs out on his bed, his sock feet dangling off the edge as he ate. Cary leaned on the edge of Jon's desk, polishing three sandwiches off in as many minutes.

He was finishing his juice when Jon said, "Everything doesn't mend. You have scars."

Cary set his empty cup on the desk. He tugged his sweater sleeves over his wrists without looking at Jon.

"Was any of that skateboarding story true?"

Cary was silent a moment. "I broke my wrists. They put pins in."

"Are you going to tell me what really happened?"

"Why do you want to know?"

Jon's forehead wrinkled. "I guess because you're my friend. And those scars are something that happened to you."

Cary held still. He thought he could say it—Jon kept his secrets. "My father threw me down the basement stairs. The floor down there is concrete, same as a skate park." He didn't mean to tell the rest, but once he started it just came out. "He left me down there and locked the door at the top. I climbed back up and I couldn't—" His hands closed. He flexed his wrist just to feel it work the way it was supposed to. "Anyways, that was a long time ago."

Jon slid forward and his feet thumped on the floor. Anger came off of him like heat. "That never should have happened to you. Your dad should have protected you. He should have loved you."

The room suddenly felt too small. Cary watched him sideways. "So he didn't. I don't feel anything about that shit. It would be stupid if I did."

Jon curled on the edge of his bed. He ducked his head and all the fight went out of him. "It wouldn't be stupid," he said in a low voice.

Cary shrugged. His body was trembling, remembering. But he didn't feel anything on the inside. All his feelings were in his skin and bones. He bent to cut the last pieces out of the cardboard.

Jon dragged his sleeve over his face, sighing. He lowered himself to his knees to adjust the walls of their project, pressing his lips in a thin, sad line. Cary glanced at him, frowning. He guessed Jon felt a lot of things inside and that's why he cried so much. How come he had nothing inside? He had the memory of kneeling at the top of the stairs, trying to open the door. It had hurt then, but it didn't hurt now. There was just a blank, like a whole chunk of himself was gone.

His hands were sweating so he couldn't keep working with the knife. He put it in his pocket. He felt like he was suffocating.

"I'm going to the washroom," he said.

Cary ducked out of Jon's room and into the bathroom in the hall. He locked the door and thumbed the knife blade up.

He stripped his sweater off and did it, quickly.

He dropped onto the edge of the tub and watched the blood go out and run down the drain. He could catch a breath again. He shut his eyes, one breath catching after another. Maybe crying felt like this, like washing something toxic out of your body forever.

His hand was numb. Cary cleaned up the tub and put his sweater on. He didn't look for bandages. He didn't care if he kept bleeding.

"I gotta go," he told Jon.

Jon looked up from the nearly finished house, puzzled. "I thought you were staying for supper."

"Can't," Cary said and left.

{Jon}

Jon finished the house alone. When it was complete, he sat back on his heels to survey their work. He didn't feel proud. He felt like crap.

He stretched on his bed and put his arms over his face. He had been so stupid to ask Cary questions about his scars, like his friend wanted to chat about climbing the stairs with broken wrists. Like there was anything Jon could say that would make him feel better.

There was a knock and his door opened. "Supper time," Pete said.

Jon swung his legs over the bed without looking at his dad.

"You okay?" Pete asked.

"Yeah, I'm fine." He used to be able to smile when he lied.

"Did you and Cary have a fight?"

"No. We finished early. He had to go."

Pete crouched next to the model, touching the sharp crease of its roofline with a finger. "Wow son. This is pretty impressive."

"Don't be patronizing," Jon muttered. "I'm not four."

Pete's smile tucked in at the corner. "I'm not. This is really fine work."

"Cary did most of it."

Pete looked closer. The roof was cut away so you could see the rooms laid out inside. "You have rooms here for everyone?"

Jon had forgotten about the labels above the doorways. There was a big room for *'Cary~Jon~Liam,'* another for *'Tabby~Bea,'* and a third bedroom with nothing above the door. They hadn't talked about it; the writing was in Cary's hand. Jon didn't give anything away. "Yeah, I guess."

Pete got to his feet with a smile. "Suppertime."

Jon followed him silently out of the room.

///

Jon let his sisters carry the dinner conversation. He was full of things he couldn't say to his parents; it was easier if he just kept quiet. He finished first and began washing up. His father joined him, taking up the dishtowel to dry. When the girls ran out to play Jon's mother began gathering up the food to put away. Pete took the dishes out of her hands. "The guys got this," he said with a smile.

When Jon was washing the last dish, Pete dried his hands and rustled through the perpetual mess of papers next to the phone.

"I picked this up on my way home today." It was a do-it-yourself guide to building a garage. Jon's eyes widened and he looked at his dad.

Pete smiled. "When we moved here, I said I wanted to put in a garage. The ground is thawed now. I could use a hand—a couple of hands."

Jon's face lit up. He'd dreamed of the day he would be old enough to use his dad's power tools. "I got a couple of hands."

Pete took the guide back without looking at him. "Do you think Cary would be interested?"

Jon grinned. "Yeah. That would be *great.*"

They put away the last dishes in a hurry and went out to the backyard to look at the open space where they would lay the concrete pad and build the garage. Jon couldn't keep the smile off his face.

"When can we start?"

Pete was pacing off the dimensions of the garage. He looked up, his eyes crinkling in a smile. Sun sparkled on the red in his hair and beard. "How soon can you free up your busy schedule to head to the hardware store?"

Jon answered a little too quickly. "No youth group, no worship practice—my schedule's all freed up."

Pete looked down again. Jon didn't think he appreciated his humour.

Jon kept talking like he didn't notice. "Cary's really good at this stuff. I'm glad you're asking him to help."

"Can you answer a question honestly, Jon?"

That stung. "Yeah."

"Is Cary involved with anything that I wouldn't want in my house?"

"No." Jon took a breath. He needed to answer this well. "He smokes. But so does Grampa White." Pete was sitting on his heels in the grass, watching him. Jon met his dad's look across the thick evening light filling the yard. "I know you don't get why we're friends, but dad—you don't know what it was like when we moved."

"Tell me what it was like," Pete said evenly.

Jon stuffed his hands under his arms. "Nobody at school would look at me. I thought it would just take a few weeks to make new friends, but when Todd started— nobody wanted to get in his way. He would be pushing me around and nobody cared."

Jon tried to smile. "Remember in Sunday school how, like, every lesson you taught us was about making friends with the kids who didn't have any friends?"

"Huh." A smile ghosted over his father's face. "That was years ago."

Jon lifted his shoulders. "When we moved—that was me. And Cary was my friend when I didn't have anyone else. He didn't need to be partners with the loser new kid. Everyone at school respects him because he's tough, you know?" He could see his dad's worried expression deepening. Wrong words. "And I know you don't agree with him punching Todd, and I know I should have told you about Todd sooner so that never happened and I'm sorry. I'm really sorry."

Pete straightened with a sigh. "Thank you for apologizing son. I forgive you."

Jon's shoulder bumped his father's arm as they walked back to the house.

At the door, Pete said. "Jon? Please ask Cary to leave his knife at home. I would hate for the girls to get a hold of something like that."

That touched off a little spark of anger in his chest. As if Cary would be that careless. Jon ducked his head. "Sure." He didn't speak again.

10

The hole.

{Cary}

Cary's father was gone when he got home—gone for a couple weeks to teach at some important university. Beverly told him this while scrambling eggs for dinner in the kitchen.

Cary dropped his coat and backpack in the corner, feeling twenty pounds lighter. The eggs smelled like they were burning. He moved her aside. "Mom, let me do that."

Beverly drew a stool up to the counter and pulled her glass of wine towards her. "The nanny is upstairs with Liam. Phillippa. She speaks very good English, you know. Your father would not have someone foreign speaking bad English to his son." She giggled and Cary wondered how many glasses she had poured before he came. In Conall's absence, she was like a planet missing the gravitational pull of its sun.

He took the eggs off the heat and dug in the bread box for something to make toast with. He plated the meal with a garnish of parsley and presented it to his mother, relaxing his face in a smile. "Ta-dah."

She giggled again, then spun off her stool and across the kitchen to flick on the stereo for some dinner music.

They were in the middle of eating when she caught his wrist. She turned his arm over, pushing the sweater sleeve to his elbow. The cuts still bled sluggishly. "What is this, Ciaran? What were you trying to do?"

Cary met her eyes, mouth shut, his tendons jumping as he clenched his fist.

"You promised," she said. "You promised me you would stay."

He jerked free. "I am."

She was pale, her eyes boring into him. "So what was that then—a mistake? A little joke to scare your mother?"

Cary got up and scraped his meal into the garbage. "No. Not a joke."

He should have kept his mouth shut, but since he was already bleeding he thought she couldn't hurt him any worse. "Did you ever think we could go?" he asked without looking at her. "Every night could be like this, just the two of us and Liam." He held still, his fingers curled over the cool metal edge of the sink, listening to her silence while the music crooned.

"You want me to leave my husband. Your father. Our home." Her soft, cold voice made him turn and look. Her cheeks were flushed and the tips of her teeth showed under her sneering lip. "Let me tell you something, Ciaran. Your father could have put you out with the garbage. He could have turned us out into the street. You should be grateful he saw more in you than a baby-killer."

Cary hands flew up, like her words were shards of glass thrown in his face. "Mom," he gasped. "Stop. I'm sorry."

"You should be." She got down unsteadily from her stool and swayed out of the kitchen.

Cary put his fingertips against his eyelids, where he felt the prick and burn of tears that couldn't fall. He stayed still, trying to breathe. Of course she could still hurt him. She knew all his secrets.

He left the dishes and climbed the stairs. Liam's door was open, but he didn't turn his head to look. Instead, he went to his room and climbed out the bedroom window.

The shingles were rough under his palms. He imagined sliding forward to the edge of the roof, then kicking off into the sky, leaving the dead weight of his body and everything behind.

He grabbed the window frame with one hand. For a second that had felt so real, he thought he was going over. He hung on tight and swung around to drop back into his bedroom. There was a reason he should stay—if he could just remember what it was.

He reached into his backpack for his smokes and put his hand around Jon's Bible. He drew it out. Somewhere in this book was the story of the bleeding man. Somewhere in this book was the answer to the peace in Jon's house. It made no sense that those two things would go together.

Cary sat on his bed and used the ribbon to open to the stories about Jesus. He hunted for the part where they killed him like he was pressing a bruise. He read it all: the blows, the scourging, the nails pounded into Jesus' hands.

It was different in Jon's book. Jesus wasn't surprised when they arrested him and he wasn't afraid. He never broke when they beat him. He never begged. He never said he was sorry. He said, "Father, forgive them," when they stretched him on the cross. He died with a shout—"It is finished!"—that made Cary rock back and put his hand over the page.

How did You do that?

He held still, his heart beating double-time, thinking of what it would take to absorb that much hurt and stay yourself. Jesus was strong.

Cary wanted that to be a true story. He wanted to face his own shit with half that strength. Cary covered the cuts on his arm without looking. He was sure that he couldn't.

He shut the book and went to the washroom to bandage his arm. He felt like the Jesus in Jon's book was watching him. He didn't look up at the mirror. Jesus was totally different than him. Jesus didn't deserve to hurt.

Cary turned off the light and climbed into his bed, curling with his face to the wall. He didn't open the book to read to the end—the part where Jon said Jesus came alive again.

///

He was in a hole in the basement, digging. The ground was hard and the light was poor. He struck his shovel into the dirt and chucked another clod over his shoulder. The hole went up to his chest; he'd been digging all night.

The plastic hanging from the ceiling rustled. Someone had opened the door at the top of the stairs. Cary hunched his shoulders. He climbed out of the hole and gathered the dirty bundle of blankets into his arms. He watched the figure coming down the stairs, tall and shadowed.

The stranger from the campfire stepped into the light of the single naked bulb. Cary drew in his breath. It wasn't who he expected, but he was still afraid.

"You have something that belongs to me," the man said.

Cary's arms tightened around the blankets. "Who are you?"

The man's lean face opened in a smile. There was a couple days growth on his chin. If he said a name, Cary didn't hear it. His ears were packed full of white noise like cotton. He was down here for a reason. He turned and picked up his shovel, dropping back into the hole and propping the bundle in the corner. One smudged little arm fell free of the blankets, limp in the dirt. Cary tucked it back in. She was cold. He turned his back and dug his shovel into the dirt again.

The man's bare feet dangled over the lip of the hole, then he dropped lightly in. His clean clothes and hands made Cary aware of the mud caked on the knees of his jeans and under his fingernails. "Get out of here," he said.

The man lifted his face, looking around. "How long do you think you can go on like this?"

Cary hefted the shovel in his hands. The way the man looked at him made him feel something. His skin sizzled: it was anger. "Get out."

The door at the top of the stairs bounced off the wall and Cary flinched. "That's him. Get out."

The man acted like he hadn't heard, looking at Cary with that stupid, open face. Cary swung the shovel at him. "Out!" He beat the man in time with his father's footsteps coming down the stairs.

"Where are you, Ciaran?" Conall called softly.

Cary whimpered and crouched in the hole, reaching to check that the bundle of blankets was safe.

The stranger got to his feet, blood pouring down over one eye. "Hide," Cary said. "Don't let him see you."

The man glanced at Cary, then put his hands on the edge of the pit and climbed out. Cary put his face in the dirt and covered his head with his arms. There was a din of noise, then silence. The door at the top of the stairs swung shut.

Cary lifted his head. There was blood everywhere: dripping down the plastic and pooling on the concrete. His breath hitched. There was also blood on his hands and spattered up his arms. He crawled out of the hole. His eyes jumped away from the body smashed on the floor.

The body moved. The man got up to his knees. Cary pressed his hands against his chest, frozen.

The man stood up. He stood in Cary's basement with blood sheeting his face. "You're bleeding," he said.

Cary pulled his hands away from his chest. They were sticky. "You shouldn't have come down here," he whispered.

"Give her to me," the man said. He held out his hands and said her name. There were scars on his wrists so deep they went through to the other side.

Cary couldn't breathe. He knew the answer to his first question. He got into the hole and gathered the blankets in his arms. He uncovered her blue-white face and kissed her stiff cheek. He passed her up into the waiting arms of the man. Jesus.

When Jesus held the baby to his chest, she was alive. She turned her head and looked at Cary with pink in her cheeks. Cary's heart thundered as if it would burst out of his chest and he woke up.

He sat up with a gasp, his heart still thudding. His cheeks were wet with something. He put his hand to his face. Had he been crying in his sleep?

He saw the man with the scars and a fresh cut splitting his lip bleeding red down his chin. He made a noise and lay down, covering his face. He wanted one more minute to say he was sorry for everything. God, he was such a fuck-up.

11

Where he is now.

{Jon}

Jon had never been friends with someone who was suspended, so he didn't know what to expect. Cary wasn't at the north doors in the first break, so Jon left Mike and the others and went back into the school before the break was up.

The Eastglen administrative offices were encased in glass like an aquarium. Jon could see Cary at a student's desk pulled up outside the principal's door. Cary leaned his head on his hand, pressing a book open to read. He looked tired.

Jon waited until the receptionist had turned away with a call, then slipped past her desk.

"Hey," he said.

Cary looked up. He glanced at the receptionist and frowned. "You shouldn't be here."

"You don't get a break?"

Cary shook his head. "Lunch."

"Okay. I just wanted to see if you can come over after school today. My dad wants to start building a garage. He's wondering if we can help this week."

The look Cary gave him was so flat and strange that Jon checked over his shoulder to see if someone was behind him.

"He wants me to help?"

Jon nodded. "Yeah. And then, you know have supper with us or whatever."

Cary looked down at his book. "She's done her call."

Jon straightened up, darted a look at the receptionist and hurried out.

///

Todd didn't even look at Jon in English class. At lunch time, Jon ate his PB&J sandwich on the grass outside the north doors, imagining the burger he was going to buy the next day. The days of Todd frisking him for his lunch money were over.

Cary came out the doors partway through the break. Jon thumped the grass. "Pull up a seat."

Cary arched in a stretch. "I sat all morning." He lit his cigarette and drew deeply with a sigh.

"This the only smoke break you get?" Jon asked, watching him.

Cary nodded. "I'm quitting."

"Cool," Jon said. "Did you think about the project? The garage?"

"No." Cary didn't look at him.

Jon's forehead wrinkled. Cary had walls up again and he didn't know why. He looked down the corridor between the buildings at the slice of blue sky touching the sports fields. "I really want you to help."

Cary didn't move. Jon watched him in the corner of his eye. Was it hard for Cary to come to his house and see how different it was? He wanted Cary to have a break—to give him that at least.

Finally, Cary said, "Okay. I don't need supper."

Jon's smile didn't feel all there. "Sure."

Cary sat on the edge of the grass next to him and finished his cigarette. When he was done he reached into his jacket and pulled out the last thing Jon expected.

"Hey, my Bible. I was looking for that."

Cary handed it over without looking at him. "Sorry I took it."

"That's okay." Jon looked at the side of his face. What was Cary doing with his Bible?

"I read it," Cary said.

Jon was startled. "All of it?"

Cary gave him a look. "The part about Jesus, when he died."

Jon stayed quiet, hoping they weren't going to fight about this again.

"You said he came alive again. Is he still alive?"

Jon felt a smile start on his face. "Yeah. He came back with like a new kind of body that doesn't die. The kind we'll all get in the end."

Cary's hands plucked up blades of grass, one by one. He frowned. "But he still has scars on him."

Jon's eyes went to Cary's wrists—the thick scars just visible beyond the cuffs of his jacket. He slowed up, trying to listen for Jesus. This felt important. "Yeah. I think that's just him. His scars are special because he died for us."

Cary's hands closed. He looked at Jon from under his eyebrows. "He what?"

"Um—he died so we could come to his Father—God—without being afraid. Before, we were far away because of sin—the bad things we've done—"

"I know what sin is," Cary said.

Jon took a breath. If he knew anything about Cary, he would say he was angry. *Okay, help.* "So we all have sin. And God loved us and wanted us close instead of far away. So Jesus came to die and make a way for us to have a relationship with him."

Cary's voice was soft and flat. "Did his Father make him do that?"

Jon swallowed. "No. Jesus wanted to. He loves us too. They're like the same person—everything Jesus did the Father would do too."

After a long moment, Cary shook his head. "You sound crazy."

Jon made his voice light. "You think this life is all we get? That's crazy. That would suck."

Cary looked at him again. "Huh." He stretched out on his stomach in the grass. "Time is it?"

Jon checked his watch. "12:35."

"I need to be back before the second bell."

They were silent a few minutes. Jon thought Cary had gone to sleep.

"If he's alive, where is he now?" Cary's voice was muffled with his face on his arms.

Jon looked at Cary's shoulders. He could practically hear Jesus' answer. "He's right here," Jon said.

"Like invisible?"

"Kind of. His Spirit is here, in me. With you. He never leaves."

Cary turned his head to look at him. Jon couldn't read the expression that rippled over his face. Jon thought about the way Cary's shoulders looked under his jacket and swallowed. He didn't look away.

The first bell rang. Cary got to his feet and knocked the grass off his jacket. "See you after school."

Jon smiled. They were still friends. "Yeah, see you."

12

Hope.

{Cary}

Cary sent his mom a text when school was done, just a couple of words to say he was at a friend's and would be back for supper. She texted back almost immediately with smiley faces and exclamation points, something about going out for dinner and have a fun time. He stuck his phone in his jacket and rolled his shoulders. Probably she didn't remember what she'd said last night. She had to be pretty tight to open her mouth about the baby.

He wanted a smoke so bad his head was splitting. He fiddled with the pack in his pocket, thinking about how he told himself this morning he would cut back to one a day and then quit. Two cigarettes a day was still half what he used to smoke. He lit up in the shelter of an alcove, waiting for Jon to come out of the school doors. A moment later, Jon came swinging through the crowd of kids with his head up and a smile on his open face. Cary concluded that asshole in English was leaving him alone. He ducked his head to hide his own smile and stubbed the smoke out on the brick. He pushed off the wall and fell into step beside Jon.

"Hey." Jon's smile brightened. "My mom's picking us up, so we don't have to catch the bus."

"She doesn't have to do that."

"Monday and Wednesday Bea has preschool, so she gets her then me."

"Oh." Cary tried to smell if his jacket smelled like he'd just had a smoke. Shit, of course it did.

Mrs. White turned to smile at him as he climbed into the backseat of the minivan. He noticed her eyes were the same colour blue as her blouse. "Hi Cary. Thanks for coming over to help today."

He ducked his head, mumbling, "Sure, you're welcome."

Jon's little sister was buckled into a car seat next to him. She turned her head away, playing shy. Cary was happy to do the same. He could see Jon's mother in the rear-view mirror, the corner of her temple where she'd missed a hunk of hair making her ponytail and one eye sparkling as she bantered with Jon. A couple times he saw her look up, checking him and Bea in the mirror.

There was no way to be invisible in Jon's family—everyone got noticed. He was a different Cary to Jon; he was somebody who helped and somebody who had things to say that were worth listening to. Cary sat back in the seat and let his shoulders relax. He liked himself the way Jon saw him.

Jon's dad knew less and saw more than his son. Pete was patient with both boys, even and fair in divvying up jobs, but Cary had a lifetime of experience reading the signs. Pete White did not like him. Pete saw the things Jon didn't pay attention to: Cary didn't talk freely, he didn't look grown-ups in the eyes, and he looked like the kind of kid who would pull a knife on someone without thinking twice.

Cary didn't blame him—that was all true.

He let Jon ask the questions, watching Pete's hands as he went over the blueprints. The garage was simple enough—one door, one window, and a sloped roof. Cary paid close attention so he would remember everything Pete said the first time he said it.

They measured the ground, dug out the foundation and built the form to pour in the concrete. When the afternoon was done Cary was sweaty, dirty, and his hands were blistered. He couldn't think of any way he would rather have spent his time.

Pete surveyed their work, wiping sweat off his face with his wrist. "Thanks boys. Nice work on the corners, Cary. You have a real accurate eye."

Cary's ears got hot and rang faintly. He thought he could have been more careful with his angle cuts; he'd only used a chop saw a few times in shop class. He didn't say anything.

As they went inside, Pete put his arm around Jon's shoulder. He had his head tipped to his son, listening with a smile while Jon described something from his day. Cary dropped back to pick his jacket up from where he'd left it in the grass. He looked one last time at the dark clay rectangle they'd dug and framed. He was happy. He went out the back gate and headed for the bus stop.

Jon caught up with him on the street. "Hey, leaving already? You sure you don't want to stay for supper?"

"No," Cary said. "Thanks. My father's gone for a bit."

"Oh." Jon's face brightened. "Well, can you come again tomorrow?"

Cary looked in Jon's smiling face and let his own face make that smile. "Yeah. Tell your dad—" Words got stuck in his head a second. *Tell him I won't fuck this up.* "Tell him I'll be there."

Jon peeled off to jog back to his house and Cary stuck his blistered hands in his jacket pockets. Back to the White's' house tomorrow. He put his head down and made his feet go slowly. *Careful now*, he thought to himself. Nothing was free. Happiness usually cost more than he could afford.

///

Cary worked on the garage with Jon and his dad almost every day after school. He kept his head down and his mouth shut, even though his father had drilled into him that this was disrespectful. Cary couldn't do different. The more he knew Pete, the more he was afraid that if he lifted his face and opened his mouth, Pete White would crack him open and everything inside would spill out on the grass like a hot pile of garbage.

He put all his respect for Pete into the work. His hands were good at building things—and they were strong enough to break a bone or press the life out of someone. Maybe Pete didn't know why exactly he didn't like Cary around, or why he was nervous when his little daughters were in the backyard with them, but he was right. Cary wasn't safe. He didn't belong in a house like Jon's. Cary knew that, but he couldn't make himself quit going.

13

Snap back.

{Cary}

On Thursday, Cary bussed home from school, instead of taking the bus to Jon's house. He had an essay to finish, and Jon said that if he had a rough draft done he would come over and edit it the next day.

He expected the main floor of the house to be empty and to eat cold leftovers out of the fridge. Instead, he found Phillippa in the kitchen with Liam tied securely on her back in a broad blue-and-green striped cloth. She smiled when he came in, her cheeks high and round as apples.

"Mr. Douglas, you are just in time. Your mother said you need supper, so I made chicken and rice."

"Don't call me that," Cary said. "Just Cary." The kitchen was filled with the smell of garlic, ginger and soy sauce. "You don't have to cook for me." His stomach growled in disagreement.

Phillippa *tsk'd* disapprovingly. "I have brothers. I know boys need good food to grow. You are much too skinny."

Cary flinched away from her hand, shrugging his shoulders to cover his involuntary response. Phillippa snapped her fingers instead of pinching his arm. She bent to take the bubbling pan of chicken drumsticks out of the oven. Liam surveyed his new view—the kitchen ceiling fan—with the same puzzled expression he gave everything.

Cary opened the fridge, hunting for a Coke.

"You were at a friend's house today?" Phillippa asked.

He slung a leg over one of the stools at the island counter. "Nope." He cracked open his pop. "Homework."

Phillippa set a plate of curry chicken and rice in front of him, smiling into his face. Cary looked away. "Thanks." He took a bite, then closed his eyes—it was amazing, hot, sweet and spicy.

Phillippa laughed and his face colored. One side of his mouth wanted to smile with her, but he didn't do that here. He watched her clean up out of the corner of his eye as he ate. Phillippa was younger than the other working women he had seen slipping in and out of side entrances in his neighbourhood. He didn't think she would last long in this house. But he was starting to hope.

Liam made a little complaining noise, and Phillippa hefted him around onto her hip and lifted him out of his wrappings. Cary got up to help mix Liam's bottle.

Phillippa smiled again. "Thank you, Mr....Cary. Do you want to feed him?"

Cary stepped back, crossing his arms tightly. "No." As she settled Liam in the corner of her elbow, he remembered the baby's warmth and weight in his arms. He stayed to watch Liam eat until his brother's eyes drooped with sleep, and Phillippa took the baby upstairs to settle him for his nap.

Cary went to his room and sat at his desk, pouring music from his headphones into his brain and writing one painstaking sentence after another on his essay. He vaguely heard the front door open and close; a few minutes later his mother came into his room carrying Liam. He took his headphones off, watching her sideways.

"Look Liam, it's your big brother. I know, we never see him anymore. Take a good look." Beverly brought Liam close so his blurry eyes focused on Cary's face and widened.

Cary leaned away. "Mom, I have homework."

She put on a pout. "You're so boring—homework here, homework at a friend's house. Liam my love, lie here." She laid the baby in the center of Cary's bed. Liam kicked his legs and gurgled.

"Where's the nanny?" Cary asked.

His mother was rummaging in his closet. "I asked her for a turn." She flashed a smile, sharp as a knife blade, around his closet door. "She's going to do some laundry."

She came out with an armful of Cary's clothes. "Darling, these are filthy." She gave a pair of pants a shake and a shower of wood shavings fell on the floor. "What have you been doing?"

He hadn't lied to her; he just hadn't offered any information. "Framing a garage."

A neat wrinkle appeared between her eyebrows. "Should I assume we are not talking about a work of art?"

"Jon's dad is building a garage. That's what it's called when you make the frame of a building out of wood."

For a second, she was speechless. She looked again at his clothes. "Ciaran, if you wanted a hobby, I would have been happy to pay for lessons or sports—or something other than construction." She made a face.

Cary turned back to his desk. "It's what I'm good at."

She sighed. "Well, for God's sake, don't let your father find out." She left with her arms full of laundry, muttering to herself.

Cary stole a look at Liam. His brother was holding up his fist like he had never seen anything so bizarre. Cary turned his desk chair so he could see Liam above the edge of his notebook. He reached in his pocket and pulled out his drawing pencils.

When Beverly returned, she curled on the bed with the baby. She let Liam catch her finger in his tiny fist and grinned over at Cary. "Let's do something fun tonight. The three of us."

Cary lifted his pencil. Almost anything would have been preferable to carving another fifty lines on *'Brian's Winter.'* "Like what?"

"I don't know—let's rent one of those old movies we used to watch and have popcorn in our pajamas. There's a place that still rents them in Strathcona."

Cary looked at her sideways. "What about Liam?"

She gathered her son in her arms, ready to go. "He'll just sleep. I want some time with you."

Cary shrugged and got up from his desk.

///

When they got back from the movie rental store, his father's black sedan was in the garage. Cary turned his head to watch its smooth side slide by as his mother pulled in beside it. She turned the car off, and they sat silently in the dark.

"Is he supposed to be back today?" Cary finally asked.

She shook her head. "Something must have happened."

"I'll take Liam upstairs?" He waited without looking at her.

"Yes, do that." His mother flipped the visor down and checked her face in the mirror. She made an irritated noise. "No lipstick."

Liam was asleep in his car seat and Cary hated to disturb him for this. He took the keys out of the ignition and went in through the garage door. Beverly went in the front entrance.

He found Phillippa in the nursery, reading with her feet up on the stool. She stood when he appeared. "Mr. Cary? Isn't it Liam's bedtime?"

Cary held out the keys. "He just fell asleep in the car. Can you drive?"

She nodded, half-smiling in amusement and curiosity.

"My mother wants you to drive him around for another 45 minutes so he'll be out for the night."

She took the keys and went out by the back stairwell. Cary hoped that would be enough time.

He went down the hallway to listen from the top of the stairs. His parents were fighting in the front entryway; their voices bounced off the cavern of space above them, making the glass sculpture shiver and shake.

" –come home hungry and find the house empty, the kitchen a mess. Would it be too much to ask to have dinner ready at the end of the day?"

His mother said, "Darling, we had no idea you were coming back today. You told me—"

The *'slap'* made Cary's whole body tighten. He saw his mother fall back a step, her eyes wide, red printed across her cheek. She brushed it with the back of her hand, lifting her chin. "Why don't I order in, a nice meal from Ginos?"

"Why don't you do that," Conall growled. "God, my head is splitting."

Cary didn't wait to hear any more. He ducked into his room, threw his window open, and climbed onto the roof. He sat against the house gripping his knees while the sky melted from blue to black.

The light went on in Liam's bedroom. He turned his head and watched Phillippa's shadow pass across the curtain as she tucked Liam in. Nothing disturbed the peace of that scene. It was like looking into another world—a fairy tale he would never be a part of. Cary kept his eyes on Liam's window until the light went out. He shut his eyes. Somehow, he had to keep that peace for Liam.

He was numb with cold, and starving when he slid back through his window. Phillippa's curry chicken seemed like another day entirely. He decided to risk a trip into the kitchen for food before he tried to sleep.

When he stepped out of his bedroom, he found the house dim and quiet. He thought the kitchen was empty until he snapped on a light. His mother was leaning against the cupboards, holding an ice pack to her cheek.

Cary held still. "Are you okay?"

Her eyes darted to his face, then away. She nodded.

"Where is he?"

"His office. The university sent him the wrong assignment. He had all the wrong material to teach from. It was an awful week."

Cary turned aside. "That's not an excuse."

"And you've never had a bad day and taken it out on someone else." She tossed the ice pack back in the freezer and thumped it shut.

It was a low blow; she knew it was. He poured cereal without looking at her.

She sighed and touched his shoulder. He flinched and she rested her hand there, holding him steady. "Same as me, I'm sorry."

It wasn't the same and Conall never said sorry. Cary kept that to himself and ate his cereal. He didn't want to fight with her tonight.

She leaned against the counter next to him while he ate. Her shoulder was level with his. They were the same size now; he hadn't noticed before.

"Can you help me tomorrow?" she asked in a low voice.

Cary swallowed. "With what?"

"I need you to look after Liam, just for an hour. Phillippa's off for Easter weekend. I wanted to go to a Good Friday service."

He was silent. Finally he said, "Like that?"

She turned her face to him; one side was swollen, angry and red. She brushed a strand of hair back. "I'll wear make-up. People see what they want to see. You know that."

First rule of camouflage. He blew out his breath. "Yeah. I'll look after Liam."

He held still while she kissed his cheek. Her lips were dry and cool. "Thank you."

"Good night, Mom," he said softly, as she retreated into the shadowed hallway.

14

Everything that's wrong with this family.

{Cary}

Cary was carrying the baby and she was cold. He couldn't find her blankets—he looked for them everywhere, hurrying. Jesus was after them. Cary was terrified and desperate with hope at the same time. Jesus was going to rip his heart out. He hoped he would have enough breath left to see his sister alive in Jesus' arms again before the end.

He jerked awake at a *'tap'* on his door. His room was light—it was morning. His mother slipped into his room.

"Cary? Are you awake?"

He pushed sleep and the nightmare away with effort, sitting up. "Yuh. You can turn on the light."

She was wearing her Sunday clothes and holding Liam in her arms. "Is he home?" Cary said.

She nodded. "In the conservatory. I think he was up all night."

Cary registered the rise and fall of piano music coming from the downstairs. He shoved his blankets back. "Okay, I'm up."

Beverly looked at him strangely. "Do you always sleep in your clothes?"

Cary took Liam out of her arms without answering. His heart thudded in his chest at the feel of Liam's soft weight. "He's growing."

She smiled. "Don't drop him." He shot her a look and she held up a hand. "Just teasing." She set the diaper bag on his desk. "There's a bottle and diapers in there. He just woke up, so he'll need to eat in a few minutes."

Cary held Liam tightly. "Okay." He tried on one of Jon's reassuring smiles. "See you in a bit."

She threw a smile over her shoulder as she left. She was right, he could hardly see the bruise.

He left the door open a crack behind her. If it was shut, his father would push it open to see what he was trying to hide. He laid the baby on his bed and dug in the diaper bag to mix a bottle. His hands shook. He clenched them against his chest and closed his eyes.

I don't want to hurt him. Please please let him not be hurt.

He didn't know who he thought he was talking to. The man with the scars was in his mind, holding the baby girl. Jesus would know how to do this. Cary took a breath, made the bottle, and cradled Liam to feed him.

Liam was still hungry when the bottle was empty. He fussed, gumming his fist. When he lost it, he waved his fists and fussed louder. Cary walked his brother around his room, rubbing his back and jiggling him up and down. He even tried singing what he could remember of 'Twinkle, Twinkle Little Star.' That made Liam start to cry for real.

There was no more formula in the bag. He checked the nursery—there was nothing there. Liam was red-faced from crying, burrowing against Cary's shoulder.

Cary swore softly. The can of formula was downstairs in the kitchen cupboard. He touched Liam's head, stroking his dark, silky hair. "Okay, we'll get some more. Don't cry. Please don't cry."

He rooted around in Liam's crib and found a soother. Liam sucked it hard, sniffling quietly in the hallway and down the stairs. Cary got a breath into his tight chest.

The sound of the piano was loud on the main floor, crashing around the high ceilings. The baby startled and started to cry again before they made it to the kitchen. Cary worked as fast as he could with Liam in his arms, trying to measure formula into the bottle with one hand. He was making a mess, but that didn't matter right now. His ears were full of the din of Liam's cries; he didn't hear the piano stop.

He put the bottle in Liam's mouth and the cries cut out. Instant relief.

When he turned, Conall was in the kitchen with him. His father's eyes were bloodshot and his hair was wildly disheveled. Cary bumped back against the counter, getting a better grip on his brother.

"What are you doing with him?" Conall asked.

"He's just hungry Father. I made him a—"

The blow snapped Cary's head to one side.

"What are *you* doing with your hands on my son?" Conall was right in front of him, huge and crackling with anger. "Give him here."

Cary tasted blood. There was no way out. "No. Not when you're like this."

Conall hit him again. Cary twisted, sheltering Liam with his shoulder. Conall grabbed a barstool and swung it, dropping Cary to his knees. Cary turtled up with Liam under his body. The bottle skidded away, spattering formula on the floor.

Cary held Liam tight but he couldn't keep Liam's head from knocking against the floor with every blow. His teeth locked around a scream: Liam was going to be smashed. They both were.

Conall grabbed Cary by the hair and dragged him out from under the counter. His father twisted his fingers tighter and flipped Cary onto his back. Cary's eyes watered and Liam spilled out of his arms. Conall dragged Cary away from the baby and threw him through the doors into the dining room. For a second, Cary thought his father forgot about the baby screaming bloody murder on the floor. He fought free of the dining room chairs to get back in the kitchen with Liam.

But Conall didn't come after him. Instead, he gathered Liam into his arms and fished for the bottle on the floor by the fridge. Liam refused to take it, twisting his head and yelling.

Cary's breath went in like a knife and he bent until his forehead almost touched the floor, spitting blood.

Conall burst through the swinging doors. "What did you do to him?"

Cary lifted his head. Conall was jiggling Liam up and down to try to soothe him. "He's afraid." His voice cracked. "Father, please don't hurt him."

Conall snapped his black glare to Cary. "You hurt him. You're everything that's wrong with this family. I want you out of my house. If I have to abide your presence one more minute, I'll be sick with it."

Liam finally latched onto the bottle, his tiny body still shuddering with sobs as he ate. Conall turned his face away from Cary, watching his baby son intently.

Cary was frozen. Wasn't his father right? Wasn't Liam safer without him there making his father angry? He got up and staggered out of the dining room, falling against the wall in the hall. Shit, something was broken. The blood was drumming in his ears so loudly he couldn't think. His mother had left him to take care of Liam; he couldn't go. He needed to stay close even if all he could do was get in the way of Conall's anger until it beat him into the ground.

He went to the basement. The door at the top of the stairs was closest to the kitchen and within earshot of Conall's study. He slid inside and dropped onto the top step. It was dark and cool. He rested his head on his arms.

///

He heard his parents fighting as if it were a long way away. His father was shouting; his words were clear through the door: "How could you leave the baby with him? Did you forget what he is? He can never, never be trusted with Liam." He couldn't hear his mother.

Conall's voice broke and got quiet. "Look at him, Bev. He has bruises. I can't..." The next words were indistinct. "I want better for Liam. Don't you?"

Cary wrapped his arms over his head. Then his father was in the hall, standing directly behind Cary on the other side of the door. Conall's words went off like shots fired through a silencer. "Deal with your son. I'm finished with him. If I see him again, I'll kill him."

Cary pressed his face into his knees, not breathing. His father's footsteps went past him and up the stairs. Cary's lungs cried for air, but he wanted them to stop. He wanted to reach into his chest and just stop everything.

"Cary?" His mother called softly.

Breath sobbed in his chest. He reached behind to open the basement door a crack. She stepped inside and shut the door on them both. He could feel her standing, looking down on his bent head.

"I didn't mean to hurt him," Cary whispered.

She snapped on the light. "Look at me."

He squeezed his eyes shut and turned his face to her. The smell of her Sunday perfume wafted toward him as she crouched. Her fingers were cool against the heat of his cheek where his father had struck him. He opened his eyes and looked at her.

She was crying. At least, tears were sliding down her cheeks and dripping off the edge of her jaw. The rest of her face stayed still and lovely as a china doll's. "Do you have someplace to go?" she asked. "You can't stay here tonight."

He couldn't look at her again. She was making a choice; he got that. He had to make his own choice not to care. It took a minute to bury everything under stone. "The youth shelter will take me. If I'm kicked out."

She was silent beside him. He knew what she was thinking.

"I'll tell them I got in a fight at school."

Her cool voice filled in the rest. "I'll tell them you were scaring us. That you left bruises on your baby brother."

His drawn breath stabbed him. "Please don't tell them that."

"Every lie needs a little truth," she said.

He covered his eyes. She ran a hand over his back and his skin shuddered all over. "Go wait in the car, I'll pack you a bag."

He waited until she was gone to pull himself to his feet. He moved slowly down the hall, listening and hanging onto the wall. He got his jacket from the bench in the boot room and checked the pockets for his smokes, his knife, his drawing pencils, and his phone. He put the jacket on. It felt heavy.

They were silent on the drive to the shelter in old downtown. Beverly pulled into the bus lane to drop him off in front of the yellow-brick building. She didn't look at him or speak. Cary braced a hand on the glove compartment, getting ready to get out without giving away what it cost him. "You'll be okay?" he asked.

"Of course." There was nothing real about the smile she put on. He looked at her from under his eyebrows and they both knew she was lying. She lifted her hands and let the smile drop off her face. "I think your father is right. You bring out the worst in him. I was never afraid before you... before."

She drew in her breath and shut her eyes. "I want that back," she said, so softly it was almost lost in the sound of passing traffic.

Cary ducked his head and opened his door. Beverly caught his wrist, her fingers wrapping around his scar. "Ciaran."

He looked back, his arm tensed to pull away.

"Be good. Be safe. Call me when you can." Her voice almost disappeared.

He couldn't say any of the things that were in him to say. He got out of her car and walked away without looking back.

15

Shelter.

{Cary}

A staff person in shorts and a hot pink t-shirt looked up from his magazine when Cary came, blinking, through the doors. The guy smiled, but his eyes were uninterested. "Hi, are you looking for a place to stay?"

Cary nodded.

"Come on back. I'll give you a run-down of the shelter rules and do the paperwork on you."

Cary followed him into the main office, a big open space, with phones and computers and a window looking into the rec area. He wanted a smoke; he had to do an intake interview before he could go out back and light up.

The staff guy took his name and age and vital stats and explained the long list of shelter rules. Cary tuned out. He'd been here before; it was pretty straightforward— keep curfew, respect the staff, do chores when it was your turn. The youth shelter was temporary housing, which meant after thirty days he needed to find someplace else to stay. Most kids didn't make it past day ten. After living on your own, even if it was just sleeping under a bridge, the shelter rules and structured routine quickly became an impossible price to pay for three okay meals and a bed.

After Cary's own house, the shelter was easy.

When the guy finished talking, Cary said, "Is there a nurse or something?" He brushed his hand over the bruise on his cheek. "I think those kids broke my ribs. I'd really like a Tylenol."

The even way he spoke seemed to throw the guy off. He looked closely at Cary for the first time. "Um—no. There's no nurse. I'll ask my director about a Tylenol. Sorry, how did you break your ribs?"

"The fight with some kids from school. You wrote it down in your notes there." Cary pointed at the notepad between them. "When you call my mom she'll tell you all about it."

The staff guy nodded. "Right. I'll send someone with the Tylenol, if my director says that's okay."

"Thanks." Cary got up. "I'll be in the smoke pit." He headed through the office doors to the concrete yard at the back of the building where residents were permitted to smoke.

///

There were a couple kids already in the back, clustered together and goofing off while they passed a cigarette around. There was a girl Cary knew from the north doors, laughing loudly with her mouth wide open while two or three guys looked on hungrily. Cary kept his distance.

There was a storage shed making shade on the other side of the yard. Cary put his back against it and gingerly lowered himself to the ground. He didn't care about the kids or the phone call to his mother that was probably happening in the office. He lit his cigarette and turned his attention inside himself, checking the damages to try to figure out how long he needed to recover.

His hands remembered how hot Liam had been as he'd screamed and twisted underneath him. Cary stuffed his fists into his armpits. He knew exactly where Liam had bruises: every place Cary's fingers had touched him, holding him so tight. The stone lid scraped back a crack and there was a hole in him dark to the bottom. He heard his mother saying, *I wasn't afraid before,* and what she meant slipped up out of that crack, clear as if she had said it out loud: *You scare me like he does.*

He sat still watching the shadows lengthen in the yard, noticing the shape of the light and the dark as if he were planning to make them into a drawing. It worked; after a few minutes he was blank again. There was nothing inside him except the things his body told him: he was hurting and he was looking at light and shadow—one didn't matter more than the other.

His phone rang. He took it out and looked at the screen. Jon. His stomach twisted. They were supposed to meet this afternoon to work on their essays. He picked up. "Yeah."

"Where are you?" Jon sounded completely freaked out. "I went to your house and your mom said you didn't live there anymore—What the hell is going on?"

Cary looked at the brick wall of the shelter, trying to find it in him to make up a story that would calm Jon down. He scraped bottom: he didn't have anything left for Jon just now. "I'm at the youth shelter on Strathcona. "

"Are you okay?"

"Yeah." He covered his eyes. The jagged edge of his rib slid in and out on his breath. "I'll be okay in a couple of days."

There was a beat of silence. He could hear talking in the background on Jon's end. "Who's with you?" he asked sharply.

"No one," Jon said. "I'm on the bus. My dad dropped me at your house and then you weren't there. Cary. Are you going to tell me what happened or just leave me with the pile of lies your mom told me about how you hurt your brother? Because I know that's crap."

It made him feel something that Jon didn't believe her. It was a tiny spark of warmth. "My father came back early. He was—like he gets, and I fucked up."

"I'm coming there. I'm changing busses."

"You can't; the shelter doesn't take visitors."

"Then meet me at Gazebo."

Cary started to get to his feet. He made an involuntary noise of pain; his whole left side had stiffened up and he would be lucky to make it to the dining room for supper. "I can't. I can't walk that far."

He had never heard Jon sound so close to scary. "Tell me. Exactly. What he did to you."

Cary wrapped his free arm around himself, pressing the palm of his hand against the bruises on his ribs. The counter had sheltered his right side, but the left side of his body had the shit kicked out of it. "I think my ribs are broken," he said evenly. "He hit me with the kitchen stool to try to—crack me open and get Liam. I had him under me. That's how I hurt him—holding him too tight."

Jon sucked in his breath. "You have to let me tell my dad."

He went rigid. "No."

"Cary, *please*."

"No! What the fuck good would that do if your dad even believed you?"

"You can't leave Liam there with him!"

Cary laughed sharply and then had to hang onto the corner of the shed while black pressed all around the edges. When he could breathe he said, "You don't get it, Jon. I'm the problem. If I just keep out of Liam's life he'll be better. They're good now. It's over."

"Then what about you? What are you supposed to do?"

"I'll be fine." The phone fed the words back to him, faint and echo-y.

"Cary—" Jon's voice broke.

"Jon, if you tell I will lie my fucking face off, and you will look really stupid."

He heard Jon take a breath. "Okay." He sounded soft, like he was crying. "I won't. Please call me if you need help, okay?"

"Sure." Cary closed his eyes. He'd done it; Jon was shut up. He couldn't do anything about how his friend sounded so sad. Jon just needed to get tough. "I gotta go for supper."

"'Kay," Jon said. "Bye."

Cary hung up. He wrapped his arms around himself, holding still. The other kids were going inside; the dining room was open. He needed to go with them and eat something to stay strong enough to sit and stand and act like everyone else. He needed to pull it together, to shove the stone lid over the basement full of rooms with shit inside and go on. He was too tired to move.

There was a boy coming across the pavement toward him, his crown of blond hair shining in the sun. Cary frowned. He recognized this kid from somewhere, but not from school.

"Taylor said to find you with these." The boy's high, sweet voice took Cary back to the church steps, the last time he ran away. It was the kid who'd been with Mike, the one who said crazy shit about seeing what was going on with people.

The boy's round face lit up in a smile. "Care, I didn't know it was you." He crouched, holding out a couple of Tylenols and a plastic cup of water. Cary took them, watching the boy sideways.

"You work here?" Cary asked.

"No, I just stay here a lot." The boy's friendly face didn't cloud over; this was just a fact of life. "The dining room is open. Leftover church potluck: turkey and mashed potatoes. It looks pretty good."

Cary started to push himself to his feet. The boy stuck out his hand and hauled him up. His eyes touched the bruise on Cary's face, then politely slid away.

"What's your name anyways?" Cary asked.

"Leonard. Most of the kids call me Down Low. You can too if you want. I don't mind."

Cary took another look at his child-like face and open expression. Downs—that explained a bit. But Cary didn't plan to call him anything. He was hoping entire days would go by where he didn't have to say anything to anyone.

Leonard held the door open for Cary; that was a little annoying. The boy followed him to supper and sat next to him at the empty table, smiling around the room like there was something lovely about the scratched table tops and concrete walls.

Cary kept an eye on the other two tables of kids. The dining room was only half-full and, with the exception of one thick-chested older boy, he was pretty sure he could take any of the others in a fight—at least, if his left side wasn't so fucked up. Head down, mouth shut until he was healed. Probably after that, too.

He looked at his half-eaten turkey, pink and rubbery in a pool of gravy. He swallowed, sick again. His body would mend, blindly repair itself and keep on: heart beating, lungs breathing, brain making his eyes blink and his legs and arms move. But Cary didn't know what for. Tomorrow and every day after that unfolded blank and white, empty as death. In fact, he was pretty sure being dead would hurt less.

He put his knife and fork down, finished. His mouth was dry and tacky. He drank his cup of powdered Tang juice to the dregs.

"Are the dorms open?" he asked without looking at Leonard. He didn't want to go to the effort of getting up until he was sure he knew where he was going.

"Yeah, and I have my own room. Do you want to stay with me? I'll make sure it's okay with the staff."

Cary shot a look at the guys at the other table. The bigger guy was teasing the girl with the teeth, snapping her bra strap on her shoulder. She caught it back, glaring at him. Good chance if he didn't bunk with Leonard, he'd be with one of them.

"Sure," Cary said.

The boy's dorm was one floor: six rooms with four or five bunks each. Leonard's room was closest to the bathrooms. His bed was neatly made up, with the blanket tucked in at the foot and the corners folded like a present. Cary set his backpack at the foot of the lower bunk across from it, then dropped onto the bed, exhausted.

He got out of his jacket and stretched out on the bare, plastic mattress. He slung an arm over his face, intending to shut his eyes for just a second. He was asleep before Leonard came back with the sheets.

///

He woke up with a sharp intake of breath, looking up at the bunk hanging low over his face and then at the dim room around him. Where was he?

Leonard looked up from where he sat propped in the corner of his bed, reading by the light of a flashlight. Cary rolled over to sit up, still disoriented. His rib punched him in the side and he caught the bunk above him to keep from tipping out of bed onto his face while the wave of pain slammed into him.

"You okay, Care?" Leonard asked softly.

"In a sec," Cary said through his teeth.

"Do you want me to get more Tylenol?"

The wave receded, rippling on the edge of Cary's awareness, ready for him should he move too quickly again. He kept his breaths shallow and careful. "Sure," he said.

Leonard swung his feet out of his bed. He was wearing big furry slippers, so worn and dirty they were more grey than white. "I'll be right back." His worried face flashed in the dimness and he was gone.

Leonard had made up the bunk next to his for Cary. The blankets were tucked in at the feet, exactly like his own. Cary painstakingly moved his backpack to the foot of that bed. He was going through its contents when Leonard returned.

Cary took the cup and the white pills, touching Leonard's eyes with his own for just a second. "Thanks."

The boy sat across from him, watching Cary drink with a worried expression. He had his feet lined up exactly side-by-side, the twin flop-eared doggies panting up at them in the dark. "Did someone do that to you? You're pretty..." he moved his hand to Cary, the bruises showing on his bare arms. "You're pretty banged up, Care."

"It's Cary," he said. He set the empty cup on the desk beside the bunks. He didn't think anything would turn Leonard's worried look aside except some kind of truth. "I don't like to talk about it, okay Down Low?"

Leonard curled his shoulders in. He went to his bed and slid under the blankets. "Okay," he whispered.

Cary re-packed his backpack. His mother had swept everything from his desk into the bag: his drawing book and the homework he'd been working on. She'd also put money in his wallet. He fingered the bills, then touched the edge of the razors tucked into the card pockets. She'd

been in a hurry to not notice them. He buried the wallet at
the bottom of his bag. He was a little too glad to see it.

16

Trade you.

{Cary}

The shelter had an eight AM wake up call, one of its least popular features. Cary dragged himself down to breakfast and nursed a cup of coffee, feeling like shit. Leonard joined him with his bowl of porridge and bright quarters of orange.

"Morning," he said cheerfully.

The fierce girl with the laugh was with him. Cary shot her a frown. She looked different with no eyeliner and her dyed and fried hair pulled back in an elastic. She huddled in her baggy sweater like it was what passed for a hug in her world.

"Cary, this is Karmin." Leonard said.

Cary nodded and didn't bother looking at either of them again. She was giggling at Leonard before breakfast was over. Cary endured it in silence because he didn't want to move. He was thinking about sneaking back into the boys' dorm to crash.

He spent the morning buried in an armchair in the shelter lounge with his drawing book and pencils. He lost track of time. Leonard came for him with a fresh dose of Tylenol exactly four hours since the pills he'd had at breakfast. Cary didn't have the heart to tell him they barely took the edge off.

"It's lunch," Leonard said. He sat on the arm of the chair next to Cary, leaning over his shoulder. "Hey, did you draw that?"

"Yeah." Cary flipped the book closed on the picture of his mother and Liam curled together on the bed. He had finished it.

"You're really good. I bet people would pay you to draw for them."

"Huh." The last thing Cary wanted to do was spend time with people doing their drawings.

He was starving. They were the first two in the line for lunch. The rest of the kids trickled in from the bus stop, or the smoke pit, or the ravine out back. Karmin came to sit next to Leonard again. Her lipstick looked like the slash of a wound on her face.

"Hey Leonard." She ignored Cary. Her eyes darted around the room at the other kids in line.

The guys she'd been with the day before set their trays down at the table around them. Cary held still in his jacket, keeping his stone face blank and hard like he would give as good as he got if it came to that.

Leonard chatted and joked but the guys' laughter felt more like they were laughing at him than with him. Karmin snugged her chair so close to Cary that her arm touched him. Cary ate quickly, got up and left.

///

He was in the smoke pit when Karmin came out the doors, flicking her hair back, her mouth sneering. "Oh my god what an asshole." She stopped next to him with her hip cocked. "Not you. Can I have a drag?"

He looked at her from under his eyebrows. She rolled her eyes. "I'm sorry, but if I don't get a cigarette I'm going to tear someone's face off, know what I mean?"

He passed her the smoke he'd half finished. "Keep that." He didn't want it back with the red crap from her lips on it. He lit another one.

"Thanks. Nice to finally meet someone decent in this shithole. For a while there I thought Down Low was the last nice guy in the world."

Cary frowned at her. Whatever she was angling to get from him, he didn't have anything except that smoke.

"Not much of a talker, are you?" she remarked, after five minutes of smoking in silence.

"No," Cary said.

She flicked the cigarette onto the concrete and straightened her shoulders. The tank top was back. "We're hanging out in the ravine just back there if you want to come chill," she said, sticking her thumb at the tangle of bushes and trees growing across from the parking lot.

Cary shrugged. He was pretty sure there was no one there he wanted to "chill" with, and the way she tucked her hand into the waistband of her jean shorts and stroked her thumb over the strip of pale skin above her hip made him uncomfortable.

"Come find us if you change your mind." She went back inside, waggling her hips.

Cary shifted and turned away. Girls. It was a mystery how they went from sweet and innocent as Jon's sisters to shit-full of secrets as his mother. The pouty in-between stage confused the hell out of him.

When he went inside, he discovered the dorms were open for the afternoon, supposedly so the residents could clean their rooms. Cary rolled into bed with his jacket still on and crashed to sleep.

///

He would have slept through dinner if Leonard hadn't gotten him up, patting his shoulder with his freckled hand. "Suppertime, Cary," he said in his light voice.

Cary pulled the blankets over his head. Leonard had been gone for a couple minutes before he was ready to sit up and face the dorm room. He looked at the metal bunks with their identical grey plastic mattresses and the tiny window with flaking trim. He felt as bleak as the room. He could already predict what would happen tomorrow and the next and the next after that. It led to nowhere at thirty days, a dead end.

His family would close around the place where they had cut him out, and there wouldn't even be a mark. Maybe they would laugh more and go on vacations together. Liam would get big and be their son. Cary made a sound, like something wrenched loose. He pressed the heels of his hands against his eyes.

He wanted them to be happy. But that left him here, alone with nothing except the basement and his scars. His body could mend and keep going, but there was something inside him that couldn't. That couldn't mend.

He dragged his sleeve across his nose and pulled his backpack toward him. He dug deep and pulled out his drawing book, his pencils, and his wallet of razors. Something was taking shape in his mind. He wanted to say sorry—that meant blood. Then he wanted to be done.

His heart missed a beat, then sped up. God, if he could be light. If he could cut free from this broken body and all the shit he'd done and had done to him. The basement was heavy; he'd been carrying it so long it had crushed him until he almost didn't recognize himself. He didn't give a shit about anything anymore—just Liam and Jon. He dug the heel of his hand into his chest. They weren't enough.

Cary let out his breath slowly. He had one chance to do this right. He opened his drawing book and carefully tore out the picture of Liam and his mother. He folded it once and wrote, "For Liam Douglas." He tore out the picture of the house he and Jon had built together, folded it, and wrote, "For Jon White" and Jon's phone number and address. He left the drawings on his pillow.

He took out his phone and opened a new text to Jon. He shut his eyes and took a breath. He imagined Jon was sitting on the bed across from him with his open face and easy smile. He put all the things into his fingers that he could never make his mouth say out loud.

<Jon I wanted to say thanks. You're like a light in a dark place. I never had someone try to push the dark back for me. you cried for me when nobody noticed.

this is not your fault the dark in me is just too big. I'm sorry.>

He had to stop because his hands were shaking. He put them into his armpits to warm them up. He realized his whole body was shivering. There was so much to say and now he was out of time. He picked up his phone again and punched in the rest.

<tell my brother about me when he's old enough. just tell him i loved him. cary.>

He sent it, and when it was gone he turned off his phone and left it on the pillow with the drawings.

Everyone was at supper. No one saw Cary leave through the back doors and head for the ravine. He went in the opposite direction he'd seen the other kids coming and going; he didn't want to meet anyone.

Once he fought his way through the bushes, the way was open. Evergreens stretched tall and gloomy, carpeting the ground with their soft needles. There was a small creek running over stones, chatting quietly. Cary followed it, looking for the right place.

He walked a long time. Sometimes he could hear traffic above him; once, a helicopter thudded in the distant sky overhead. The stream ran out of a culvert in a tall, weedy bank. Traffic rumbled above it, covering the noise of the water falling from the man-sized pipe. Cary doubted anyone in the passing cars even knew there was a stream here. He stepped up the bank, pushing through the weeds and tucking in to a sandy spot next to the culvert. Its metal side was cool and rough. If he stayed down, the weeds hid him from any unlikely passers-by.

Cary put his back against the bank, taking a breath. This would do. His eyes caught on the black shapes of the evergreen branches reaching for the evening sky. It was even kind of beautiful.

He took his drawing book out from under his arm and his pencils out of his pocket. He turned to a clean page. He shut his eyes a second, flipping the stone lid aside and dropping into the basement. There was a room in his mind he kept tightly locked. He opened it.

It was a nursery done in pink and yellow—his baby sister's room. He was just big enough to climb into her crib when she woke up from her nap and make her laugh and laugh. He was drawing her like that—laughing. While he drew, he remembered being there in their hiding place with the crib blankets pulled up over their heads. He was holding her in his arms and they were not afraid. There were no shouts in the other room and she was quiet and content. He drew her closer and put his face against hers.

He whispered: *Renae. I should have held you like this.*

But he hadn't. He had held her tightly enough to smother her cries while his mother's screams came through the wall. When he opened his arms, she was dead.

The hand holding the pencil dropped to his side, and Cary bowed his head. Maybe if there was some kind of life after death he would see his sister there—before he went to the dark place that was for people like him. He hoped it didn't hurt, that there was just nothing. That he would be erased with everything he had done, and all his scars wiped blank.

He couldn't kick free of the memory of the nursery. He had tucked her blanket against her cheek—maybe she was sleeping and she would wake up. Her body had rolled out of his arms, limp. Nothing he did could make her open her eyes again. Cary took his wallet out of his jacket pocket without looking. He was so sorry he couldn't breathe. He cut the lines across his arm, watching his sister's still, blue face. This time he was going to draw the line that crossed them all, wrist to elbow.

He was gathering his strength to finish it when someone else stepped into the room. Cary balled into the corner, trapped. He could see a pair of hands reaching into the crib. They had scars; he recognized those scars.

Jesus lifted her tiny body, cupping the back of her head with his scarred hand. He kissed her lips and said her name. Renae's eyes opened and when she saw His face, she laughed.

Cary choked and wrapped his hands over his mouth. Jesus was holding his sister, alive in his arms and joy came off of him like light. Cary hid his face, waiting for him to look up and that joy to change to anger like a lightening strike. Blood ran, soft and cool, down his arm.

He heard Jesus ask quietly, "What did you want to say?"

Cary swallowed, risking a look. Was he talking to him?

Jesus touched him with a look and Cary shrank back like he'd been slapped. "Ciaran," Jesus said. He was still smiling but his mouth pressed in at the corner like something hurt him.

"I'm sorry," Cary whispered. He put his head down and his hands up, like his palm-full of blood was enough. "I'm so sorry. I know I can't take it back. But I would. I would trade—if I could pay you—" He strangled those words. There was no way to pay back a life. He was going to hell.

There was a laugh so quiet and near that Cary opened his eyes. Jesus was hunkered down, face-to-face with him in the nursery, waiting for him to look up. "You don't know me very well yet."

They were quiet, looking at each other. Cary's understanding expanded like a drawn breath. His sister was alive. She wasn't dead in her crib or cold in the ground. She was with Jesus now. He couldn't see her, but he knew that was true.

Jesus touched Cary's hands and he shivered while Jesus uncurled his fists, smoothing Cary's fingers open. Cary had cut across every part of his arm that had held her, right down to his fingertips. Jesus made a small, hurt noise.

Cary's other fist was full of razors. Jesus saw them too.

"Can I take those?" Jesus asked.

"What do you want them for?" Cary asked.

"What do you want them for?" Jesus returned.

Cary couldn't look him in the face. He lifted his shoulders, then let them drop. His jacket felt like a hundred pounds. "I can't—carry this anymore."

Jesus held out his hand. The scar on the inside of his wrist was pink and puckered. Cary tipped the razors into

Jesus' palm. Jesus touched the sleeve of Cary's jacket. "Can I take this too? Will you give it to me?"

Cary shook his head. "You don't want it."

"Yeah I do." Jesus wore that smile, the one that opened his face so everything underneath shone out. "It's hurting you. I want it."

Cary pulled his jacket off his shoulders and he held it out.

"Thank you," Jesus said softly. He slipped it on.

The hairs on Cary's bare arms stood up. He felt like a rag bag of broken bones and scars wrapped up in black and blue skin. He didn't think he could hold together without that jacket. He wanted his razors back.

Jesus pushed back the jacket sleeve and turned his forearm up. He closed and opened his hand until the tendons showed in his wrist. In a second, he had drawn the cuts across his arm, over and over. He turned the razor and cut his arm open right down the middle, wrist to elbow.

Cary was screaming before the blood started to come out. He collided with Jesus, slapping the razor out of his fingers. Jesus fell back and Cary's hands slipped on his bloody skin. He wrapped his fingers around the cuts, swearing frantically while blood beat out of Jesus' body. The last cut was deep, too deep. He bent, touching his forehead against his red hands.

"Jesus, why did you do that?"

Jesus laughed that soft laugh. "Trade you," he said, and he died.

Cary's breath caught strangely and his eyes were hot. He took one hand then the other off of Jesus' opened arm. The knees of his cargos were soaked black-red and his face was wet. He put the backs of his hands to his eyes; they were crying.

He looked at Jesus' dead body wearing his jacket and a part of him knew he could open his eyes and be crouched by the culvert instead of here. He didn't want to leave Jesus like this, splayed in a pool of blood.

He gritted his teeth and dragged the jacket off Jesus' body. When his arms came free of the sleeves, Cary sucked in his breath. There were bruises on Jesus' arms and there was one on his face. Jesus' shirt was rucked up above his waist. Cary lifted it with freezing hands and saw that his body was shadowed with bruises. He touched Jesus' left side. Jesus' ribs were broken.

"Oh God," he whispered, his tears falling on Jesus' broken body.

When he could see again, Cary smoothed the shirt down and laid Jesus' scarred hands across his chest. He straightened his legs, and when he didn't know what else to do, he covered that still face with his jacket.

Cary drew a breath and opened his eyes on a sunset streaming gold and red above the evergreens. He was still crying. He dragged his jacket sleeve down over his cut-up skin, and pressed his bloody palm against his chest, curling and choking on his tears. He wanted Jon here to ask him, *He comes alive again, doesn't he?* It felt urgent.

He knew what Jon would say, though. He could see Jon's smile brighten as he said it: *Yeah, he does.*

Cary caught his breath and wiped his eyes, the salt-water stinging his cuts. He dug a hole in the bank and buried his razor wallet, down deep. The thing that killed Jesus wasn't an option anymore. He hated to even touch it to drop it in the hole. He climbed down the bank and walked back to the shelter.

17

How to live.

{Cary}

Leonard was sitting at the picnic table in the smoke pit when Cary climbed out of the ravine. Cary glanced around. There were no other kids out and Leonard didn't have a cigarette. He smiled as Cary crossed the concrete, but he looked sad and distracted.

"Hey, Cary."

Cary closed his fingers on the cuffs of his jacket. His cuts prickled, clotting and closing. "Hey." His voice was husky from crying. "What are you doing out here?"

"Watching," Leonard said.

Cary frowned. After a minute, he sat on the bench beside Leonard. He still felt naked, like he wasn't wearing his jacket even though he was. He took his cigarettes out and lit up for something to do. The scribbled lines he'd made on his palm looked black in the fading light. He closed his fingers, hearing the hurt sound Jesus made when he saw his hand—the Jesus in Jon's Bible. The Jesus Pete prayed to. He felt like the ground had shifted and everything was oddly unfamiliar from this new angle. Jesus was real.

It was purple and dusky when Cary and Leonard heard laughter floating up from the ravine. Leonard stirred, like this was what he'd been waiting for. A handful of kids emerged out of the dark, staggering out of the bushes and into the street light. The biggest guy had his arm slung over the girl next to him, walking so close to her they were one shape in the dim light. Karmin. Her hand was a white shape splayed on his body, steadying herself as she walked.

Leonard got up. "'Kay, let's go in."

Cary looked from Leonard to the approaching kids. He stubbed out his cigarette and followed him back to their rooms.

When the door was shut Cary shucked off his jacket and tossed it under the bed. Leonard's face was wrinkled like he might cry. "He's not good for her." He sighed deeply.

Cary didn't know what to say to make him feel better. He guessed *quit caring so much* wouldn't work on Leonard.

His phone and the drawings were neatly on the pillow where he'd left them. He sat on the edge of the bed, looking at the names he'd written. His heart beat slow and steady in his chest, pushing his blood around his body to feed and mend all the broken parts. He was still alive to give a shit. He wasn't sure what to do with himself since it basically hurt every day to be him. Maybe seeing Jesus changed something about that. Maybe it didn't.

"Did you have supper?" Leonard asked after a moment.

Cary shook his head.

Leonard's smile was back. "Ha, thought so." He lifted the pillow off his bed and produced a danish and an apple streusel, wrapped in a napkin and only slightly smashed. "Saved these for you."

A laugh puffed out before Cary knew it. "You're something Leonard."

Leonard slid back into the corner of his bed, a pleased smirk on his round face. Cary ate every crumb of the supper, and licked the sugar off his fingers when he was done.

He was stretched on his bunk, a hand behind his head when another kid rapped on their open door. "I'm looking for a kid named Care?"

Cary just gave him a blank look. Leonard smiled and said, "Yeah, this is him."

The kid jerked his thumb over his shoulder. "Mike's outside for you."

Cary frowned and got to his feet. What the hell was Mike doing here?

Cary came out the front doors of the shelter, blinking in the dark. Mike was a hulking shape leaning against the bus stop sign. Cary stepped into the circle of light thrown by the street lamp above them and crossed his arms. "It's Cary," he said flatly. "'Care' is not a name. It's a thing you do."

"Sure it is." Mike's gravelly voice came out of the shadows. "Gotta package for you Care."

There was another shape unfolding from the bus bench. Jon stepped into the light, his eyes wide in his white face.

Cary blinked. "How did you get here?"

Jon was tense as a drawn bow, checking Cary all over like he was looking for the hole. "I got your text and I got on a bus and then when the busses stopped, I started walking."

"Alone? At night?" Cary couldn't believe Jon had left the safety of his home to find him.

Mike said, "Picked him up on Strath with a couple punks tailing him, looking to score. Course there's nothing in his pockets but they didn't know that."

"What?" Jon was momentarily distracted, turning to Mike. "What just happened?"

"You're a doofus," Cary said. "That's what."

"You can take him from here, Care," Mike said. "I'm out." He shambled off.

Jon stepped within reach, grabbing a handful of Cary's shirt and pulling him close. "Do you know how freaking scared I was I'd get here too late and they'd be asking me to ID you in a bag? Jesus, Cary." He let him go, and Cary rolled his shoulders, his hands stuffed safely in his pockets.

"You would go on," Cary said dryly. "You have your family. You would make new friends."

"None of them would be *you*!" Jon snapped. "Do you have any idea what it's like, losing someone you care about so much, it's like they cut a piece out of you? That never closes and never stops hurting."

"I have some idea," he said. His hands were sweating; one was stinging. He thought Jon might actually punch him. Another time it might have been funny.

"Well I can't do it again," Jon growled. "So figure out how to *live*."

Cary ducked his head in a nod. "'Kay."

Jon slumped, exhaling. "Okay."

"Good talk," Cary said.

Jon's laugh was unsteady. "Yeah, thanks. I worked on that the whole way here. Between begging Jesus to stop you..." He drew in his breath and shut his eyes.

Cary held still. The world had just tilted again. "You what?"

Jon's voice was small. "I didn't get your text in time and I couldn't get here fast enough, so all I could do was ask Jesus to stop you." His voice broke. He wiped tears off but they kept coming, and he covered his face, making a sound like he was lost.

Cary's chest hurt, watching Jon cry. He took his hands out of his pockets, standing there awkwardly, then he put his arms around Jon. He held Jon like that for a second just to tell him to be still, that he was okay. He stepped back again, checking Jon's face. Did that help? It was the best he could do.

Jon drew a shuddering breath, pulling his sleeve over his face. His tears had stopped. "It matters to me," he said in a low voice. "You can't just leave. It matters to me that you're here."

Cary lifted his shoulders, the shelter at his back. "Here I am."

Jon looked up at the brick building and around the abandoned street. His laugh was a little strangled, but closer to the real thing. "Can I sleep over, or how am I supposed to get home?"

"They won't take you," Cary said. "You have parents."

"You should come home with me," Jon said suddenly.

Cary took a step back. He couldn't breathe. He shook his head, mute.

Jon came after him. "I'm serious. You could stay with us."

It hurt like Jon had punched him. He wanted to. He wanted to be the kind of person who could who could say yes to staying with Jon's family. "No." His voice was rough and uneven. "I'm too fucked up for your house. They'll ask questions."

Jon was quiet a moment, looking at him. There was something hard in his face. "What would be so bad about someone asking questions?"

Cary shook his head, crossing his arms tightly. He could feel the cuts on his arm pull and open again. "Please, Jon. Please leave it."

"I hate him," Jon said.

"I don't," Cary replied. There was a strained silence. He made spit for his dry mouth. "Call your dad, or I can get the shelter to do it."

"What do you want me to tell him?" Jon asked.

"Same thing my mom told you."

"That you hurt Liam? That you're kicked out for scaring them?"

Cary knew how that would sound to Pete: *Cary is violent—Cary is dangerous.* Everything inside him balled up small. "Yeah. It's even true, so you can make it good."

He sat on the bus bench while Jon made his call. It sounded like Jon and his dad were fighting. When it was finished, Jon sat heavily beside him. "He's mad."

Cary nodded. He kept his eyes straight ahead, watching the traffic light change from green to yellow to red to green over an empty street. "Thanks." He meant it and he didn't think it sounded like he did. He bent his head. His shoulder touched Jon's shoulder beside him. "Thanks for coming, Jon."

Jon let out a long breath, knuckling his eyes. "I'm grounded for like—eternity."

Cary made a dry noise, kind of a laugh. "I'll be here when you get out."

"You better," Jon said.

They sat in silence. Cary's heart beat and his breath went painfully in and out. He tried to trace the shape of the feeling inside of him, since it didn't have words. It had to do with Leonard saving him supper, and Mike up the street looking out for strays and most of all with Jon beside him. The feeling was a thread holding him together, keeping him back from the edge of the hole.

As soon as Jon's dad pulled up in the van, Cary got up and walked back to the shelter. He didn't want Pete to see his face. The bruises on his cheek were a note, from one father to another, that he was a fuck-up. He could make Jon tell his dad that story over the phone, but if he had to watch Pete's face fill with disgust when he saw him, Cary thought he would fall apart.

"See you around, 'kay?" Jon called.

Cary lifted his hand without stopping or turning, and went inside the shelter.

///

When Cary came into the room, Leonard's face lit up like he'd been gone for hours. He had a deck of cards laid out on the hills and valleys of his blanket. "Hey Cary, do you want to play 'War'?"

"Um—I'm pretty tired." Cary said. In truth, he'd slept almost all day. He just didn't think he could stay upright any longer. He crawled onto his bunk, and lay down with a sigh. Leonard went back to flipping his cards down, humming to himself. Cary turned his head so he could watch his stubby fingers sort his cards.

"Hey Leonard?"

Leonard looked up. Cary liked the way his face was never wary; Leonard had no secrets.

"How come you were watching the ravine tonight?"

Leonard folded and unfolded a corner of the card he held. "I was worried about Karmin. I thought they might hurt her."

Cary saw the group coming up from the ravine again in his mind. All guys, and Karmin. He thought Leonard was right.

"We're friends, kind of," Leonard said. "Even though I'm different."

Cary frowned. "You're not that different."

Leonard stuck his lip out, his forehead deeply creased. He lifted his shoulders. "I know I am."

"I guess if that means nicer than most people, sure." Cary turned his head to look at Leonard.

That put a little smile on Leonard's face. "'Kay."

Cary shifted, curling on his right side with his arm tucked under his head. He shut his eyes, feeling his body relax. With the weight off his bruises he was almost comfortable. "How come you're here, Down Low? Where are your parents?"

Leonard put his cards down and clasped his hands together in his lap. "My mom was in high school when she had me. I see her sometimes. I don't know my daddy." He was quiet for a bit. "I think about him sometimes—if I'm like him. Mom says he liked cars like me and he had yellow hair like me. She doesn't have any pictures."

It was quiet except for the sound of traffic outside their window and a dog barking in the distance.

"Do you have family, Cary?"

"Yeah. My mother and my baby brother."

"That's the picture you drew." He could hear Leonard's smile. "Your mom is real pretty."

"Yeah she is." Cary said. Maybe when she was their age she thought that would mean she'd have a happy life. "They still—they all still live together with my father."

"Do you miss her?"

Cary was quiet, feeling his heart thud inside the hole. He was going to have to figure out how to live without her—how to live with a hole that never closed. "Yeah I do. I wanted her to come with me. She loves him."

"Is it your real dad she's with?"

Cary's laugh hurt him. "Yeah, he's my real father." Cary tucked his cut up hand under his side, holding his ribs. He shut his eyes. He didn't want to talk anymore.

After a moment Leonard got up and turned out the light. "Have a good sleep, Care. Thanks for being in my room."

"Yeah you too," Cary said.

18

Cross my heart.

{Cary}

Cary had a crap sleep and not enough of it. He woke up early, too stiff and aching to fall back asleep. He made himself get up; if he moved around he might feel better. He went to the showers. It was so early no one else was up and the hot water went on and on, beating on his skin until he could have tipped against the tile and passed out from bliss.

One of the staff was in the common area, tidying up when Cary came in looking for a place to draw until breakfast. She flashed him a smile.

"Happy Easter. There's Easter eggs in the basket for everyone."

It was Sunday—Easter Sunday. Cary's face lifted in what was almost a smile back. He peeled the foil off a candy egg and went back to his room with the taste of chocolate in his mouth. He was going to see his mother today.

He had changed from his jacket into a clean sweater from his backpack when Leonard rolled over and rubbed his eyes. Cary frowned, wishing he had another pair of pants besides his green army cargos. He took his cash and his smokes out of his jacket and put them in his pants pockets.

"Where are you going?" Leonard asked.

"My mom's church service," Cary said.

Leonard sat up. "Can I come? I like church."

Cary hesitated, looking at him. Probably he would only see his mom for a minute and it wouldn't matter if Leonard was there. Jon White had taught him that it felt good to have a friend at your back. "Do you have something nice to wear?"

"Oh yeah, I do." Leonard jumped out of bed and rummaged through his locker. He held up a wrinkled button-down shirt and a string tie. "How's this?"

"Huh." Cary couldn't help laughing. "Yeah, okay."

Leonard did a little dance of joy between the bunks. He put the shirt on over the T-shirt he'd worn to bed, the one with pictures from the latest teen vampire movie. Cary had to re-do his buttons so they lined up over the preternaturally pale, pouting faces on the front. Leonard jiggled with impatience.

"You're worse than Jon's kid sisters." Cary muttered.

They were the only ones in the dining room for breakfast before wake up call. Leonard's excitement to have an outing was infectious. Cary could barely eat; his stomach was turning nervous flips. He hoped his mother had Liam with her. He wanted to look in his brother's face and know he was alright—that his little body mended too.

They got bus tickets for the short ride across old downtown. They were an hour too early for his mother's service and took a park bench to wait. Leonard jiggled for twenty minutes before he sagged against Cary's shoulder, exhausted.

"I'm just gonna sleep a minute, 'kay?" he mumbled.

Cary sat still, his eyes on the road his mother would drive up while Leonard drooled on his shoulder. He found words running in his head, over and over. *Let them be okay. Let them be better now. Please Jesus.* He didn't know where that left him and it hurt a lot, but maybe he could move through that pain if they were happy.

Her car didn't come. Couples and families in their Easter best went up the steps into the church, and Leonard sat up smacking his lips.

"Is it time? Cary, let's go in!"

Cary caught him back. "Wait."

She was there, coming up the street with her hair tucked under an elegant white hat, her lavender dress swinging as she walked. His father was beside her, Liam's car seat hefted on one thick arm.

"There she is!" Leonard shouted. Cary was too frozen to tell him to shut up. Leonard caught a look at his face and drew back next to Cary. "Is that your dad?" he asked in a small voice.

Conall had his hand on the small of her back as they climbed the steps together, heads bowed. Cary couldn't tear his eyes away from his father going with his mother into a church. It was as impossible as the dead walking.

Down Low searched his face. He had taken one of Cary's hands without either of them noticing. "Are we still going to go in?"

"No." Cary's answer sounded scraped.

"Are you afraid?"

Cary got to his feet, wiping his sweating hands on his sweater. "Let's go."

Cary walked so fast to the bus stop that his breath stabbed him. Leonard trotted at his heels, panting and making worried little noises.

Cary pressed into the corner of a bus seat, wrapping his arms around himself. Was his father praying to God right now? Was he taking that cracker in his big hands and putting it in his mouth? Was he saying sorry for staying away so long, and can I come home?

Would Jesus listen if his father asked for mercy?

Leonard was silent until they got to their room at the shelter. Cary yanked his sweater over his head and threw it under the bed. He hung onto the top bunk while he dug for a different shirt.

Leonard stood where he'd stuttered to a halt, his chubby hands against his cheeks like a cartoon of someone in trouble. "Cary, why did they—why did they kick you out like that?"

Anger was keeping him up. "Because I'm not a good person Leonard. I fuck things up. I hurt people." There were no more clothes in the bag. He chucked it against the wall with a *'smack'* and stood breathing hard, trying to hang onto himself before he blew apart like a bomb.

Down Low was stammering like his tongue was in a knot. "If you hurt them, how come you... you're the one who looks like that?"

Thinking was like running into a wall. "What?"

"They don't—they don't look hurt, Care. Just you. You need a doctor."

Cary's breath caught like a hook in his side. He made a sound and pressed his hand against his ribs, holding still while the hook slid back out. He said through his closed teeth: "I don't need a doctor. They'll just say—rest. And tell me how to breathe so I don't get shit in my lungs. Same as last time."

Leonard wasn't looking at him now, pulling at his lower lip like he was afraid. "He did that to you. Your dad. And he did that before."

Cary sank onto the bed. *Fuck.* He was too tired to hide. "Yeah."

"How come you let him?" Leonard was close to tears.

"I didn't…" Cary shut his eyes. That wasn't true. He dug the heel of his hand into his chest where it hurt. "You know how you feel about your dad, even though you never met him?"

"Yeah," Leonard whispered. "I love him."

Oh God, he was in the basement now, down deep. Cary said, "When I was a little kid, I used to… run away so he would miss me and want me back." He could still feel how hot that hope had been in his chest, riding home beside his mom thinking that this time his father would smile and hug him.

"He didn't." He almost couldn't get the words out. "But I still…" He closed his hands into fists. In the blackened crater that was left of his chest something alive was trying to beat, to shine. His laugh hurt him and tears fell on the knees of his cargo pants. "Jesus. That is so fucked up, right? I tried—I couldn't cut that out. I tried."

He couldn't get his breath in to talk anymore. Leonard's eyes were full of tears, shining blue. He put out a hand, hesitated, then patted Cary gently on his head. "Okay. Okay Care."

The stone lid was gone; he was just an empty hole with wind slicing past the edges.

Cary let out a long, shuddering sigh, wiping his eyes on his wrist and thumbing the tears off his scars. "Can I borrow a shirt?" he asked in a low voice.

"Yeah you can. Of course." Leonard dug in his locker, sniffed the shirt he pulled out and handed it to him. "This one's clean."

Cary pulled it over his bruises and got up. He caught a look at Leonard's face, creased with misery and blotchy from crying. He touched Leonard's cheek with his fist.

"Hey. I never should have told you that shit. Quit thinking about that, okay?"

Leonard lifted his eyes to Cary's face.

Cary put on his best Jon smile, shrugging his shoulders. "This is going to mend and it'll all go into the past—a done thing."

A shadow of his smile flickered in Leonard's face. "You promise?"

Cary drew an X over his heart—over the hole. His mother had done that when he was small enough to believe her. Leonard would never know the difference. "Cross my heart. Good as new."

19

Try.

{Cary}

The dining room was half empty for lunch. Leonard set his tray down next to Karmin and after a second Cary joined them. He ate without tasting much and he didn't speak to anyone. He couldn't help picturing his mother and father in their church clothes, eating lunch at the dining room table with Liam in his swing next to them. He had to quit thinking about them as his family when they didn't want him.

When he went out for a smoke, Karmin joined him. Cary lit one for her and passed it across. "Where's your boyfriend?" he asked without looking at her.

"Omigod don't call him that." Her red mouth sneered and she flicked her hair over her shoulder. Her sweater was too short for her arms; her angular wrists stuck out three inches. "We just, like, fuck around and whatever. Something to do."

The smudge of purple on her wrist caught his eye as she lifted the cigarette to her mouth. He looked away, wishing he hadn't seen it.

She tilted her head at him. "What did you say?"

Cary blinked. He had spoken out loud without meaning to. He looked for cracks in her made-up face, for any sign there was a real person in there.

He spoke softly, his voice flat: "He left marks on you. You shouldn't let him do that."

He got up and left her open-mouthed. She was cussing him out before he got the shelter door open. He rolled his shoulders as it banged shut behind him. Not his problem. It took a couple minutes to figure out he was angry. He seemed to have caught Leonard's bug for caring, and it was pissing him off.

He went to the main office. The staff guy swivelled his chair to face him, in a day-glo blue shirt today.

"You should be watching the ravine," Cary said. "Kids are screwing around down there."

The guy's face was regretful. "Yeah I know. We mostly can't stop it. I mean, we'll try but…"

"Try," Cary said, and left.

///

He didn't want to spend the afternoon surrounded by the dinted concrete walls of the shelter. It was the first hot day of spring, the warmth teasing the barely formed new leaves with a promise of summer. It was the first day Cary could imagine slinging his backpack on and wearing it for any length of time. He passed Leonard playing solitaire in the common room and turned on his heel.

"Hey, Leonard."

Leonard looked up with a smile.

"Karmin is in the smoke pit. Maybe she'd like to play cards with you." She was definitely bored enough. Leonard's smile brightened and he gathered up his deck. Cary hit the sunny sidewalk hoping he hadn't just set his friend up for a chilly rejection.

He got on a bus without thinking much about where it was going. When he arrived at the west side depot he realized he was close to home—to what used to be home. He walked the length of the concrete island in a sea of traffic, trying to convince himself to turn around and go back and hang out at Gazebo Park for the afternoon.

He did the stupid thing instead. He caught the same bus he used to get home from school and texted his mother on the way.

<can you talk?>

A couple minutes later his phone buzzed in his hand. <yes. meet me?>

<YES> Cary couldn't help the caps, he was smiling. He waited a second before answering: <I'll be at the bus stop> with the street address.

<be there when i can> his mother answered.

Cary got off the bus just a block and a half from his house. He wished for a ridiculous moment that he had a hat and a disguise. He sat small at the end of the bus bench, buried in his drawing book.

He worked on the drawing of his sister laughing in Jesus' arms. While he was working on it the world around him was as invisible to him as he was to it. He didn't try to draw Jesus' face; he didn't think he could capture the way he was gentle and joyful and scary all at once. But he paid careful attention to Jesus' hands. They were as strong and well-shaped as his father's, but they would never leave marks on Renae's skin.

He finished with a sigh and sat looking at what he had done. He wanted to see Jesus again—to see him alive and hear him speak—but he didn't know how to let Jesus know that. Jon just opened his mouth and spoke like Jesus was there, listening. Cary was embarrassed to try. So he just sat in silence, letting his heart fill with the face he hadn't drawn.

When he lifted his head, he was surprised by how far the sun had progressed across the sky. He checked the time. Little waves of anxiety lapped him. He turned to the picture of Liam and his mother, which he had tucked back into his drawing book.

He swallowed. That drawing had gotten smudged and the graphite fingerprints looked like bruises on their skin. He shut the book and shut his eyes. He wasn't good at thinking in words, but his head was filling with something he needed to understand. He saw his father's hand on his mother's back going up the church steps. He saw Leonard's face when he said, *They don't look hurt. Just you.*

He remembered his head pounding while his father said, *You are everything that is wrong with this family.*

Cary's ears buzzed. This was why he didn't like to use words. His bruises were already better, but those words hurt more now than they had then.

His mother's sedan slid up alongside the bench and Cary jumped to his feet, stuffing his drawing book in his backpack and pushing those thoughts away. Beverly flashed him a brilliant smile as he got into the passenger seat.

"I have reservations for two at Ginos. I told them we were the Smiths." She laughed as she pulled away. He checked the backseat; the car seat base was empty.

"Liam?" he asked.

"Your father has him. They were reading stories when I left."

Cary drew a quick breath, hiding his face from her. He hadn't thought about how this would be when he wasn't wearing stone. It hurt already.

"And how are you darling? Are they treating you well?"

He tried to be as casual as she was. "It's fine. The food kind of sucks. I have a good roommate. Leonard."

She laid her free hand on his arm. "I'm glad." That, at least, sounded sincere.

He sat silently the rest of the way to the restaurant. He'd spent all his effort at making conversation in one go.

She parked on the street and stepped out, looking like a movie star on the red carpet, in her white pant suit, bright scarf, and wide sunglasses. "Let's eat on the patio; it's such a lovely night."

When she didn't take off her sunglasses to talk to the hostess in the dark cavern of the restaurant, a warning bell went off in Cary's head.

They were the only ones on the patio as the rosy evening light fell through the latticed walls and roof. Beverly glanced around, smiling. "This is lovely, don't you think, Ciaran? A dinner date for two."

Cary spread his hands on the table. "Mom. Take your glasses off."

Her lipsticked mouth pouted at him. "It's bright out. I don't want to."

They were alone. He reached across the table and pulled the glasses off her face, fingertips brushing her powdery skin. She lifted her chin, daring him to say something. The skin around her eye was black and swollen.

He tossed the glasses on the table. "How's Liam?" His voice sounded rough; he was holding back a shout that would do his father proud.

She flipped her hand. "Oh Ciaran, he's fine. I just—"

"Burnt the toast? Left the laundry on the floor?"

She looked hard at him, her nostrils flaring. "Ran into a door," she said coldly.

Cary tried to keep breathing like he was a normal person with a normal life, out for dinner. He wanted to yell and turn the table over. It wasn't going to end; his father wasn't going to change. It didn't matter if Cary was there or not—except if he wasn't there she was the only one left to cover for Liam.

He didn't know how to say any of that.

"What are you going to order?" Beverly asked pleasantly as the waitress approached.

Cary couldn't look at her. "Whatever. Don't make me talk to her."

But she did. She ordered a half plate of pasta and salad and diet iced tea and when she was finished she looked expectantly at him, her eyebrows lifted behind her glasses.

"Spaghetti," Cary said. The waitress bent to hear him, and then he had to answer a barrage of other questions: Salad? Garlic toast? Meatballs? Coke?

When she was finished with him he had found something close to stone. He was angry.

"Did he tell you how Liam got hurt?" he asked.

Beverly made an annoyed noise. "Ciaran, if you're determined to spoil our evening—"

"He was hitting me with a kitchen stool. Liam was in my arms and he was hitting me like he forgot Liam was there."

She went silent, looking at him. One hand turned her soup spoon over and over, making light glance and flash around their table. She looked aside. "Your father is changing. He came to church with me today."

"Before or after he blacked your eye?" Cary asked.

"Enough," she snapped. "You've said quite enough on the subject."

He shut his mouth and sat back, stuffing his fists under his arms. She was better at stone than he was; if she didn't want to hear something, then nothing got through to her.

Their food arrived and they ate in silence. Cary pushed his plate aside half-finished.

Beverly smoothed her napkin over her lap. "What I wanted to talk to you about is how we can be a family again. I think if you would truly apologize and make more of an effort to please your father, you could come back home." She smiled. "You belong with us, Ciaran. Your father will see that. This situation is temporary."

He braced his arms against the table edge, staring at her. It took a couple seconds for him to find his voice again. "Mom, that will never… I can never please him. He is not going to stop—" he drew in his breath and shut his eyes. Things were getting ragged. He was going to fall apart here, and he still had to try to reach her.

"For once in your life please… look at what is really real. He is the smartest man we know—except when he loses it—" He shut his mouth, battered with memories from the basement. They never talked about this. He didn't know if he could even find the words.

He dug into his backpack and pulled out his drawing book. He didn't have to find the words; it was there in heavy strokes of 2B pencil. He opened to the pages he was thinking of and passed it over.

She looked, white and still, then turned the page. And the next. She pulled her hands away, holding them up like he'd asked her to do something dirty. Criminal.

He wrapped his arms tightly around himself, watching her. "Mom, those things happened. To me. I covered for you, and I can't—" He swallowed, sick with the memories he'd let out. He wanted to vomit up darkness until he was empty.

He tried to catch her eye, to get her to look at him and hear. "I want him to stop hurting you. I want my brother to have a normal life. I want him to break his first bone falling off a bike—" his voice broke. "If you leave him we could have that. You and me and Liam—we could all have that. Please, Mom. Look at me and say yes."

His heart was beating in his throat like it wanted to jump out of his mouth and throw itself at her. She didn't look at him or his drawing book. Instead she picked up the wine list, opening and closing it like her thoughts were far away.

"Cary, darling, you know I love you, but sometimes the things you say—"

He bent his head, whispering, "Don't—Mom, don't do this."

"—are positively crazy," she finished. "I'm really not sure what to do with you."

He put his elbows on the table and his hands over his head. He was trembling. That was it. All his words didn't make a dent in her stone-cold denial. He had no more tries.

He was one breath—one touch— away from blowing apart right here on Gino's patio. He shoved back from the table. "I'm done. I'll bus back."

She stood up, frowning. "All right, there's no need to be dramatic. I'll just pay the bill and drop you there myself." He wouldn't look at her so she took his hand and dropped the keys in his palm. "You can wait for me in the car."

He snatched his drawing book off the table and went.

///

After that, Cary was wound up so tightly he could barely speak. He blew through the shelter and out the back door. He propped himself against the yellow brick and lit his cigarette. When it was finished he lit another one. He wanted to burn a hole right through his chest.

Karmin and her not-boyfriend were head to head, arguing in undertones. Cary ignored them until the guy slapped her. Karmin screamed names at him and slapped him back, leaving claw marks on his cheek. She stormed inside and the guy moved to follow, glowering.

Cary flicked his cigarette away and pushed himself off the wall. All the hurt and anger pressing inside him suddenly had a place to go. The guy noticed him for the first time and his face got even uglier. "What are you looking at, fuckhead?"

Cary threw himself at the guy with no thought for what would come after.

THREE

One thing I ask of the LORD,
this is what I seek:
that I may dwell in the house of the LORD
all the days of my life,
to gaze upon the beauty of the LORD
and to seek him in his temple.
For in the day of trouble
he will keep me safe in his dwelling;
he will hide me in the shelter of his tabernacle
and set me high upon a rock.

(Ps 27:4-5)

1

Trust.

{Pete}

Pete was already in bed when the phone rang. A pool of light spilled onto the open pages of his book as Melanie snored lightly beside him. He checked the call display. It wasn't anybody he knew; he let it go.

Jon appeared in his doorway holding out the phone from the kitchen, his hair rumpled over his pale face. "Dad, I think you should take this. It's Cary. He's in trouble."

Pete took the phone, searching his son's face as he said, "Hello?"

"Is this Mr. White?" The woman sounded stressed and annoyed.

"Yes."

"This is Marissa from the Youth Emergency Shelter. Ciaran Douglas gave us your number as a possible contact person. We've asked him to vacate the premises before midnight tonight. Will it be possible for you to come pick him up, or should I give him a bus ticket?"

Pete tried to put this all together. Jon was watching him, gripping the doorjamb tightly. "I'm sorry Marissa, could you hold on a minute?" He covered the phone, frowning at his son. "Jon, the Youth Emergency Shelter wants me to pick Cary up tonight. Do you know anything about that?"

Jon's face was tight and secretive. "No."

"So Cary is kicked out of his house, and the youth shelter in the space of three days and you don't know why?"

"No, I don't."

It took an effort not to react when Jon was so obviously lying to him. "And why should I drive out there tonight to play taxi for Cary?"

Jon turned his face to the darkened hallway, like there was someone there with the answer. "It's not what it looks like, Dad." His voice was strained. "Please believe me."

That at least sounded like the truth. Pete put the phone back on his ear. "Hello, Marissa? Could you please put Ciaran on the line?"

There was a rustle and a mutter of voices. "Hello?" Cary's voice sounded thick and slurred. Pete couldn't help wondering if he'd been drinking.

"Cary, what do you want me to do for you?"

There was a silence. "I'm sorry Mr. White. I told them not to call you. I don't need to go to the hospital. Sorry to wake you up."

"Okay, just wait a minute. What do you not need to go to the hospital for?"

Cary was infuriatingly slow to respond. "I was in a fight. It's just some bruises. Please don't trouble yourself Mr. White."

Pete put his feet on the floor. "I'm already troubled, Cary. I'll be there in thirty minutes. Stay there."

///

By the time he'd gotten dressed and spoken with his wife, Jon was waiting at the door with his jacket on. "I'm going with you," Jon said.

Pete gave him a level look. "What are we doing right now Jon?"

"Cary needs our help," Jon said. "He's my best friend. I'm coming."

Pete took his time putting on his jacket, thinking. When he faced Jon again, his mind was made up. "Son, you can come. But hear me very clearly—I will do this for Cary once, but if he continues the way he is, your friendship with him is over."

Jon's lips quivered and he bit them together, silent.

Jon was silent for the entire drive, staring at the dashboard with his hands clenched together and pressed between his knees. It took Pete two tries to find the youth shelter parking lot in the back. He frowned as he got out of the car. The concrete yard was a mess: there was a picnic table on its side and broken glass everywhere.

Pete went around the side of the building to the front door, Jon following closely at his shoulder. Cary was slouched down in a chair in the tiny waiting area. He looked up when Pete came in and the breath of cool night air moved around them both. Cary pressed back in the chair, his battered hands curling into fists. His face was bruised and his mouth was swollen. To Pete, the boy looked hell-bent on self-destructing.

The staff person opened the main office door and both Cary and Pete flinched in the slice of bright light.

"Are you Mr. White?" The woman asked.

"I am." Pete tried to relax his face. None of this was her fault. "Are you Marissa?"

She seemed annoyed that he remembered her name. "Can I get you to sign off on these release forms for me?"

Pete passed Cary without looking at him and went into the office.

{Jon}

When the office door swung shut, Jon dropped into the chair beside Cary. He opened his mouth to speak.

"Don't," Cary said. He couldn't meet Jon's eyes. "Don't say anything. I already know."

Jon's hunched his shoulders. "I can't lie to my dad anymore," he whispered.

Cary shut his eyes, swallowing like he might be sick. "I'll do it. I'll tell him. Just don't say anything."

{Pete}

In the office, Pete said, "Can you please explain to me what this is about?"

Marissa passed him a clipboard and a pen, tapping her finger on the line for him to sign. "We have a zero-tolerance policy for violence on shelter property. We had to call an ambulance for the other boy. Cary is suspended from staying with us for thirty days." She was all business and more than a little irritated. "He gave your name and number as a possible emergency contact during intake. His file says don't call home."

Pete flipped through the forms. "What am I signing here?"

"In the absence of a parent or guardian you take responsibility for the client's well-being on their departure from the shelter…"

By the time he had heard her out and signed the paperwork he was well and truly angry. It was way past his bedtime, and this was not his problem. He went back into the waiting room, blinking in the near dark. Cary touched him with a look and his face went still.

"Ready to go?" Pete asked.

"Yes sir," Cary said. He got to his feet with some difficulty and put his backpack over one shoulder. Pete held the door for him and Cary went past with his head down. At the car Pete pulled the passenger door open for Cary and turned. Cary flinched aside like he expected to be struck.

The motion was a bucket of cold water on the heat of his anger. Pete opened his hands and tried to make out Cary's face in the darkness. The boy was rigid, his hands clenched around his backpack strap. In that second of stillness, Pete realized Jesus was trying to get his attention; his anger had kept him from noticing. *Okay Lord, what do you want? What am I missing?*

His heart burned as he stood in the orange street light, an arm's length from the boy holding still. Pete made a decision: he might not be able to help Cary if Cary didn't want his help, but he was not going back home before he'd done everything he could.

"Son, I am not going to hurt you," Pete said. "Can you listen to me for a minute?"

Cary slowly turned his face to him.

"I don't know what kind of trouble you're in, but I came out here because you're my son's friend and... helping people is what I do. But for me to do that, I need you to trust me." Cary's face was still, and it occurred to Pete that word might not mean anything to him.

"Trust means when I say something to you, you can know it's true. I'm not going to hide things from you and I'm not out to get something for myself. That's my promise to you. And I want you to do the same for me. I want to know I can believe the things you tell me. Can you do that?"

Cary put his eyes on Jon, standing white and still on the other side of the car. Jon's lips formed two soundless words: *Cary please.*

Cary bent his head. His fists were still closed. "You don't have to help, Mr. White. It's my own fault I'm kicked out."

Pete looked over his head at the night sky, blotted with city light. "I know that, Cary. Thank you for telling me the truth. Now, where am I taking you?"

Cary lifted his shoulders. His voice was barely audible. "I don't have anywhere to go."

"I would really like a coffee." Pete said. "How about you?"

Cary ducked his head and got in the car.

///

Pete went through the drive-through at an all-night place. Just the smell of the bitter black liquid woke him up. He smiled to himself, sipping from the paper cup with one hand while he drove over empty streets. "Jon and I used to do this when he was a boy. Drive all night to his grandparent's cabin to fish and camp. Those drives were our best time to talk." He checked the rearview mirror. Jon had his elbow up on the door with his face turned away. His hand was wrapped over his mouth. Pete burned the roof of his mouth and winced, setting the cup back into the cup-holder between them. "We haven't done that in a while. He has a few more secrets now."

He glanced at Cary, sitting still as stone with his backpack between his feet. "I think some of his secrets belong to you, actually."

Cary didn't seem to be breathing. It started to rain; fat drops splashed on the windshield and the swish of their tires filled the silence.

"Does the YMCA still have emergency beds?" Pete asked. "Are you old enough to stay there?"

"I've stayed there before," Cary said.

"So that's an option then," Pete said. He let the white lines slip away beneath them, praying without words. He was on the edge of the thing; it was dark and dense, and Cary was in the middle of it. He needed to know its shape, even while he was afraid he was about to wade into an ugly mess. "So why am I not dropping you back at your house?"

Cary spread his hand on his knee like it took some effort to open. "My father doesn't want me." He said it carefully, like each word might break, or break him. "He said he would kill me if he sees me again. He almost did. I'd be afraid to go back."

The beat of the wipers and the rain on the car made it hard for Pete to be sure he was hearing what he thought he was hearing. He pulled into a deserted parking lot and stopped.

"That's the truth, Mr. White." Cary's voice was pressed to a whisper. He put his eyes on Pete and they were dark as the night outside the window. "Do you believe me?"

Pete held his look, praying that he wasn't being played. "Cary, if someone tells me they're being hurt in their house, I have to act on that even if I'm not sure it's true. So I need you to be really clear about what you're telling me right now."

Cary made a small sound, closing his eyes. "I'm telling you... in my house when my father is angry, someone gets hit." His voice dropped into the dark, soft and dry as sand. "It's usually me. And if he can't—hit someone—it just piles up until it needs to get put. Onto. Someone. Like me." He spoke with difficulty, like he was picking his way in the dark. "There's a place where I go in the basement. And he—uses his belt until—he's done. And I'm. Done." Cary caught his breath like he'd just cut himself and shut up.

Jon was pressed back against the seat, clenching his fists. "That's what he did to you the day you fought Todd for me?" His voice was rough.

Cary nodded once.

"You had bruises all over your back. He didn't leave an inch of skin that wasn't a bruise."

Cary shifted. "When did you see that?" he asked in a low voice.

Pete caught Jon's eyes in the mirror. His son smoldered with anger. "The day I came over. The day I met your father. He stood there making fun of you for not talking when he'd just done that to you."

Cary rubbed the palm of his hand against his knee like it itched. "I'm not exactly his favourite person."

Pete looked at Cary like he saw him for the first time. One thing after another clicked into place: Cary's silence, his secrets, and the violence that seemed a drawn breath away from him any given moment. He should have seen it.

"There's scars," Cary whispered, curling his shoulders. "If you don't believe me."

Pete gathered the scattered pieces of himself together and found his voice. "Cary, can you look at me?"

Cary dragged his eyes up to Pete's face.

"I believe you," Pete said. "I'm going to do everything in my power to make sure that never happens again."

Cary sucked in a his breath and turned his face aside like he couldn't bear the look he gave him. It was a minute before he spoke again. "I don't care about me, Mr. White. I just don't want my brother to grow up in that house and get broken like I did." He pushed his hand beside his face. If he hadn't moved Pete wouldn't have known he was crying. "My mother doesn't believe me. She won't leave. And I can't—I can't go back."

"I'm ready to call Child Protection tonight," Pete said evenly. "Do you think your brother is in danger right now?"

Cary put the heels of his hands against his eyes. "No. I don't know." He took a gasping breath like someone going under for the last time. "You don't have to call, Mr. White. I'll do it."

Pete pulled out his phone and hunted through his contacts. This was a phone call he was grateful he didn't have to make more often. He handed it to Cary. "Here. Just press send."

Cary took the phone in shaking fingers. He gave Pete a terrified look, then put the phone to his ear.

Between gusts of wind and the patter of rain on the parked van, they heard someone pick up and greet Cary.

Cary said, "I need to talk to someone about my father? I'm kicked out, but my mother and brother are still living with him. My brother is a baby. I have bruises and a broken rib from when he hit us the last time."

Pete watched Jon while Cary made his call. His son had his head bent, his fingers opening and closing like he was talking to himself. He caught a whisper of Jon's voice, praying. His forehead wrinkled. How long had Jon carried that secret? How much of their conflict had been the stress of covering for his friend?

Cary was silent, listening to the person speaking on the other line. "What happens now?" he asked.

Quacking came from the phone; a shudder went through Cary's body. He hung up before the other person was finished speaking.

Jon lifted his face. "What did they say?"

"Someone is coming to your house tomorrow. For me to talk some more." Cary wrenched the door open and staggered out of the van. The sound of falling rain filled the van while Cary fell to his knees and threw up.

He didn't get back up. One arm was splayed to the side, his hand spread on the wet pavement. Rain plastered his shirt against his ribs, heaving in and out in jerky movements.

Jon climbed out before Pete could move and crouched beside his friend. He bent to speak into Cary's ear, putting his arm across his shoulders. Jon's grip tightened and he lifted Cary back to his feet. He got Cary into the front seat and did up Cary's seatbelt like he was a child. Cary curled over his knees, shivering.

Jon met Pete's eyes across the front seat. Water plastered his hair against his head and ran down his face like tears. "Can we go home now?" Jon asked.

Pete nodded.

The car heater pounded out warm air while they drove. Pete met Jon's eyes once in the mirror. "Thank you for coming, Jon."

Jon nodded. "Glad you're my dad." he said softly. He turned to look out the window and was silent the rest of the trip.

2

Open heart.

{Jon}

Whatever adrenaline or determination had kept Cary going was spent by the time they pulled into Jon's driveway. He got out of the car with difficulty and went up the steps with his head down, like the dark was battering him back. When Jon got inside he found Cary swaying on the mat, like he didn't know where to put his feet to come in.

"Hey, you're sleeping in my room tonight," Jon said. "I'll take the floor."

That started Cary moving again. He leaned against the wall to pull off his socks and shoes, then stood in his bare feet with his shoes dripping in his hands, looking for the place to put them. Pete took them out of his hands. "Go on," Pete said.

Cary went up the hall, steadying himself against the wall. Jon followed, wrung with worry. He'd never known a situation that Cary wasn't strong enough to take and stay standing.

Cary sank onto the bed, as if he would burrow under the covers still soaked to the skin. Jon caught him by the shoulders, keeping him upright. "Care, come on—don't make me undress you. You gotta take off your wet things."

Cary bent his head and dragged his shirt off his back. He held it out to Jon with a look that asked, *What do I do with this?* Jon took it and turned aside, his eyes stinging with tears. He balled the shirt up and shoved it deep into his laundry hamper. He wished he could wring Cary's father's neck as easily.

He was digging through his drawers for clean pyjamas when Pete came in with spare blankets and the foam mat for the floor. He took in Cary's battered body slumped on the edge of the bed and Jon on the verge of a breakdown. "Dad can you help?" Jon asked. "He's pretty out of it."

Pete took the pyjamas out of Jon's hands and knelt in front of Cary. He had to take Cary's wrists to thread them into the sleeves, like he was a child. He pulled the shirt over Cary's shoulders, hiding his bruises again. "Lie down son," he said softly, and Cary obeyed, burying his face in Jon's pillow.

It took two of them to tug Cary's soaked cargos off his legs. There were more bruises, faded yellow across the back of his legs, and one hot purple and black bruise across his hip to match the ones on his ribs. Jon got him into the pyjama pants, muttering under his breath. "We are never talking about this moment in our friendship, Cary Douglas."

He covered Cary with the blankets and Cary curled into a ball, covering his head with his bent arm.

Jon took a breath, looking at him. His heart hurt, stretching to get bigger and he wished he could wrap it around Cary to hold him together and keep him safe. *Jesus, we need you.*

Jon and Pete stepped into the hall. Jon sagged against the wall. His father was watching him, his mouth a grim line in his beard. "Did Cary get those bruises in the fight tonight?"

Jon shook his head. "I don't think so. He looked the same… yesterday. I think his father did that to him before he kicked him out." He couldn't move; the thing that had just happened was so heavy it held him down.

"Jon," Pete said. "You should have told me."

"I wanted to," he said brokenly. "Cary asked me to keep quiet and I thought he—I thought he knew what he could handle." He was crying now. He'd never seen anything worse than Cary's body when his shirt came off.

Pete came in close and put his arms around Jon, and Jon hung onto him. His face was full of the smell of his father: rain and clean laundry and the salt of his sweat. Or maybe the salt was just his tears, making his dad even more wet than he was already. Pete kissed Jon's forehead like he used to. His bearded face was lined with sadness. "Praying for you tonight, son. Try to get some sleep."

Jon nodded. He thought of the things he had said to his dad this past year and his throat was too tight to speak.

He went into his room and started arranging his sleeping bag on the floor, without looking at Cary. Finally he asked, "Can I get you anything? A…an ice pack or… a drink of water or something?"

"No," Cary said. His voice was thin and tight as a wire over a long drop.

Jon sat back on his heels, looking at his friend. "Does this mean it's over, you don't have to live in that house with your father anymore?"

"It's over." Cary made a hurt noise and spread his hand over his face. The skin on his knuckles was broken, the fresh scabs looked black. "Please turn out the light," he whispered.

Jon did that. He slid into the sleeping bag and lay in the dark, listening to his friend's breath go in and out unsteadily. Was Cary Douglas crying?

In a second, Cary had strangled the tears and was silent.

Jon swallowed and shut his eyes. Cary had seemed kind of okay, yesterday at the shelter. But now, up close and in the safety of his own house, Jon could see how badly broken he was. There wasn't a thing Jon could say to make it better, and he was afraid whatever he tried to do for Cary would just hurt him worse.

Jesus, you asked me to be Cary's friend, but I don't know how to do that now.

Jesus said, *You know me.*

The hair on Jon's head lifted, and he put his hand on his side where he'd seen Jesus' wound tear open. He had promised to follow Jesus, like a hundred years ago when he was four, and now it was time to say yes again to living like him, with his eyes and heart open to the people Jesus loved.

And that meant being an open-hearted friend to Cary even though it broke his heart already, watching Cary hurt and not knowing what to do or how to help. And it was going to hurt tomorrow and the next day and the next, as long as Jon cared, as long as it took for Jesus to put the pieces back together.

He realized the truth was he was more afraid of getting hurt himself than making a mistake and hurting Cary.

Jon's pride in himself snapped off with that realization. *Jesus, I'm not like you at all. I'm sorry. Please help me to be like you. Help me to be like you for Cary because he needs you so much.*

As that prayer went up, Jon felt his heart lift with it. He took a breath; that was the right thing to do. Jesus wasn't angry with him and he wasn't going to leave. He didn't know how things would work out but at least he wasn't alone.

He turned on his side towards the bed, making his voice quiet in case Cary was already asleep. "I usually pray before I go to sleep. Can I pray for you?"

One word came out of the dark: "No."

Jon's face got hot, but he wasn't going to quit. "I know it doesn't seem like this could be true but—I know God cares about you."

"Jon—" Cary's voice shivered into fragments, and it was a few seconds before he gathered them together again to speak. "If he looks at me I'll break. Please don't tell him I'm here."

Jon felt like Jesus was so close in the dark, he could hear his heart beating. He decided to just say it. "He knows already." His voice was low. "He's right here, even if you don't say anything. He never left."

3

How he is.

{Cary}

When Cary woke up the next morning, his mind was mercifully blank. He rolled onto his back, registering Jon's room, his posters and comic books, and Jon himself asleep in a nest of blankets on the floor. This was the safest place Cary knew: this room with that person in it. He wanted to put the blankets over his head and hide here the rest of the day.

The gears of his thoughts started to grind and anxiety stroked his stomach. He remembered getting turfed from the shelter, the surreal car ride through the rain, and Pete believing him. One conversation—one phone call had set in motion the thing that would wrench his family apart. Whatever hope he'd had of making a life with his mom and his brother—he had to bury that like a dead thing. At the end of this the police would come for his father, and his mother would never forgive him for that. The only thing he'd been good for was how much he could take and still stay silent.

He put his hands over his face, trying to keep breathing. His knuckles were swollen and hurt to bend. He'd punched the hell out of something last night. He ran his tongue around the inside of his mouth. The cuts were bumpy and tasted like blood. The kid at the shelter must have decked him a couple times too. All Cary could remember after pushing off the wall was a haze of red and then three shelter staff hauling him off.

He sat up carefully, closing his fists. That fight was another thing to shove into the basement with the other scary shit and close the door. He did that as best he could. It hurt more than it used to. He got up, dug his clothes out of the laundry hamper and got dressed, shivering at the damp touch of his shirt on his skin. He straightened the blankets and folded the pyjamas on top of Jon`s bed.

Jon never even woke up, sleeping with one hand flung above his head and his mouth open. Cary filled his pockets with his smokes, his cell phone and his pencils, and then he slipped into the hall.

It was spring break; Jon's sisters were on the couch in the family room, wrapped in blankets and watching cartoons. He ducked his head and went to the kitchen. Jon's dad and mom were there, reading the newspaper with the remains of their breakfast on the table around them. Cary stopped in the doorway, frozen. There was no place to hide here, and he'd left his jacket in Leonard's room.

Jon's mom looked up first. Her smile dimpled her cheek: Jon's smile. "Morning, Cary. Can I get you some breakfast?"

Cary shook his head. He darted a look at Jon's dad. Pete looked tired.

"How are you holding up?" Pete asked.

Cary stared at him, swallowing. He had no idea how to answer that.

Pete sighed and rubbed a hand over his beard. "I spoke to Child Protection this morning. They're sending someone this afternoon."

The impact of that set him back on his heels. This was really happening. Today. He turned his face aside and edged out onto the back deck before Pete could ask him any more questions.

It was cool and misty. A heavy dew bent the blades of grass in the backyard. The sun was just touching the lumber frame of the garage, turning it from grey to yellow. Cary took out his cigarettes and lit one, watching the sun slide up the two-by-four ribs. It seemed like forever ago that he had spent his afternoons building that garage with Jon and his dad and been happy. He had been right; happiness didn't belong to him.

Jon found him curled over his knees and sat down on the steps next to him. "Morning." His hair was standing up, and he still had his pyjamas on under a hooded sweater. Cary took out his cigarettes to light another for himself and offered one to Jon.

Jon waved it away. "So are you going to be able to go back to your mom and Liam after today?" he asked.

Cary shook his head once. "She won't take me back after this. I'll go with the social worker wherever." Wherever they put fuck-ups like him.

Jon frowned. "You don't belong in foster care."

The word made Cary's stomach roll. He pressed his lips tightly shut. He could do it. Nobody was going to want a kid with his record, but he already knew how to put his head down and survive someplace toxic. He would shunt from one house to another until he was old enough to live on his own. If he had a problem with that, there was no one to blame but himself.

His hands shook as he jammed the smokes back in his pocket. On second thought, he felt too sick to smoke another.

Jon said, "Cary, I want you to stay with us. We could be your family."

The word, the idea, reached into his chest and yanked him tight. "Shut up, Jon. You don't know what you're talking about."

"We have room for you," Jon said. "If you're not too proud to share. At least here you would be with people who know you."

Cary's fists clenched so his battered knuckles ached. No fucking way.

Jon got up. "I'm going to ask my dad for you."

Cary shot to his feet and hit Jon so hard he went head over heels onto the grass. Cary was on top of his chest with his fist pulled back to hit him again before Jon got his breath.

Jon's nose was bleeding. His arms were flung wide, gripping the grass. He looked up at Cary with the same terrified, stubborn face he'd used to face Todd.

All in. All that was left to do was pound every ounce of hate he had inside him into Jon and get the hell out.

Cary stood up and dragged Jon to his feet. He had a handful of Jon's sweater; they were face to face. "Hit me."

Jon tried to pull away, wiping his bloody nose on his sweater sleeve. Cary yanked him close and slapped his cheek with his open hand. "Hit me. Come on, do it."

Jon threw his hands out like he was falling. "I won't. Cary. I don't know why you're mad, but I'm not going to fight you back."

He was crying. Cary shoved him away, out of his reach. Jon turned from him and stumbled, lifting an arm to protect his head as if Cary would be on him again if he fell. Cary watched him go, wrapping his hand over the cuts in the crease of his elbow. They itched and he hated himself so fiercely he could have torn the skin off his arm with just his fingernails.

Cary looked around the yard, at the garage, and the back alleyway that led to the bus stop. He couldn't stay here in Jon's house with Jon and his sisters and mother. Pete was the only one he didn't think he could hurt. His fingers slipped on his skin; he was scratching and he couldn't help it. He made himself stop, clenching his arms around his body until he could find a hiding place where nobody could see he was bleeding. He went to Jon's room to pack his bag.

{Pete}

Pete heard the back door bang open and leaned back in his office chair to check the hallway. Jon blew by with his hand cupped under his nose. Pete found him bent over the bathroom sink. The sight of his son's blood running crimson down the drain jolted Pete with adrenaline.

"Jon, what happened?"

Jon didn't look at him, hitting the tap on full. "It's nothing."

Pete stared at him, appalled. "Your nose just started bleeding?"

"Dad, I'm fine. Just leave me alone."

He tried to think what had just been going on to explain what he was seeing. "Did Cary hit you?"

Jon straightened, pinching the bridge of his nose hard. He didn't answer but he didn't need to. The truth was in his face. Pete's eyebrows lowered as he turned to find the other boy.

"Dad." Jon caught his arm. The strength of his grip surprised Pete. "He made a mistake. Don't—don't go do what you're thinking."

Pete looked at him. They were standing face to face, and they were almost the same height. "What do you know about what I'm thinking?"

"Don't kick him out. He's my friend. I can handle it."

"You can handle it." Pete couldn't keep his voice steady.

"Yeah, I can. I'm not a kid anymore."

"And is that why you lied to me about Cary's family? Because you thought you two could 'handle it'?"

Jon dropped back against the sink. It was a second before he could speak. "No, that's not why. I wanted to tell you. But it was... Cary's secret to tell. And you would have called the police."

"Which is exactly what you should have done." The words came out like a slap. He'd been awake most of the night, haunted by the shapes beaten into Cary's skin, and how things could have been different if he'd paid attention when Cary first came to their home.

Jon went a little whiter, and put his eyes straight ahead. "I know that. Cary wouldn't—look the way he does if I had. I have to live with that now." He straightened his shoulders with some effort. "I know it doesn't make sense, but Cary stayed in that house because he wanted to. Because… that's his family. He doesn't have anyone now. Except us." They locked eyes. "Nobody at Social Services will do a better job taking care of him than you."

Pete wanted to touch his son's face and check the bruise. He closed his hands at his sides. "And what about you?"

Jon didn't flinch. "This is more important than me."

"Not to me," Pete said.

Jon drew a breath, glaring at him. "Look, you can't have it both ways. You can't make me give up my friends and my home for you to follow God and then keep me from following God myself because you think it's too hard. I want to do this. Cary has a chance with us."

Pete felt like he was seeing a different Jon—not the child who had moved here, and not the angry teenager he'd been living with the past few months. For a moment, he saw the man that Jon would become—bigger on the inside than he was on the outside. Strong enough to carry this.

He let his anger go and found that mostly he was afraid. And sad. "Let me look at your face." Jon stayed steady while Pete examined the bruise. Pete sucked his breath through his teeth. This wasn't play-fighting; Cary had hit Jon hard. The whole left side of Jon's face was swelling. *Jesus, this is my only son. What do you want me to do here?*

"Jon, this is not okay. We are not keeping Cary if this is how he is going to behave."

Jon's face was thunderous. "He's not like a dog you can just take back to the shelter because he's too much work."

Pete withdrew his hands, looking helplessly at him.

In a moment Jon's anger had turned from a thunderclap to rainfall as soft as tears. "I'm sorry. I just...I know him. I've seen him look after his little brother, and this is not how he is." His voice stretched almost to breaking. "I don't think he'll make it a week with people who don't know him, who don't know that he's not tough like he looks, that he's just—barely holding together."

Pete pressed his finger hard against his top lip, thinking about how long it would take before Cary wasn't so hurt and angry he didn't just lash out at anyone who came close. How long it would take him to heal, if he could. And if Pete didn't have children of his own, he would have stepped up to attempt it—to be a safe place for Cary to fall apart and maybe help put the pieces back together.

But he had children. And his only son was standing in front of him with a bruise so fresh it made Pete's own face hurt.

"I want you to think seriously about what you're asking me, son," Pete said. "Cary would be sleeping in your room and going to your school. You're talking about bringing a stranger into our family to live with us with no end date."

"Not a stranger," Jon said. His clear-eyed expression reminded Pete so vividly of Jon as a child that his eyes stung. When his brother died Jon had looked like half of himself had been torn away and put in the ground. He had grown up and filled out, and somehow Pete had forgotten that there was still a hole where Jon's brother used to be. He guessed Cary had a hole where a family should have been. They fit. How had he missed seeing that before?

He sighed. "What do you want me to do?"

Jon's face filled with painful hope. "Can you talk to him? Can you get him to stay?"

Pete thought of Cary's white, tight face as he'd edged into the kitchen this morning. "I don't know." He turned aside and his heart burned like it had under the orange streetlight. "I will try."

4

Mercy.

{Cary}

Cary wiped his hands on his shirt before he touched the White's back door. His blood was caked under his fingernails and sticky between his fingers. He just needed to get across the kitchen and down the hall without being seen. The bathroom door was closed and Jon's voice came through it, low and angry:

"He's not like a dog you can just take back to the shelter because he's too much work."

He turned into Jon's room, shutting the door quickly before he could hear any more. He dropped his head against the door with a '*thump.*' He did not in a million years deserve a friend like Jon. He went to the bed and grabbed his bag, wrenching it open to make sure all his stuff was there before he left. He had closed the last zipper when his phone rang.

He startled, digging it out of his pocket with cold fingers. It was his mother's cell number. He picked up: "Yeah?"

"Ciaran, get your things." It was his father's voice, the one you never argued with.

Cary froze, his mouth open, staring blankly at the wall of Jon's room.

"Are you there boy?"

He snapped his mouth shut. "Yes," Cary said.

"The car is outside. Whatever you told those people, you are my son and you belong with your mother and me. We will fix this. Get your things and leave. I'm waiting." His father hung up.

The impulse to obey his father was so strong that Cary picked up his backpack and slung it over his shoulder, steadying himself against Jon's desk. His hands were sweating. Conall could do it. His father was strong-willed enough to pull them all back from the brink, make Child Protection believe his call had been a mistake, and put the pieces of their family back together again. Just like it had been before.

Cary threw the phone onto the bed like it was red-hot and shed the backpack to burrow into the back corner of Jon's closet. The phone rang again, over and over. He curled with his face in his knees, shaking.

The doorbell rang. Jon's house was so small that Cary could hear everything that happened in the hall from the bedrooms, even from the back of a closet.

The front door opened. "Mr. Douglas," Pete said. "We weren't expecting you."

"I'm looking for my son." His father's voice was more pleasant than it had been on the phone. "Perhaps he didn't tell you that he ran away from us some days ago. His mother has been sick with worry, trying to find him."

Cary barely breathed, sweat trickling down his ribs as he waited for Pete to come in here, drag him out, and throw him back.

There was a pause. "He's here," Pete said. "The boys had a sleepover last night and made plans for the day."

"This is terribly awkward Peter, but I need him home," Conall said.

Pete's voice was cool. "I think he'll be staying with us a little longer."

There was a beat of silence. "I respect you, Peter so I'm going to be honest. I don't feel comfortable leaving Ciaran here with your family. Whatever he's told you, you should know that Ciaran is a practiced liar. He can also be extremely violent. I can't count the number of times I've been called away from work or woken up in the middle of the night to retrieve him from the scene of some violent altercation, which he almost invariably started."

Cary put his fists against his mouth for silence. He saw Pete's face from the shelter last night, shadowed with anger, looking down on him. He saw Jon's cheek spattered with blood. That blood was still on his hands. He couldn't squeeze himself small enough to disappear.

Conall went on, sounding at once frustrated and regretful. "I have been humiliated by my son's regular appearance in juvenile court, and his mother and I are deeply concerned about his future after high school. I appreciate your impulse to offer Ciaran your hospitality, but I really think he is the last person you want staying in your home with your children."

"I look after the safety of my children, Mr. Douglas," Pete said.

Cary crawled out of the closet and got to his feet. He was heavy and aching. His father was right; he didn't belong here. He picked up his backpack and went into the hall.

"I'm here Father."

Conall didn't spare him a look; he just started down the steps. "Then good day to you, Peter. Ciaran, your mother is waiting."

Pete put out his arm, catching Cary across the chest. "You've punished him enough."

Cary's father turned, a dangerous look in his eye.

"Mr. White—" Cary whispered, pushing against his grip.

"Stay where you are Cary," Pete said. Cary held still, his heart drumming against Pete's arm. He looked from Pete's face to his father. He didn't know whom to obey.

Conall drew himself up. "I'm not sure what you think you're doing here, Peter. Ciaran is fifteen. I am his father. If I say he's coming home, then I expect you to turn him over to me."

"*I* am a father." Pete said. "I don't think we agree on the meaning of the word."

Conall sighed, pinching the bridge of his nose. "Please. That self-righteous attitude wouldn't last two weeks with Ciaran in your house. He can tell you himself."

Cary dragged his eyes up to his father's face.

"Have I lied about the things you've done, boy?"

"No," Cary said hoarsely.

Conall shrugged, like that answer hurt him. "I wish I were lying to you, Peter. I wish I could say that you and your beautiful little daughters are safe with him. But you're not." His face was lined and heavy. "Violence is Ciaran's language. He demonstrated that from an alarmingly young age. The only way he can be reached is through his skin. If you plan to have him in your home, you can learn that the hard way."

Cary's ears rang and the edges of the room went dark. He hung onto a fistful of Pete's shirt between Pete's shoulders; Pete's arm was the only thing keeping him up.

Pete didn't move—he was solid as a rock. "You've said enough," he said softly. "Get off my doorstep."

Conall drew himself up to his full height. His dark eyes bored into Cary. They said, *You know what you've done now, boy.* Cary made a noise with his mouth locked shut; even from three yards away, his father had him by the throat.

Pete stepped into the doorway, blocking the sight of Cary from his father. "Good day, Mr. Douglas."

Conall nodded stiffly. "Peter." He turned and marched down the walk without a backward look. Pete thumped the front door shut.

Cary's shoulders hit the wall and he stood pinned there, trying to breathe. He realized how big a lie he'd told Pete when he'd said he could be trusted.

Pete sighed. "Cary, what am I going to do with you."

Cary couldn't lift his eyes off the welcome mat on the floor. "I shouldn't have come here, Mr. White. I lied to you, and I'm sorry." He held still, waiting for Pete to come at him and hit him hard like he'd hit Jon, like he deserved.

Pete stayed where he was. "I knew or suspected those things about you already, Cary. Your father spoke openly about you the day we met with the principal about your suspension. I knew what I was signing up for when I picked you up last night." On the edge of his vision Cary could see Pete's arms crossed over his chest; the hairs on them glinted red and gold. There was a measuring silence.

"But I don't think you did," Pete said. He came closer and Cary dug in his heels to keep his legs from dropping him onto Pete White's floor. "Do you understand what your father meant when he said violence is your language?"

Cary had to think about it—about the things his father had drummed into his skin because he was too stupid to learn. "That it's the way I talk. And how he has to talk to me."

"Well, it's not a language I speak, and I do not permit it to be spoken in my house," Pete said.

There was a movement in the kitchen doorway and Cary looked up. Jon was standing there, his eyes fixed on his father. The bruise on his face was spreading purple under his eye.

Cary twisted his hands behind his back like he was in cuffs, pressing them in place with his body. He could have cut them off at the wrists.

Pete let out his breath. "I'm going to give you a choice now, Cary. I think you've forgotten you have choices like anyone else. When the Child Protection worker comes, you can go with her and do whatever you like when you get angry. I think we both know how that will end for you."

Cary held still, his fingers closed over the cuts on his hand. He had to end it before he became his father. If it wasn't too late already.

"Or, you can stay with us and learn the rules of my house. I want to help you do that. It's your choice," Pete said.

Cary listened to that again in his head. *You can stay with us.* The words his father had just said buzzed faintly in his ears: *I wish I could say that you and your beautiful little daughters are safe with him.*

"There's more you don't know," he whispered.

"I'm sure there is," Pete said. "All I need to know is whether you are willing to obey my rules when you live in my house."

Pete's even patience was like a hand pressed against Cary's throat. If he could have done anything for Pete, he would have. But he didn't know how to do this.

"I'll go. When this is done today." He couldn't even show Pete his face like he was supposed to. "I won't make any more trouble for you, Mr. White. I'm sorry." The words were empty against everything he owed the Whites now. A bucketful of his own blood couldn't pay them back.

"I forgive you." Pete sounded tired. "Why don't you clean up before lunch." He went past, and since he wasn't looking, Cary could look in his face. Cary had never seen a face like Pete's up close: the face of a grown up man, tired and vulnerable. He couldn't tear his eyes away. He sucked in his breath.

"What are the rules?" he asked quickly, before he could change his mind.

Pete turned back, lifting his eyebrows. He considered a moment, then said, "If you stayed with us, I would expect you to behave like you were a member of this family. When you hurt my family, you hurt me." Cary shrank into himself, pinning his eyes to the button on the top of Pete's faded red and white flannel shirt.

"Please hear me Cary," Pete said. "You're allowed to be angry. You have good reasons to be. But your hurt doesn't make it okay to hurt others. In this family, we treat each other the way we want to be treated."

"What happens when I mess that up?" Cary asked in a pressed voice.

"I will not treat you any differently than I would treat my own children."

Cary's eyes went wide. "What will you do?"

"To you?" Pete asked.

Cary nodded. He pressed his trembling hands flat against the wall.

Pete looked over at his son. Jon was listening with his eyebrows drawn down. "That depends," Pete said. "Sometimes I think you want me to kick you out and prove all grown-ups are worthless. And other times…" He looked back at Cary, closing his mouth.

Cary waited, his eyes fixed on Pete's.

Pete's mouth tucked in at the corners. "Other times, I think you've been crying for mercy so long your voice is gone. So I guess I would do whichever of those two things you wanted me to, if I could figure that out."

Cary watched Pete go into the kitchen and saw him touch Jon's arm on the way by like he didn't even know he was doing it. He ducked his head. He felt like Pete had turned him upside down and shaken him; everything was tumbled about in his head. He couldn't imagine what it was like to be Jon. He couldn't imagine being a person

{274}

who could live here, in the upside-down world of the Whites.

"There's blood on your shirt," Jon said.

Cary lifted his shoulders. His skin felt grimy and he couldn't tell if the shirt stank or he did. Probably both. "You got anything clean I can wear?"

Jon went into his room; Cary stayed by the door. Jon dragged a large black garbage bag out of the back of his closet, where Cary had been hiding. "These are hand-me-downs from my cousin. They're too big for me, so probably they'll work for you."

"I don't need all those," Cary said. "Just something while I wash my clothes before I go."

Jon straightened up, a pair of jeans and a t-shirt in his hands. His mouth was a straight, angry line in his bruised face.

Cary didn't know where to look. Finally he asked, "Did you ice that?"

Jon glared at him. "No."

Cary closed his hands, keeping them tight at his sides. "You should have fought me back."

Jon snorted. "You have a really messed-up way of saying sorry, you know that?"

That stung. He knew how to say sorry. He just needed to get out of Jon's life before he fucked it up anymore. "We're not friends, Jon. Okay? In case you're too stupid to figure that out."

"Well screw that, because I say we are." Jon balled up the jeans and shirt and tossed them at Cary's feet. "There you go."

Cary bent stiffly and gathered them up. Jon was still glaring at him.

"We're friends because we're the same," Jon said. "In case you're too stupid to figure that out."

Cary was speechless a second. "We're nothing the same."

"You have scars," Jon said. "That's the only difference—how much it cost you to be a person who cares."

Cary held the clothes tightly against his chest like he could staunch the blood. "Shut up Jon."

"No. If your father gets to say that about you, then I get to say this. You're not a person who wants to hurt people. You covered for me when Todd made my life hell, and you covered for your mom all that time, and now you're losing everything because you're covering for your brother." Jon scrubbed his hands through his hair. "I don't know how you're so freaking strong that you can just keep loving people after all the shit that happened to you."

He was one step away from being crushed under everything he was trying to carry. "I'm not strong."

"Yeah, you are. Anybody else would have given up a long time ago."

The hair stood up on Cary's arms. "What if that's what I want to do."

"Then you should," Jon said. "You should give up and let someone else cover for you for a change." He looked levelly at Cary and Cary thought he knew exactly what he'd meant by "giving up." Jon tipped his head and his mouth softened. "Care, why do you think I want you to stay? I know you're done. I want... I want you not to have to be strong."

Cary drew in a slow breath and his eyes stung. He meant to say thanks for the clothes, but he was afraid to open his mouth. He got out before Jon could say anything else.

5

Cover.

{Cary}

Cary ran the bath as hot as he could stand and gingerly lowered himself in. He felt his whole body release and let out a shaky sigh, closing his eyes and sinking up to his chin. He wanted to stay here forever.

That thought slapped him like a bucket of cold water. His eyes snapped open, and he stared at the bottles of shampoo and conditioner and body wash already crammed into one corner of the bathtub.

What if he did what Pete said? What if he could live here?

He ducked his head under the water, scrubbing his fingers into the thick tangle of hair at the nape of his neck. Once he'd had that thought he couldn't stop picking at it. He added up the cost to himself and the cost to the Whites. He would have to say sorry to Jon, he would have to let Pete and Jon close enough to hurt him, he would have to keep his hands from hurting anyone back, and he would have to tell the truth when he talked.

He would have to stay alive, even on days when it hurt just to breathe. Leaving Pete with a dead kid to explain to Child Protection would be a hell of a way to say thank you.

Maybe if Jon covered for him he could do that.

He sat up gasping, wiping his streaming face. Shit. He'd just broken his own rule and wished for something for himself. When Pete changed his mind, it was going to hurt like hell, because Cary wanted to stay.

He reached for the soap and scrubbed himself clean until his skin was raw and his hair squeaked. When he got out of the tub, the water was pinkish-grey. He put on his shorts and pants, frowning at the short-sleeved shirt Jon had given him. The cuts on his arm were bleeding sluggishly. He should have washed and treated them two days ago; now their edges were red and inflamed.

The drawers in Jon's bathroom weren't stocked with first aid supplies like his bathroom. He had opened all of them when the doorbell rang. He froze, looking at the bathroom door. He heard Pete in the front entry greeting someone—a woman. Child Protection.

He caught a glimpse of his face in the mirror and backed up so fast he almost fell back into the tub. His mouth was sloppy, swollen with bruises, and his father's hard, black eyes looked back at him. He couldn't scrub hard enough to get the bruises off his body. The scars over the mended bones in his wrists looked like thick, pink worms crawling over the backs of his hands. He was going to have to explain these things to someone he'd never met. Right now.

The room tilted. He caught himself on the back of the toilet and threw up. He spat, hanging onto the cool porcelain with his eyes squeezed shut. *I am not strong enough for this.* He straightened gently, turning on the taps to rinse his mouth and wash his hands. There was a light knock on the door.

"Cary," Jon said. "Child Protection is here. Can you let me in?"

The cold water bit the cuts on his palm. Cary shut his fingers and turned off the tap, avoiding his face in the mirror. He opened the door. Jon slid inside and shut it behind him.

"You ready for this?"

Cary shook his head. His throat was raw. "I need some—I need something to cover this." He turned his arm out.

Jon sucked in his breath. "What the crap did you do?"

Cary met his eyes. He couldn't speak.

Jon shut up, but he looked furious. He reached into the back of the cupboard under the sink to pull out a shoebox of first aid supplies, flicking packaged squares of gauze onto the counter.

"Arm." He held out his hand. Cary set his arm in Jon's palm and Jon squeezed a tube of first aid cream in a white line from Cary's elbow to his wrist.

Cary stiffened. "What is that?"

Jon didn't pause. "I don't know, medicine cream. The stuff my dad uses on us. It's for infection; these look infected."

Cary frowned. The stuff his mother used hurt more.

In spite of his sharp tone, Jon held Cary's elbow so carefully he didn't even wrap his fingers all the way around, spreading the cream in smooth strokes from the corner of Cary's elbow down to his wrist. He put his thumb against Cary's knuckles. "Open this."

{280}

Cary held his breath and uncurled his fingers. Jon's hand tightened around Cary's elbow and his lips went white.

"You didn't think you'd been hurt enough?" His eyes flashed to Cary's and Cary had to look away, shivering in Jon's grip. Jon let him go, nearly throwing Cary's arm out of his hands. He tore open the gauze packs with shaking fingers. Cary held his arm out again without being asked and Jon lined up the gauze squares on his sticky skin, clumsily wrapping a bandage over the whole mess and taping down the ends.

"There," Jon said in a strained voice. He let out a shaky breath. "You need long sleeves." He pulled off his own shirt and held it open for Cary to get it over his head. Cary threaded in his arms and pulled the shirt down. It was still warm from Jon's body, and he was freezing. He wrapped his arms across his chest.

There was a knock at the door. "Cary?" Pete called. "She's ready for you."

His stomach clenched and he covered his mouth with his hand, swallowing over and over. His hand smelled like the soap in Jon's shower; that settled his stomach a little. Jon put the hand-me-down shirt on himself. "I'm coming with you for this."

Cary shook his head, unpeeling his hand. "No." His voice was hoarse. "I can't cover for you when I'm in there."

"I know—you have to cover for Liam."

Cary shut his eyes, and got in a breath. His best memory of Liam floated up out of the dark. When he left, Liam was just getting the hang of smiling; his whole mouth would gape in a toothless grin, and then he would look so surprised, like he had no idea how his face did that. Liam was perfect; there was still a chance for him. All Cary had to do was talk. All he had to do was go down into the basement and drag that shit up and hope the dark didn't swallow him whole.

"You can't cry," Cary said.

Jon set his face. "I won't."

Cary swallowed and lifted his shoulders. "Okay." Jon probably couldn't keep that promise but he didn't care. He was cold and heavy as stone, and Jon reminded him that his heart still beat and he still had a reason to stay alive. He opened the door, and they went out.

{Pete}

Pete was pouring the woman from Child Protection— Karen? Sharon? usually he was good with names—a cup of coffee when Cary edged into the kitchen. Jon followed close behind him. Cary had the sleeves of his shirt drawn down to his knuckles and his arms crossed tightly in front of him.

The caseworker stood up with a smile, looking from Cary to Jon, then stuck her hand out to Cary. "You must be Ciaran."

Cary acted like her outstretched hand didn't exist. "Where are we doing this."

She glanced back at Pete. "Here, or, if you prefer, I'm sure there's someplace more private."

Cary pulled out a chair and dropped into it, pushing it as far from her as he could, until his shoulders almost touched the wall. "This is fine."

Pete stood in the middle of the kitchen, holding the pot of coffee and wondering whether he should leave them alone. He saw that under his stiff abruptness, Cary was terrified and he wanted one person in this room to care about that.

"Cary, do you want me to go?" he asked.

Cary didn't look at him. "It's your house, Mr. White. Stay if you want."

"I'm staying," Jon said, challenging his dad with a look.

Pete met his eyes. This wasn't like a horror movie that he could tell Jon afterward was all made up. But of all the choices Jon had made to cover for his friend, this was one of the better ones. Pete nodded—that meant he was staying too.

He turned to set the coffee pot back in its place and took a second to say a silent prayer for each one of them. He was still vibrating like he'd grounded an electrical charge in the encounter with Cary's father. He had been standing right there with Cary hanging onto him while Conall nailed his son again with just his words. Pete had wanted to take the other man by the throat and throw him into the street.

He'd had time to ground that anger in prayer, but it was still there, close. He turned and leaned against the counter with his arms crossed. The Child Protection worker took a notepad and pen out of her bag. She crossed her legs and looked expectantly at Cary.

"So Ciaran, what can you tell me about life at home?"

Cary's black eyes were intent on the woman. "If I tell you this, will you take my brother away?"

The caseworker fiddled with her pen. "That depends. We would never remove a child from his home unless we were certain there was cause. Child Protection Services is about helping families stay together."

Cary looked at her from under his eyebrows, silent.

The woman smoothly took another tack. "You have a brother, Ciaran? How old is he?"

Cary shifted. "Six weeks."

"It sounds like you have some concerns about him. Do you want to tell me about that?"

Cary said, "I don't think he'll hurt Liam like he hurt me." He put his eyes up in the corner above the cupboards. His face was still and flat. "But he doesn't always know what he's doing. When he's doing it."

"He?"

Cary licked his lips. "Our father."

Jon had his elbows on his knees, watching Cary. He was jiggling his leg like he did when he was angry and trying to keep quiet.

The caseworker said, "Are there specific times you can tell me about?"

"How much do you need to know?" Cary asked.

"What was happening the day you called us?"

His black eyes snapped at her. "I beat the shit out of some kid at the shelter. I broke his jaw and they kicked me out."

She tapped her pencil against her notepad, waiting. Cary twisted like he wanted to duck out of the room.

"I saw my mom," he said finally. He turned his face to Jon like they were the only two in the room. "She took me to dinner to tell me, if I would say sorry—I could go back. She said that with…" He put his fist to his eye. "He hits her more when I'm not there to take it."

Cary bent his head, hiding his face behind a dark wing of hair. Jon shut his eyes, not moving a muscle.

"That's why I stayed." Cary's voice was hammered thin and flat as a strip of metal. "Because I could get him to put it on me. I deserved it. But I can't—" His voice hitched and it was a second before he could find it again. "I can't cover for Liam and her, I can't…" He fought for words. "Just tell me what the fuck you want me to say to take my father away from them."

The caseworker tapped her pen against her page, looking at Cary. "Alright," she said. She went to work on him. She was relentless and exact, using question and silence like a scalpel and forceps to spread open the history of Connall's abuse on the kitchen table. Cary's narrative was disjointed; there were gaps in time where he couldn't remember anything. There were gaps of silence where he couldn't find speech for what he could remember. She didn't let up, digging for connecting details and waiting, intent, for Cary to find the words for her.

Pete felt like the top of his head was lifting off. When the hour was up, Cary was wrung out, his hands hanging limp between his knees. Pete could hear the dry click of his mouth swallowing. He took a glass down from the cupboard and filled it with water from the tap. When he came near, Cary put his shoulders back against the chair and checked Pete's face, like he didn't know if Pete was going to take him by the throat or hand him the glass of water.

Pete set the glass on the table and went back to the counter, propping his hands on either side of his body, open. He had never in his life had a child draw back from him in fear. He shut his eyes, trying to breathe Jesus in since he didn't have any words left to pray.

Cary lifted the glass. His hands were trembling as he took a drink. When he set it down he wrapped his arms tight around himself. "Is that enough? To put him away— is that enough?"

The woman crossed her last 't' and capped her pen. "I'm not the police, Ciaran. It's my job to start your file and pass it along for their investigation. I have what I need to do that, and I'll make you an appointment to visit the police station to talk to the detectives there. They'll want you in forensics to take pictures of any scars or bruises you have related to their case."

Cary's face went white and blank, as if she'd told him he would face a firing squad the next morning. He put his eyes on Jon, and a whole conversation seemed to pass between them in a moment.

The woman's smile was thin. "But I can give you my opinion. You did everything right. Your father should get used to living in four feet square."

She gathered her things and got to her feet. "I understand your family will keep Ciaran while this investigation goes forward?"

Pete realized she was talking to him. Cary looked at him; his eyes were full of pupil, huge and dark.

Pete tried to smile. "We're still working that out. We can. Unless you have something better in mind, Cary is welcome to stay with us."

She nodded, relieved. "That would be our preference. We have a real shortage of emergency beds for young people like Ciaran."

Pete thought, *I'm sure you do,* and walked her to the door. He shook her hand and did the niceties until she finally left, and he could shut the door and take a second to breathe. He was battered with memories of Jon as a boy, his son's skinny arms and legs and his big, infectious grin. Jon had been small enough for Pete to scoop him up in his arms to swing around in a hug. He could not for a moment imagine completing that swing by opening his arms to throw his son against the wall. He wanted to go into his room, put his face in the corner and cry.

When he turned, Cary was standing in the doorway of the kitchen, looking at him. "What if this doesn't work?" Cary asked. "What if they leave Liam with him?"

Pete shook his head once. "You heard what she said: Your father is going to jail." *And Jesus have mercy on his soul.*

Cary dropped back against the doorjamb. "Then what about me."

Pete heard the weight of what Cary was asking; somehow this boy carried the blame for the things his father had done to him. Pete made his voice light. "Nine years is not an insignificant sentence, Cary. Whatever you think you did, I think you did your time."

Cary's whole body shuddered, and Pete thought he might finally cry. He didn't. He said in a low voice, "I'll stay and keep your rules, Mr. White. Until you tell me it's time to go."

Pete looked across the hall at the slight, bowed form of some other man's son. That man had considered this boy of so little worth that he had broken him and thrown him away. Cary was nothing to anybody now, a child nobody would claim. On paper, there was nothing between them. But in Pete's heart, the papers were signed: Cary belonged to him now. If no one else would take care of this child, then he would.

Pete nodded. "Thank you for telling me. I'm glad you've decided to stay."

Cary stayed standing there with his head down, like he was waiting for something.

"Supper's at five," Pete said. "You can do what you like until then."

That seemed to be what Cary needed—permission to go. He pushed himself off the doorjamb and went into Jon's room without looking at Pete again.

6

Scars.

{Cary}

Jon's room was empty. Cary stood looking at Jon's rumpled bed, his head pounding like someone had been yelling in his ears for the past hour. He was heavy with the dark he'd talked up from the basement, and there was more pressing on the doors he had kept shut. There was a child down there who remembered how to cry, and the wall between them was getting thinner. When he couldn't keep himself apart anymore all of that boy's terror and heartbreak would be his.

He dug in his backpack for his drawing book and pencils and crawled into Jon's bed. He put his head on Jon's cool pillow and pressed the dark onto the page until the paper shone black with graphite. He drew until he felt something release in his chest. He let the drawing book fall, feeling so empty he scraped bottom. He thought he heard one of Jon's sisters crying; no one went to comfort her.

He was lying like that, with his frozen hands tucked under his shirt against the heat of his bruises when Jon came in. Cary blinked like someone had just turned on a light. "Where did you go?"

Jon touched him with a look. "Down to the ravine. There's some bike trails where I used to go when Todd wound me up." His face was still shadowed with anger and tears had left tracks through the dirt on his cheeks. He went to his closet and pulled off his filthy clothes.

Cary closed his eyes. That's what it looked like to not have scars. He said, "Is it supper time?"

"Not for a couple hours," Jon said. "Have you eaten anything today?"

Cary thought about that. He was hollow inside. He shook his head.

"Well you look like crap. Come on and I'll make you a snack."

Cary got stiffly to his feet. Dark gathered in the corners of his vision, and he kept his eyes between Jon's shoulders, following him down the hall like he was a bright planet in a black void.

Jon pulled a box of frozen waffles out of the freezer and lined them up in the toaster. "Are you thinking about staying?"

"I told your dad I would."

Jon turned; his face glowed like a light had switched on inside him. Cary shivered, watching him. If he fucked this up, he would care so much about that it was terrifying.

Jon hid his grinning face in the fridge and said, "Check it out, there's real whipped cream in a can."

As if on cue, Jon's littlest sister wandered into the kitchen. She climbed onto the chair next to Cary, watching Jon with a hopeful expression. "Jonee can you make a waffle snack for me?"

"Sure Bea," Jon said.

Bea stared at the side of Cary's face so hard that he finally turned and looked at her. "What."

She had Jon's worried crease in-between her eyebrows. "What happened to your face?"

Cary slid Jon a look. What was he supposed to say here?

Jon said, "Up to you." He grabbed the waffles out of the toaster, blowing on his fingers. He put plates in front of them both.

Cary cut his waffle into four and then cut it again into eight. He did not want to talk about this with Bea. "I made my father angry."

Bea frowned harder. "What did you do?"

Cary held the memory of that morning at a distance with some effort, sweat pricking under his arms. "I was making my brother a bottle. He thought I was hurting him." He could just say it now. "He hit me."

She drew back, astonished. "That's not true, is it Jon? Did Cary's dad do that to him?"

"Sorry Bea," Jon said. "I can tell you from personal experience that people can be really mean. Not Cary though; he'd never hurt you. Anyways, he's too banged up to even catch you. You're a pretty fast runner."

Bea giggled. She shook up the can of whipped cream. "Gimme your plate."

Cary stopped with his fork halfway to his mouth. He set the waffle down and passed the plate to Bea. She made a mountain of white foam on his waffles, and then on hers, her mouth curving as she admired her work. "There. That's better, isn't it?"

He took his plate back without comment. His mouth filled with the soft, sweet taste of the waffle. It was the best thing he'd eaten in weeks.

When Bea was finished her waffle she used her fingers to mop up her plate, licking syrup off of them thoughtfully. "Did your dad say sorry to you?"

Cary darted a look at her. "No."

She made a face. "Well, that wasn't very nice. He left a big mark on you. Next time he comes here, I'm going to tell him that."

The picture that made was so scary Cary want to shove her in a cupboard and hold the door shut to keep her far, far away from his father.

She jumped off her chair, tossing her pigtails. "Bye." Cary watched her go, his heart doing double time before he remembered who she was. Pete wouldn't let anything happen to her. He didn't have to worry about her because Pete was her dad.

"I think she likes you," Jon said.

"She doesn't know any better," Cary said. "You're so fucking lucky. All of you."

///

They spent the afternoon in Jon's room. Cary stretched on the bed working on his drawing. Jon laid on the floor reading comic books. The noise of Jon's house— his sisters playing, his parents talking, the hum of the dishwasher—washed around them like waves.

"Bea is six," Jon said, after more than an hour of silence.

It was a moment before Cary could pull himself out of his drawing and look at him. Jon was lying on the floor with his arm over his eyes. His mouth was flat and unhappy. "That stuff happened to you when you were six."

Cary put his eyes on his page. He'd had something lodged in his mind like a glass shard since he dragged it out for the social worker, and this drawing was the best he could do to get it out. He'd pushed the perspective so the child's outstretched hands in the foreground were as large as the figure raised to strike in the shadows behind him. But he didn't feel anything about it. It was like looking at the photograph of someone else's kid; he knew it was real, but he didn't care.

"I don't really remember what that was like," he said. "Like it happened to someone apart from me."

Jon sat up. "That's why you don't cry."

Cary looked silently at him. He thought about opening the door to the pink nursery, and how he'd cried then. What would happen if he opened all the doors? He dropped his eyes to the page, resting his fingertips on the paper. He didn't want to find out.

"Sorry." Jon pressed his fingers against his eyes. Tears had slipped out of them. He let out his breath slowly. "Sorry, I said I wouldn't cry."

Cary lifted his shoulders. "There's nothing wrong with you," he said. "You don't have to apologize for who you are to me."

"There's nothing wrong with you either," Jon said. "In case you're too stupid to figure that out too."

Cary's shoulders tightened. "I could have broken your face, Jon. I still could."

"That's not who you are. That's just the shit you learned." Jon's voice vibrated with anger.

Cary's face stung like Jon had slapped him. "That's the shit he carved on me and it's in me now—" He dug his palm into his chest. "—scars on my scars. I can't just—cut them out and be something different. You don't know a fucking thing about that."

Jon absorbed that with his eyebrows drawn down and tear-tracks still on his cheeks. "Just what I know from you."

Cary muttered a swear. He was responsible for so much shit in Jon's life right now.

"And not just you." Jon bent his head and drew in his breath. "Jesus has scars."

Cary watched him sideways. This was the part about Jon he didn't know anything about. "So?"

Jon was quiet for a bit, his hands cupped together in his lap, like he would use them to scoop a mouthful of water. Like he needed that water to speak. "So Jesus knows what it's like. He knows how to be good, even when he was so hurt." Jon lifted his face to him; his expression was full of light, like water held quivering in a bowl.

Cary had to look away. He had rooms full of darkness, frozen inside him, and that light was what was inside Jon.

"He says he can take your hurt and heal it," Jon said, soft and low. "I don't know how he can do that, but he wants to and that must mean he can." He caught his breath like tears were close.

Cary made a disbelieving noise. "Jesus said that to you?"

Jon shrugged, his face pinking. "Well… yeah."

What if that was true? Cary was clenching his battered hands so tightly his knuckles ached. "What would I even say to him?"

"I don't know—sorry?"

Cary caught his breath. "I can't." It was easy to picture Jesus with his face smashed in, getting back up and reaching for the shovel. He cupped his hands over his mouth, panic making him short of breath. The basement was so close, ready to drag him out of this room and into a black hole of memory.

Jon frowned at him. "Why not? Just say sorry and get another chance."

Cary could taste concrete dust and copper in his mouth and feel the electric crackle of his father's anger making the hairs all over his body stand to attention. Then the basement swallowed him whole, the force of it slamming him against the wall and pinning him there. He wanted to say sorry but his father wasn't going to let him until he'd made him twist and break and bleed.

Jesus God please

please

please

He couldn't breathe. The bed rocked and Jon said, "I'm coming over there, don't punch me in the face." His solid warmth settled against Cary's shoulder and he put his hand lightly on Cary's shoulder blade. Cary drew into a ball with a whimper.

"Jesus." Jon's hand lifted. "Cary…I'm not going to hurt you."

Cary made a wrenching noise that was supposed to be a laugh, brought back to this room by the ridiculousness of Jon saying that to him. "I know." Panic beat him back, teetering on the top of the stairs, and he fought to stay here, with Jon.

Jon took a shaky breath. "What's going on?"

Cary was still trying to scrape his mind back together. "I said sorry." His voice was uneven. "A hundred fucking times. In the basement."

"Well your father is an asshole," Jon said sharply. "Jesus is not like that."

Cary shook his head. He knew this, right in his bones. "Sorry isn't good enough."

Jon's forehead wrinkled. He still didn't get it. Quick as thinking, Cary caught his face and pressed his thumb against the bruise swelling Jon's cheek. "Somebody pays," Cary said. "Somebody has to carry it."

Jon met his eyes without flinching, even though Cary was holding him hard enough to feel the ridge of the bone in his cheek. "So?" Jon said. "Why does it have to be you?"

Cary let his hand drop. Not broken. He wasn't sure what he would have done with himself if he had broken Jon. He folded his arms over his head and rested his forehead on his knees. Everything hurt and he was exhausted. "I'm sorry," he said in a soft, dry voice. "For hitting you. I fucked up."

He felt Jon shrug against his arm. "I forgive you," Jon said. "So forget it."

Cary stayed still. Just like that.

"Was that so hard?" Jon said lightly.

Cary turned his head to look silently at Jon. That bruise would still be hurting Jon when he talked or ate or rolled over on the wrong side in bed. Sorry or no sorry, he could add that to the list of shit he couldn't take back.

Jon nudged his shoulder. "You know how my dad looked when you said sorry?"

Cary closed his eyes a moment. Jon looked like Pete when his face was like this.

"God is like my dad," Jon said. "His love is steady like my dad's. He carries the cost." Shadows passed over Jon's expression. "I have been... ungrateful and selfish, and I've hurt my dad on purpose, and he never hurt me back. He took it and still came to tuck me in and pray for me every single night until I made him stop." Jon drew a breath. "I wish I could give you all the good days I've had with my dad so you could see what it's supposed to be like."

"Don't," Cary said, low and rough. "You can't. So just—don't."

Jon set his jaw and looked at his hands spread on his knees. "At least I can forgive you. The way he's covered for me."

Cary hiccoughed a laugh, rubbing his eyes with the heel of his hand. "God, you Whites. So fucking stubborn."

Jon's smile made his whole face warm and bright. "Yes we are."

Cary let out a long shaky breath, looking at Jon's battered face wearing that smile. "If I lose it again, I need you to fight me back."

Jon's eyebrows drew together. He didn't say anything.

Cary took a hold of Jon's shirt in his fist, then opened his hand instead. "I mean it. Please. I can't hurt you again." He swallowed, feeling Jon's heart galloping along under his palm. "I need you to stop me."

"How could I stop you?" Jon asked in a flat voice. "You're bigger, and you're good at fighting."

"Look." Cary sat back and lifted his shirt.

Jon flinched, looking at the hot purple bruise where Cary's ribs were broken. "Hit me here, good and hard," Cary said. He pushed his hand against his ribs, feeling the way black tightened around him when he did that. "Get your shoulder in or your knee and I'll go down. I won't get back up. You'll be safe."

Jon drew back. "No way. I can't do that. Hit you where you're hurt."

"You have to," Cary said. "Jon, that kid I fought at the shelter—his face didn't look like a face anymore when I was finished. I don't remember anything after the first minute." He was shaking, thinking about how close he came to doing that to Jon this morning. He let his shirt drop and held his hands up. "If I did that to you... if I did that to you again I couldn't bleed enough. And I would have to leave. Please help me not fuck this up."

Jon's face got hard, and Cary folded his fingers over the lines cut into his skin. Jon got to his feet. "Fine," he said. "Whatever you say."

Cary held still, watching him cross the room. "You look mad," he said.

"I am mad," Jon snapped. His eyes flashed gold in the long afternoon light as he looked back at Cary. "I hate that you hurt yourself so many ways. I hate that you think you deserve it. If you need me to say I'll do this, to feel safe enough to stay—then okay, I will. But I want you to know, right now—I'm never going to need to. Because you won't let this happen again." Jon brushed his hand over his bruised cheek. "I know you."

Cary ducked his head, out of breath. "Okay. Thank you."

Jon sighed. "Yeah, you're welcome, Cary. That's what friends are for."

When the door shut, Cary shut his eyes and slumped sideways onto the bed. He covered his face and tried to get a breath into his aching chest. He couldn't believe he'd done such a good job of hiding from Jon that Jon thought he wouldn't hurt him again. Cary wanted to believe that the Cary Jon saw was in him somewhere, even if he was bent by scars, but he was so tired. More likely that Cary was dead and gone and Jon just saw the shape of where he used to be.

7

The door.

{Cary}

Cary fell asleep curled in Jon's bed with his forehead against the wall. He woke up on the floor in his own bedroom. He got to his feet, looking at the sun going down in the window. He had been dreaming that he was in Jon's house, that he lived there. The dream fled, and Cary made a sound as it went, taking all the warmth with it.

There was something wet on his face: he was crying. He never cried at this house anymore. If he was back here without his jacket... *Jesus-God, I'm fucked.* He slapped the tears out of his eyes and dried his face on the hem of his shirt.

His room was completely empty, and the carpets were torn up. The floor was obscured by a layer of sand, and the walls were smudged and grimy up to eye level. Cary hunched his shoulders and went to look for Liam.

Liam's nursery was bare except for his crib, standing in the middle of the room with a naked plastic mattress behind the bars. Cary's heart jumped into his mouth. He turned from the doorway and went from room to room, panic rising. There was no furniture anywhere and nothing on the walls. His mother's closet was bare except for a

{300}

tangle of hangers. The chandelier was missing in the front entrance. The rooms were all empty, and the silence pressed on his ears like water.

Cary stood in the hallway, short of breath. There was one place left to look. He went to the end of the hall and opened the door to the basement.

In this house, there were no stairs. The basement was a finished room, with another room inside it. There were no windows. The hall light made a rectangle of light on the bare floor, and there was a thread of light where the drywall of that other room didn't meet the ceiling.

"Liam?" Cary stepped through the doorway and to the side, putting his shoulders against the wall. His fingers felt how smooth and cool the painted surface was. Red. The room, the floor, and the ceiling were all painted red. Cary's head buzzed.

The room inside the red room had a white door, which was startlingly clean and bright in the dark. Cary crossed the room and tried the doorknob, but it was locked. Cary threw his shoulder against the door, yelling, "Liam!" He heard a sound and held his breath. On the other side of the door, a child was crying in short gasps like he was trying to be quiet. Panic beat its wings inside his chest. Was the light on? Was Liam in there in the dark? His brother was too small to reach the cord.

Cary swore and hammered on the door until his knuckles broke and bled. He leaned his shoulders against it, breathing hard. He lifted his face.

"JESUS!" he hollered. "WHERE ARE YOU? GET HIM OUT!"

"You locked him in," a soft voice said. Jon was sitting cross-legged next to the door. He lifted his face to

Cary, and his mouth pulled up in an unhappy smile. "That's not Liam in there, Cary."

Cary started away from the door like it was red-hot. Jon's eyes followed him, and there were whispers in the shadowed corners of the room. Cary drew his hands against his chest. They were freezing cold. "I need to get out of here."

The child's sobs rasped in Cary's ears. In every break, he hoped he was done—that he had finally curled up in the corner and died. Jon blinked, and two tears dropped, shining on his cheeks. "You have the key to this door. You can open it."

"No," Cary said. "He needs to stay in there."

"Why?" Jon asked. "Why is he different than Liam?"

The shadows in the room gathered thickly, a deeper darkness high in the corners. Cary whispered, "Liam never did anything wrong."

Jon spread his hand over the white door. "What about you?"

That was right; he couldn't leave either. This was his room, where everything was red. The shadows fell down from the ceiling. Cary could feel how cold they were, sliding over his shoulders and pressing him down. Cary was heavy as stone, bent almost to the floor. "Get out of here, Jon."

Jon said, "I just want you to look at him."

He couldn't open his mouth or move any direction except down. Cary sank to his knees and put his forehead against the floor. The weight of the dark held him there, slowly crushing him. "Help me," he whispered.

Jon's arms wrapped around his chest and lifted him to his feet. He was stronger than Cary would have guessed. He got Cary to the door and propped him against it.

Something burned Cary's skin, right over his heart. He reached under his shirt and tugged out a key on a shoelace. His hands were clumsy and numb and he could hardly see for the dark. Jon plucked the key out of his fingers and put it in the lock.

When the door opened, Cary fell into the room. It was warm. There was a window, and the room was full of light. He toppled onto his back, staring up at the ceiling in a daze.

There were model rockets and airplanes suspended above him. He turned his head: the room was larger than it had looked from the outside. There was a bed with a comforter covered with stars and planets and rocket ships, just like the one Cary had picked out of a catalogue when he was six—when Renae was going to have a matching one.

He rolled to his hands and knees, letting his head rest against the floor a moment. When he could lift his head, he found a boy looking back at him. He had dark hair, and he was wiping tears off his face.

"Ciaran," Cary said.

The boy nodded.

Cary looked for bruises. All the skin he could see was smooth and unmarked. "Are you hurt?"

Little Ciaran shook his head. "I've been in here. Where you put me. You told me I should keep the door locked and never come out." He came closer, his face full of concern. "How long have you been out there?"

Cary tried to pull himself together. He got to his feet and staggered to the bed to sit down. "I don't know."

The boy drew near, frowning. He put out his hands, then checked himself. "What is this?" He folded his hands over his chest rather than touching Cary.

Cary looked down at himself. There was a wide stain on the front of his t-shirt, black-red and sticky, where the hole was. "It's always like that." He ran his hands over the crisp softness of the coverlet, blinking around the room. The window's brightness made his eyes sting and water. There was a star chart on the wall. There was a telescope. It was exactly the room he'd wanted when he was six.

Cary slid a sideways look at the boy, afraid. Little Ciaran was smaller than he remembered, and his face was so open Cary knew he didn't know the first thing about protecting himself. "Show me your hands."

The child held out his hands, slowly opening them. Cary touched the smooth, damp palms with his fingers. Nothing. He put his own scarred hands, closed, beside him and laughed softly. "He never touched you. I hid you safe in here."

Little Ciaran put a finger, one light touch, on the scar on Cary's wrist. He withdrew his hand. "I could hear you out there sometimes," he said in a small voice. He set his face, but his eyes filled with tears. "I wasn't afraid. I—wanted to help. But I stayed in here because you told me to. I did what you said." The child stood trembling in front of him. "I have something I want to give you. Can I?"

Cary nodded, still smiling.

The boy came close and slipped his arms around Cary's ribcage. He put his head on Cary's chest. He sighed a deep, shaky sigh, like he'd come home, and then he was gone.

Cary put his hands flat against his chest. Something in that broken mess was set back in place to heal. He stood up to go, feeling stiff and old compared to that unmarked child. The red room looked black compared to the light of the child's bedroom.

He didn't make it over the threshold. He remembered abruptly how small he had been, how thin his skin had been. His breath caught like there was a hook sunk into that hole in his chest, yanking on him hard.

He woke up because he couldn't breathe. He curled, turning his face into Jon's pillow, tears scalding his eyes. He had cried so little over the years he couldn't remember how to stop. He kicked free of the blankets and fell out of Jon's bed, dragging a breath in, then another. He crawled across the floor and buried himself in the back of Jon's closet, grief pounding him like ocean breakers. He had been that small and his face had been that open and defenseless. Cary clenched his fists over his head, going under, coming apart.

The door to Jon's room clicked open, and a light voice said, "Hello? Is somebody here?"

Cary couldn't make himself silent. He pressed his face into his legs, swearing frantically under his breath.

The closet door swung open and he shut up, but his breathing was still crooked and tears kept streaming out of his eyes.

Jon's littlest sister hung onto the closet door handle, tipping her head. "Whatcha doing in here? Can I hide too?"

She squeezed into the small space without an invitation and worked her way under Cary's arm. Her bony shoulder dug into his ribs, the side that didn't have the shit kicked out of it. Cary turned his face away, trying to hold his body still except for the catch and gasp of his breathing.

Bea stretched to look into his face. "Cary, you're hurt? You're sad?"

"Go away."

Bea put her arms around his body. Her hands met on the worst of his bruises, where his ribs were broken, and Cary swallowed a cry. His hands went up, pressing flat against the walls on either side, and he would have nailed them there if he could to keep them from hurting her. She held him feather-light, her face buried under his arm. Cary's breathing smoothed out and slowed. He wiped his face on his sleeve and let out a long, shaky sigh.

Bea hugged him tighter. "All better?"

The tiny space tightened around him like a screw and a red explosion went off in his brain. He threw her off, pinning her in the corner with his thumb against her throat. The narrow ridge of her collarbone was under his hand; he knew exactly how much more pressure would break her.

She lifted her hands and stroked his arm. He could feel her trembling. "I forgot you're hurt. Sorry, Cary, sorry."

He snatched his hands back, scrambling to get away from her. "Get out of here Bea."

She came after him, her face full of concern. "Are you okay?"

He hit the wall of the bedroom and curled around his ribs. Pain beat red on the edges of his vision in time with his drumming heart. He said through his teeth, "Get away from me."

"I said I'm sorry." She put out her hands, and Cary balled up, locking his arms over his head. He did the only thing he could think of.

"Jon!" He yelled so hard it felt like his rib poked out through the muscle in his side.

Running footsteps came down the hall. "What is it? What's wrong?" Jon's voice buzzed. In between red-black slides, Cary saw him catch his little sister around her chest and turn her toward himself. "Bea, are you okay?"

"I hurt Cary when I hugged him tight." Bea was crying now. "He won't take my sorry."

Jon smoothed the hair back from her flushed, tearful face. "Okay, that's okay Honey Bee. You didn't mean to. Cary knows that. You go on. Mom wants you for bedtime stories."

Bea went, sobbing. The sound of her crying caught in Cary's chest. He'd already cried so hard his head ached—and there was more inside him. He pressed hard on his temples, trying to find a way to breathe that didn't hurt.

Jon crouched in front of him. "Are you okay?"

"I almost hurt her." He could still feel the soft skin of her throat under his fingers. "I could have snapped her in two."

It was quiet a moment. "But you didn't," Jon said.

Cary put his hands down and looked Jon in the face.

Jon startled. "You've been crying."

"No shit." Cary's voice cracked. He pulled himself painfully to his feet. He felt as if his skin were made of glass and any amount of pressure would break him. How was he going to talk about the shit his father had done to him, at the police station tomorrow? How was he going to do anything like this? He went out of Jon's room and down the hall, steadying himself against the wall.

It was dark outside. The cool night air stroked his skin and Cary took a full breath, straightening in spite of the pain. The porch light illuminated the bones of the garage, standing tall in the yard. Cary went toward it, seeing the way the corners joined neat and tight where he had hammered them into place while Pete held them steady. That was a thing he had done with his hands and he was proud of it.

He tripped a little on the edge of the concrete pad and crawled to the middle. He stretched out on his back, looking up at the night sky framed by the ribs of the garage roof. When the porch light blinked off, the stars sprung out against the dark, piercing him.

Could there be something—someone—big enough to hold all this inside his hands? If Jon was right, could the maker of something as large and dark as outer space make himself small enough to fit inside the dark of Cary's basement?

Not that He ever would. Cary shut his eyes and held his breath while that pain pulled steadily on him. No one innocent and clean like Jesus would ever come for him. That was why it was so stupid to hurt for that child who had cried down there; that was why it was so fucking stupid to want someone to care.

Someone's feet rustled across the grass. Jon hesitated in the middle of the dark backyard. "Cary?"

"I'm here," Cary said.

Jon joined him on the concrete pad, sitting with his knees drawn up. He tipped his head back and Cary could see his smile gleam in the dark. "Wow. Beautiful sky."

"Yeah." They were quiet, then Cary said, "I used to climb out my window and lie on the roof at night. To get away for a bit. To get cold, like space." His chest was hot inside, glowing like a space heater, pulsing in time with his heart like a beacon. He put his hand over that heat, like he could hide its *SOS*.

"I found him. The boy that was me," Cary said. Jon turned his face towards him. "I remember stuff I didn't used to. About... about the way I was."

"Are you okay?" Jon asked again.

Cary closed his eyes. "No."

After a moment of quiet, Jon put his feet towards the back of the garage and his hands behind his head. He tipped his face to the stars. His presence anchored Cary in the dark.

There was something Cary needed to get out, and talking was the only way he had left now. "I had a sister— did you know that?" His voice was soft and rough. He didn't think he would cry again, but it might be close.

"No." Jon sounded surprised.

"She died when I was six." He held still, measuring what he could say out loud. He hadn't told this part to the social worker—or to anyone, ever. "After..." After the wailing sirens and the funeral and the house full of strangers, his mother never got out of her bed. His father stalked about the empty house, silent, huge and terrifying. Little Ciaran stayed invisible a long time; so long his father forgot he was there—forgot he had a son who was still alive and needed the things living children need: food and words and touch.

"I wanted my mom to wake up," Cary said. "I went to try and wake her up and he caught me. He never hit me before that, not even with his hand." Cary's fists closed against his chest. "I didn't have any scars. I didn't know how not to cry. I couldn't—I couldn't hold still. He put me in the basement." He shivered all over and shut his mouth.

"Jesus," Jon said brokenly.

Cary thought about Jesus, about what Jon said about God being like Pete. The physical memory of Pete's arm catching him across his chest steadied him, so that his voice sounded even when he asked, "You think he was there? You think Jesus was there for that?"

Jon took a breath. "Yeah, I do."

Cary frowned into the dark. "I don't see where he could be."

Jon turned his face to him. "What if you… Cary what if you asked him?"

Cary looked back at him. "What?"

"Where he was. Do you think you could ask Jesus?"

Jon's question was so simple Cary didn't think it could work. He wanted it to work. He thought of the man with the blood on his face and the bare light bulb making a halo of fractured light around his hair. *Where were you?* Cary asked him.

He expected Jesus' face to dissolve like water between his fingers as soon as he grabbed too hard. Instead, the picture got so bright that Cary's eyes watered with tears. When his vision cleared, he was in the basement.

Turn around. The words whispered in his ear.

Behind him, the unfinished basement room was bright with daylight. This was the real basement in his memory; there was no door. Cary stepped to the opening. The drywall was pocked with nails holding the sheets to the studs. There was a window, and the drywall around the frame was cut jaggedly, exposing the white chalk core. Cary knew every detail of this room. It had been his hiding place to wait for his mother to open the door at the top of the stairs. He steadied himself against the doorframe and made himself look at the boy propped in the corner.

Little Ciaran had his skinny legs drawn up against his body. He was watching the light from the window where it fell against the wall. Tears kept filling his eyes and he shook his head hard to clear them. He wanted to see.

Cary's hand tightened on the doorframe, and he put his eyes on the other person in the room. Jesus was sitting against the wall beside the boy, talking softly to him. He was tracing the shapes with his finger in the air, so the boy could see them framed by the rectangle of light on the wall. Little Ciaran had his head tipped toward Jesus and his fingers moved in his lap, planning the drawing he would make when he could go upstairs again.

Cary's breath caught, and he closed his eyes. Just like that, he had slipped inside the skin of that boy, watching the light cross the wall while the blood beat in his bruises. The light turned the corner and the room darkened. He was afraid again. There was a naked bulb in the ceiling, but he wasn't tall enough to reach the string. His mother always left a nightlight on for him when she tucked him in.

He crawled to the pile of drop-cloths and plastic and burrowed into them, curling up small. Night came down like a shade over the window.

The basement room did not get dark. Light came off Jesus, rippling like he had a fire lit in his chest. Little Ciaran didn't wonder about that. He went to sleep and Cary watched him from the door. Jesus dropped his hand on the sleeping boy's hair, his eyes on Cary's face.

Jesus didn't look angry; his scarred hand was stroking the boy's hair the way Cary's mother used to.

Cary took courage from that and crept to Jesus's feet. "I remember this," Cary said. He watched the boy; even in sleep he had a deep furrow in his forehead. Cary knew he was as battered on the inside as he looked on the outside. He still had the scars from this day. "You were here, after."

Jesus nodded.

"You made it light," Cary said. "You showed me how to look at the light."

Jesus mouth lifted. "Your mother got up and bought you a drawing book and pencils the next day. You were a natural."

Cary put the heels of his hands on his eyes, holding that inside him. "Were you there for the before?" he asked in the dark.

"Yes," Jesus said.

"Show me," Cary whispered.

He was the boy again, his face full of the blankets on his parents' bed. Jesus was holding him as tight as he had held Liam. Conall's belt caught them both and Cary felt Jesus' breath shaking against his cheek. In the skin of this boy, Cary was defenseless. His cry made Jesus curl more closely around him, turning his face so his eyelashes brushed against the skin on his temple. *Here I am.*

Cary's hands on his face were wet. He drew in his breath and sat up. Apparently he could cry again.

Jon sat up with him. "What happened? Did Jesus answer your question?"

Cary turned his face to Jon. He couldn't speak. His eyelashes were heavy with tears; he blinked and more slid down his face. He nodded and got to his feet to go into Jon's house.

Bea was at the kitchen table eating cereal. Cary hesitated, looking for a way through the kitchen that would keep him away from her. She looked up, trying to smile. "Hi Cary. Are you better now?"

He nodded once and touched his fingers to his collarbone, where he had grabbed her. "Did I hurt you?"

She nodded solemnly, and something froze in his chest.

"Right here." She put her hand over her heart. "I said sorry for hurting you, and you didn't take it."

He let out his breath, a soft 'ha.' "I take your sorry, Bea."

She clasped her hands against her chest, still anxious. "Do you forgive me?"

He tucked his elbow against his ribs. The pain of her embrace had dulled to a steady throb. "I forgive you." The words felt awkward in his mouth, but important. He'd never said them or had anyone say them to him before today. "Can you c'mere, Bea?"

She climbed down from her chair and came toward him, her face bright with hope. He went down on one knee and drew the collar of her pyjamas to the side. The skin on her shoulder was peach-soft—no marks left by his fingers.

She held still, unflinching, looking into his face with a puzzled crease between her eyebrows. He withdrew his hands and made a smile with his mouth. That felt almost like the right thing on his face.

She smiled back. "Are you living with us again tomorrow?"

He looked around the kitchen, at the cluttered counter and chipped cupboards. There was something pressing in his chest, filling him up until it hurt. He nodded.

"And the next day and the next day?"

Cary closed his eyes, feeling Jon's house around him like a protective shell. "Yeah. I live here now."

Something light and warm touched his face, and his eyes flew open. Bea had her hand on his cheek, trying to cover his bruise, and her bottom lip was caught between her teeth. "Why was your family mean to you? Why don't they want you anymore?"

That went into the broken mess in his chest like an arrow and stuck there, quivering. "I don't know," Cary said. That hurt as much as thinking he knew what was wrong with him.

Bea took his shoulders, rocking him off balance. She kissed the bruise on his cheek, knocking him flat on his butt. "Get better soon, okay?"

It took a second to catch his breath. He nodded. "'Kay."

8

Hiding place.

{Cary}

Cary lay awake in Jon's room thinking about tomorrow and the next day and the next. He hadn't imagined he would live that long. If Jon hadn't been who he was at school, and if Pete hadn't come for him at the shelter, he was pretty sure he wouldn't have made it to this day, let alone hope to live through another one tomorrow. He felt like the stump of something, severed from the whole and left to bleed. Except the bleeding had stopped. The edges were sealing, and they might heal. That would just leave him with a hole in his middle he could maybe live with. And the scars.

He closed his eyes and found himself standing in the basement room with his scars drawn all over his skin. His heart shone like a fire in the hole of his chest. He put his hands against it to warm them, thinking about the other person he knew with scars.

He heard his name and turned. Jesus stepped into the room. He was taller than Cary, and light still came off him in waves. Cary barely held his ground. He didn't think he should be afraid of the person who had taken his father's beating with him, but they were in the basement and Jesus was bigger than he was—by a lot. He looked for bruises on Jesus' face and arms. "Are you okay?"

Jesus smiled. "I make everything new. Look at you." He laid his hand on his chest instead of touching Cary and opened it like a door. "That's beautiful."

The hair stood up all over Cary's exposed skin, and he crossed his arms over his body.

Jesus tipped his head, like Cary had spoken out loud. "You don't have your jacket," he said.

Cary lifted his shoulders, trying to hide his trembling. All the places he'd been hurt were open now and deeply tender, and there was nothing left to cover them with.

Jesus took a step toward him. "Can I be your jacket?"

"What?" Cary said through numb lips.

"I could hide you—inside me." Jesus lifted up his shirt and Cary blinked at the wound, hot and red, open in Jesus' side.

He put out his hand without thinking. "Does that still hurt you?" He closed his fingers and shut up, checking Jesus' face. He shouldn't have asked that. His father never told him what to do if the person he was addressing was God, but he could imagine what Conall would say—or rather, the way Conall would say it to him.

Jesus' mouth pressed in at the corners, like Jon's when he was holding tears inside. "You're still afraid of me."

Cary stayed still, watching Jesus from the corner of his eye.

"I didn't come here to make you afraid." Jesus was standing as still as he was, leaning a little toward him. "Do you want me to go?"

Cary bent his head. "You're God. Do what you like. Stay if you want."

There was a low, glad laugh, and Jesus slipped up so close he could have reached out and grabbed Cary with his long, strong hands. Cary went rigid, not breathing.

Please don't hurt me. He kept his mouth shut on those words, but they were so close to speech they shivered over his skin.

Jesus brushed the bruised skin on Cary's ribs with his fingers. Cool relief spread from his touch like the medicine cream Jon put on Cary's arm. Jesus looked down at Cary, standing there trembling, and his expression was so tender Cary could barely believe he was the object of that emotion.

"I'm not him," Jesus said.

Cary could fill his lungs again, and he dropped his head onto Jesus' chest with a sigh. He was so weary.

Jesus caught his breath. He set his hand carefully on Cary's shoulder blade, like he was afraid to frighten him away. That was all. There was space between them; the air was warm with heat from Jesus' skin. Jesus bent his head and his breath brushed Cary's ear as he said, "Think about what I said, child."

Sleep wrapped Cary up and carried him away while he was still wondering which thing Jesus meant. He dreamt of the lift and fall of Jesus' breathing and his own heart keeping slow time under that scarred palm.

END

Acknowledgements and Thanks

This book could not have become a reality without the generous, skillful editing work of Amy Robertson, who believed in this project and made time for it in her busy life. Thank you, Amy. I assure you, any remaining mistakes are my own fault for touching it after she was finished! I'm also grateful to Jess Wiberg, who gave this project the strikingly edgy cover it needed to actually be a thing. You rock, Jess!

This story was born in the creative mess of a little campus writing group shepherded by Brita Schenk. I still remember the smell of German apple pancake filling her kitchen when she told me why Cary burned his father's books. That moment gave me the key that unlocked worlds inside Cary that I had only guessed at before. Thank you, Brita.

I am deeply grateful for the providential ordering of the universe that put Kendra and I together just as I was finishing draft 2.0 of this novel. She was 16 at the time, and we came from worlds as different as Jon and Cary. Her visceral first response to the manuscript told me I had by grace bridged the gap to tell her story, as well as mine. Thank you Kendra for being Cary's first and forever fan, keeping him real and grounded to the end of this book—and into the next!

So much love and gratitude to my parents for giving me a home full of peace and love growing up, and yet leaving room for others to come into our family and get a taste of God's welcome around our table. And to Logan's folks—our time in their home only deepened my appreciation for God's welcome and grace for the broken. Thank you.

And of course to my own little family—it's not easy to live with a writing mommy who seems to be in another world half the time. Love and thanks to my children Nevin and Nora, who learned the art of knowing when to ask me twenty times before I heard them, and when ask daddy instead. I don't have words adequate to honor and thank my husband Logan who took my writing habit seriously and made it a priority in a busy season of family life. I love you and I'm so grateful God gave us to each other.

Writers always say their characters are fictional, but in truth it's real people and real stories that inspire us and drive us to the page. There are many such people between the lines of this story, especially behind the character of Pete White: my own father, my husband, Glenn, Pastor Kevin, and my uncle Peter all played a part in shaping the character of that good man. Gentlemen, it is a privilege to have you in my life.

And to you, whoever you are, whether you picked up this book on a whim or because a friend told you that you had to read it... thank you for taking the time for this story. I've come to believe that there is a God who knows each of our stories and cares about each detail. He is intimately acquainted with grief and pain. May you find Him with you on the journey.

Grace and peace,
Rachel.

41309148R00198

Made in the USA
Charleston, SC
27 April 2015